More Advance Praise for Cate Dicharry

" Cate Dicharry's exemplary debut novel *The Fine Art of Fucking Up* is the literary version of what you'd get if, say, Remedios Varo had painted 'Dogs Playing Poker', or Man Ray was responsible for Glamour Shots Photography: an honest artspace where both absurdity and ubiquity live together like the proper mates they actually are. Where the eccentricities of an artist do not exempt him from humdrum human woe: petty jealousies, university politics, the complexities of marriage, the annoyance of houseguests. Rain falls on the painter and the painting alike. Dicharry's comic timing is unimpeachable and though her characters are idiosyncratic and quirky, they are deeply dimensional and exceptionally real. A richly complicated and rewarding novel."

Jill Alexander Essbaum, author of *Hausfrau*

ABOUT THE AUTHOR

PHOTO BY MICHAEL KREISER

CATE DICHARRY graduated from Lewis & Clark College in Portland, OR with a BA in Political Science in 2003. Cate moved to China to teach English at Dalian Nationalities University and discovered a love for creative writing. Cate went on to earn an MFA in Creative Writing from the Low Residency Program at the University of California, Riverside. Cate lives in Iowa City, Iowa, with her husband and two small sons. *The Fine Art of Fucking Up* is her first novel.

The Fine Art of
FUCKING UP

A NOVEL

Cate Dicharry

The Unnamed Press
Los Angeles, CA

The Unnamed Press
1551 Colorado Blvd., Suite #201
Los Angeles, CA 90041
www.unnamedpress.com

Published in North America by The Unnamed Press.

1 3 5 7 9 10 8 6 4 2

Copyright 2015 © Cate Dicharry

ISBN: 978-1-939419-25-5

Library of Congress Control Number: 2014948159

This book is distributed by Publishers Group West

Printed in the United States of America by McNaughton & Gunn

Designed by Scott Arany
Cover art by Sara Andreasson

For Mark Haskell Smith

The Fine Art of
FUCKING UP

Chapter 1

$\mathcal{I}$ AM SITTING BEHIND MY desk watching the downpour when I catch the scent of bacon. Dunbar is in the building again, despite the restraining order.

I close my eyes as if that might enhance my sense of smell and wonder if Ramona can detect the bacon back in her office. No doubt she's sitting in her Herman Miller Aeron chair, tucked behind her computer screen, sneakered feet barely reaching the floor, her compact runner's body folded in half at the waist, not in an attempt to hide or be secretive, but trying to physically burrow into *A Beat of the Heart* or *Under the Sheets* or whatever other period-specific, euphemistically risqué bodice-ripper she has open in her lap. I know what's going on back there. Fantasizing. Role playing. Vicarious pleasure seeking. Page after page of cream-whipped breasts pressing up against bulging pectorals and arrowhead pelts of silky chest hair, heaving women impaling themselves on the swollen brawn of lust-crazed men, "shattering" in any number of adventurous positions and locales.

Ramona used to be competent. She used to be organized, precise, militantly efficient, the tireless director of the School of Visual Arts—my boss—and the sort of woman who wouldn't bother to scoff at paperback love. Now, under the screen name FlexibleTigress, she's the most frequent commenter at RomancingTheBlog.com.

Early this past fall, before she was so far afield, Ramona and I faced difficulty trying to legally bar a tenured professor from his place of employ, even a pathological agitator like Bert Dunbar. The man considers himself an edgy New York City artist-provocateur and lives in constant struggle against the geographical and circumstantial facts that he is something else, namely, a Midwestern drawing teacher. In his screwball mind he affirms his artistic relevance (to peers, students, the voices in his head) with his action art, elaborate schemes designed to upend the administration. When ignored, he cries creative censorship and then, when that backward reasoning doesn't get anyone's attention, he insists it's meta-censorship—censorship of the censorship.

Dunbar's oeuvre includes hatching ticks in the main gallery as a statement against the blood-sucking School of Visual Arts management and assigning his Performance Art II class to assemble a twelve-person Viking battleship—"my ketch, my schooner, my clinker-built knarr," Dunbar said—then take it on the river to fire what were called in the incident report, "human waste cannon-balls," at the SVA building. He requires artistically and motivationally substandard students, permitted to enroll in his courses by yours truly, to wear straightjackets for the duration of one or more class periods, depending on the degree of their unimaginativeness. He once erected a watchtower (a repurposed children's playhouse) just off campus and lived in it for a week of "anti-art reconnaissance." He kept logs and diaries detailing not only the movements of various deans and ombudspersons but also his own food and sleep-deprived delirium—page after page of anthropomorphic bananas, entire banana families, bananas in tuxedos and sportswear, and, toward the end, bananas engaged in sex acts with more tiny bananas for genitalia—all of which he made available for public viewing at the year-end faculty show.

One might think these escapades would be sufficient for restraint, but Dunbar has been at it for decades and drapes himself in the protective cloak of detailed, amended, indexed, claused, and infuriatingly air-tight consent and release forms, signed by each student in each of his courses on the first day of each semester, well before they know they're handing over their mental, emotional, and at times, physical liberties to a complete and total whack job.

What we finally busted him for was peeping on a nude model in an evening drawing class. Dunbar claimed he was on the ladder to change a lightbulb but Brandon Nichols, a generally disgruntled and once straight-jacketed undergraduate, said he saw Dunbar leering over the classroom divider, "practically slobbering on that naked chick." It wasn't a strong enough case to fire him (he did, in fact, have a lightbulb in his possession), but when a young person suggests sexual misconduct, municipal civil judges are quick with powers of injunction. We take what we can get.

I stalk out of my office, licking my lips, on the hunt. Catching Dunbar in violation of the restraining order is one of my professional charges as administrative coordinator of the School of Visual Arts. He is allowed to enter the facility only when he is teaching and under no circumstances may he communicate—verbally, electronically, culinarily—with faculty, staff, or students not registered for one of his courses. Since issuance of the restraining order, he has been sneaking into the building and firing up a hot plate in a corner, closet, or unused office and frying bacon. The scent overtakes the building, letting us all know he does not intend to go quietly. Or rather, nonodorously.

In person, Dunbar is a befuddled, incoherent, untucked goon of a man, the consent and release forms, prepared at his behest by a pricey and commensurately skilled attorney, the only indication of productive brain function. That he can do anything remotely elusive, let alone repeatedly, is astounding to me. And yet we haven't caught him in the act. *I* haven't caught him in the act. But after he vacates the building, I know where he's been; he leaves calling cards, green gourds grown into molds of his own making, carved with his initials. The first was in the shape of a painter's palette, but they've become more antagonistic, the most recent a remarkable replica of a dove making a crude gesture with its feathered wing. The time and effort it must take to prepare the intricate molds then tenderly grow gourds into those molds indicates to me the depth of his depravity. What kind of man does that to a vegetable?

I've collected the eleven gourds we've found so far and arranged them on a bookshelf in my office as motivation to catch Dunbar red-handed, something general counsel says we must do before we can take further legal action. Even if we do catch him, we're not certain it will be considered a fire-able offense, so we're working on a plan to claim the gourds and bacon constitute communication and are therefore transgressive of the restraining order—another strategy Ramona laid out before veering off into fantasy land.

Out in the atrium, the scent of prey in my nose, I walk toward the stairs and inhale, sniffing, a hound on the trail, my olfactory nerve—not to mention adrenal glands—alert. I look around the atrium for any indication of where Dunbar might be. Smokey air. A trail of grease perhaps. Gourd shavings. I am out for blood.

Ethan, my husband, is constantly telling me I shouldn't let Dunbar get to me, that it's useless to reprehend the motivations and behaviors of others, especially certifiable, tenured art faculty. "Everyone's doing their best, Nina, and you can't expect more than that." This is his mantra. Everyone's doing their best. Everyone's doing their best. Everyone's doing their best, Nina. Like he truly doesn't believe in personal malice. Like there's no such thing as gratuitous incivility. He tells me, "Dunbar is out of his gourd."

Ethan makes this little joke frequently, always looking at me like *maybe this time you'll get it*, and I tell him, first of all, I do get it, it's just not funny. And second, he can laugh only because he doesn't have to deal with Dunbar day in and day out. That's not true, though. Ethan would laugh even if he was in my position. He'd love it. He is another infuriating kind of human being, the incessantly optimistic type who actually lives his own mantra and would never be ruffled, certainly not provoked, by a man so mentally defective, so completely ridiculous as Bert Dunbar. I accept that Ethan's perverse optimism and good cheer are likely the reasons he loves me but, the fact is, hearing his voice in my head telling me to give Dunbar a break, to have fun with him ("How can you resist pranking him back? I have some ideas…"), only invigorates my bloodlust.

I take a deep bacon-laced breath and wonder about Ethan's agenda. This morning he said, "I was hoping we could meet for lunch today, at noon at the Red Herring?" We do occasionally have lunch together, but not like this, not premeditated, like an appointment. Ethan prefers spontaneity to actual plans, showing up unannounced, dragging me to the new Indian restaurant in a neighboring town. I spent much of my morning distracted by speculation. Maybe they've asked him to be chairman of the Physics Department, and, though it'll be good for his career, it'll mean a lot more time at the office. Perhaps he finally bought the Triumph motorcycle he's been eyeing and wants me to trade in the Subaru and thinks this will be problematic for me, which it will. Maybe he slept with one of his grad students.

In my imagination, I followed this last scenario all the way to the moment of confession and then on through the ensuing outrage and break-up. I'm not sure if it was the train-wreck appeal of the storyline, but I had a hard time ignoring the sparkle of energy that coursed my shoulder blades as I pictured myself bawling over Ethan's infidelity, telling him that his remorse, no matter how sincere, couldn't undo the betrayal. It was too late, the damage was done. It was over.

Standing in the School of Visual Arts atrium—a three-story-tall open cylinder with a Jackson Pollock adorning its putty-colored façade, stairs corkscrewing up along the wall—I close my eyes and take a more measured breath, trying to gauge from which direction the bacon scent is coming. Rain pounds the building's corrugated steel roof, and it's like the noise is interfering with my sense of smell. If only it was silent I'd be able sniff out exactly where Dunbar is hiding. I think of the noise-canceling headphones sitting on my desk, the ones Ethan gave me for Christmas last year—the best present I've ever received—but I wore them all yesterday and the batteries are dead. I sniff again and head for the stairs.

When I reach the second story, I turn left down a wide glassed-in hallway that is cantilevered out over the river, sticking off the side of the silo-shaped building like a tree branch. Maybe Dunbar is in the Art Library.

As I do every time I walk this corridor, I look out at the Pollock—acknowledge it, revere it—hanging high above the atrium, dead even with the second-story mezzanine. It's one of his lesser-known works, a smaller abstract, supposedly a portrait, though there's disagreement regarding commission and subject. Completed in 1947, it precedes his famous "drip stage," all those large-scale paint-flung masterpieces, though this one is by no means diminutive: fifty-five inches high, sixty-seven inches across, nearly four-and-a-half feet tall by five-and-a-half-feet wide, facts I've recounted to inattentive prospective students on countless building tours. I can't look at it without thinking of Pollock's own description. A stampede, he called it. Everything barreling across that goddamn surface.

The library doors come into view, up ahead on the right. I spent an afternoon last week mapping and categorizing the building's electrical outlets, rating them one through five—five being best, one being worst—based on their potential for clandestine bacon frying. I know there are two somewhat hidden but still accessible outlets amid the library's stacks that I rated "fours" and another one behind the graduate carrels I gave a "three." The pounding rain is amplified by the hallway's thick aquarium-glass walls, and it sounds as if the drops are falling in unison, like an enormous electric drill turning against an immovable screw. It distracts me for a half a second but when I walk farther down the hall toward the library, the smell of bacon intensifies, fueling my pursuit.

I reach for the library doors, sensing Dunbar's presence, certain I'm closing in on him, when Suzanne Betts, professor of sculpture and faculty advisor of my MFA graduation committee ten years ago, turns the corner at the end of the hall and marches toward me, purple suede clogs pigeon-toed and clomping, red sundress aflutter, canvas messenger bag yanked across her body, flopped open and practically animate, spewing papers, folders, books, some kind of miniature orange traffic cone, and what looks like a two-by-four. Suzanne and I became close when I was a grad student and are like family now. She often takes shameless advantage of our personal friendship for professional profit and I can see by her expression of pre-apology and the scraggly looking boy ambling behind her that this morning will be no exception. The boy is wearing tight tapered jeans that look like they belong on his thirteen-year-old sister, a too-small t-shirt adorned with the artificially faded graphic of some band or another, laceless red converse all-stars, an asymmetrically hacked mullet, and some kind of scummy kerchief around his neck.

"We were just coming to find you," Suzanne says. She points to the arty ragamuffin. "Nina Lanning, this is Mathias Daman, my absolute most promising undergraduate student." Suzanne says this about nearly every student at one point or another, not because she has that teacherly yearning to be adored but because, like Ethan, she is perilously optimistic and needs, simply *needs*, to believe in the talent of young artists.

"Nice to meet you, Mathias." There was a time when I knew most of the undergrads by name. These days I'm lucky if I recognize a face.

"What's up." He looks at me like I don't get it, whatever *it* might be. I have never been a hateful person so I'm surprised by an impulse to take him by the kerchief and bark, "cut your hair you little mutt." I clasp my hands behind my back.

"There's been a robbery in the third floor gallery," Suzanne says.

"Ok, well, can we deal with it a little later? I'm right in the middle of something." Suzanne looks at me like I've just said Damien Hirst is a nincompoop. Her sense of smell is perfectly intact, she knows exactly what "something" I'm right in the middle of, and evidently does not agree it supersedes a burgled student.

"Come on," she says.

"Why don't you call campus police? They'll probably be happy to have something to do. Tell them a work of fine art has been stolen. A real caper." I don't mean to sound sarcastic, that's just how it comes out.

"Nina." She glances at Mathias and I note that he is the one getting her look of apology now.

"Alright," I say. "Let's go see what happened."

I'm supposed to supervise each exhibit, check students in, walk them through their responsibilities, make myself available to assist in hanging and labeling work, but I am the only staff member at the SVA and Ramona has been useless all semester, so I don't have that kind of time. I go up to the third floor if and when I must. Upon entering the gallery, I see large hunks of what look like driftwood placed on maybe a half dozen podiums around the room. Mathias' show.

"Ok, you see all these little holes in the pieces of wood?" Suzanne says.

"Mm-hmm."

"There used to be hypodermic needles in those."

She looks at me to see how I've received that little tidbit, and when I don't reveal anything, she continues. "And there were hatchets stuck in that big piece over there. When we came up for critique this morning, all of it was gone."

Though most faculty don't know the cause of Ramona's decline, they've noticed her absence and have responded in one of two ways: either they're behaving like Mommy is out to lunch and it's a free-for-all, as in Suzanne's case, or they've sensed administrative weakness and are gearing up for a coup. Either way, I'm the only visible target. I do what I can to contain the mischief and mutiny, a certain amount of which is to be expected at a place like the School of Visual Arts, but I have no real authority, and there's really no disciplining the tenured anyway. I'm a zookeeper with no cage keys.

I look at all the holes in Mathias Daman's artwork and, not for the first time this academic year, consider quitting my job and moving somewhere far away and non-English speaking where I literally cannot be asked to resolve anything for anyone. Instead I say, "How many hypodermic needles and how many hatchets?"

"Like, three, four hundred needles. But only two hatchets. And I want to file, like, a complaint, or whatever. Like a police report or something. For robbery. This is my work, man. Plus those hatchets are my dad's." The boy smells like Bubblicious and unwashed hair. "Do you guys have insurance here? 'Cause I think if my shit's not recovered I should be, like, compensated and stuff."

I am relieved that Suzanne and Mathias Daman, most promising undergraduate student, did not call campus police—it can't possibly be permissible for a public institution to have three, maybe four, hundred hypodermic needles and two hatchets in an unlocked room in a building open to the public. At a minimum, it's a breach of university safety and sanitation policy, probably a violation of multiple OSHA regulations. Certainly it's an actionable offense of some kind. There is no way I'm going to let this kid file a police report. I don't have the energy to wage that battle, and more than that, I'm tired of being in somebody's crosshairs.

"I understand your frustration," I tell Mathias, contorting my face and voice so they suggest empathy rather than, say, contempt, "but we're on campus, so we don't actually file reports with the city police. You can file an internal theft report with the school. I'll take your statement and then work with campus police to resolve the incident." There is no internal theft report, I've never taken anybody's statement, and I have no intention of working to resolve the incident. Mathias' dad is just going to have to buy new hatchets.

"That sounds awesome," he says. "Can we, like, go do that shit right now?"

"Actually, I have another order of business I need to attend to first, but if you and Professor Betts can wait in my office, I'll join you shortly."

"Nina, Jesus," Suzanne says.

"Just give me five minutes."

We walk down the stairs and when I stop on the second floor, Suzanne and Mathias continue past me. I go back down the cantilevered hallway, past the Pollock, and into the library. There is a definite bacon smell, although it doesn't seem to be as strong as earlier. My heartbeat quickens as I simultaneously sense Dunbar's presence and fear he has eluded me yet again. I check the outlets from my map. No Dunbar. No hotplate, no smoke-filled air, no bacon grease. And no gourd. Just that savory scent, hovering in the chilled library air. I comb the stacks to see if he found an outlet I don't know about. Nothing. I make the full library circuit twice more. At the doors I take a last look around and head downstairs.

———

In the first floor atrium, I am stopped in my tracks. Sitting on the polished cement, a few feet in front of my closed office door, is a gourd. In the shape of a face. My face. With my tongue sticking out. At me. My shoulders and hands stiffen, my legs go loose. Anger flares along my hairline and earlobes. The goading, the provocation, the astounding likeness of the thing. I march over, reach down, and palm the gourd like a basketball. A growl vibrates in my throat, and in a burst of anger, I hurl the gourd to the ground.

A long fracture explodes across my gourd forehead, and my gourd brain spills out onto the atrium floor. The cracked rind-skull lolls back and forth a couple times and comes to rest, chin down. I hear chatter behind me and look around to see a couple dozen students, none of whom I know personally, and a few faculty, all of whom I know well, staring at me, half appalled, half delighted, like I've just passed rumbly gas that's now echoing about the atrium. In a flush of embarrassment, I pick up the fractured gourd, scoop the innards back into the shell, and carry the whole mess to my office where I carefully arrange it on the bookshelf in its place next to the others.

Chapter 2

ISTORICALLY, I'VE REVELED IN Dunbar's brand of avant-garde buffoonery. It's fun. I mean, it's ludicrous and distracting but almost always entertaining. And harmless—there's no real consequence to the antics of institutional art, even when mean spirited. It is, literally and otherwise, all academic. But over the past year or so, and with Dunbar in particular, I can muster no amusement, not even patience. Partly it's my growing annoyance at Ramona's lovesickness, partly the timesuck of Dunbar's special derangement. But really, I'm irritable. The truth is, our campaign against Dunbar has me thinking of when I believed in him. Of when I believed he was a true capital-A Artist.

Years ago, when I was an MFA student and Dunbar sat on my graduation committee, I found his "action art" important and original, and him, as a thought leader—a straight-faced epithet at the time—singularly inspired. He embodied all the reasons I wanted to be an artist, the reasons I believed art was a worthwhile pursuit. I was beguiled by his pretension to exceptionalism and didn't remotely doubt the purity of his intent nor his claim that others—everybody, all the people, most especially other artists and university administrators—had been, as he plagiarized it, "weighed and found wanting." Rather than recognize a smalltime charlatan resentfully fondling his own demented ego, I actually admired his contempt. It seemed to indicate a complex worldview. Moreover, it indicated consequence. What Dunbar did was not only meaningful, it was imperative. His art wasn't about beauty, it wasn't art for art's sake. No, it *did* something, *accomplished* something, something real and important, which was more than most people could say of their life's work. With each act of creative disobedience—all the same stupid shit he does now, all these years later—Dunbar was taking a stand, even if I didn't know or understand exactly what it was.

It's humiliating how easily and completely I was taken in by artspeak proselytization. There is nothing more seductive than being told your passion has value. Tell me I'm important. Tell me what I believe matters. What I do matters. *I* matter. Tell me those things and I'll happily blind myself to all manner of rhetorical failing, up to and including streams of egomaniacal hooey.

The first time I suspected Dunbar's routine was self-serving horseshit I'd been out of school three, maybe four, years and was working at the SVA. A Concerned Citizen wrote a letter to the editor of the local newspaper about there being private parts on display in university buildings. Was the community aware, Concerned Citizen wondered, that a variety of these so-called "artworks" hung in public view throughout campus hallways, including the president's own offices? Obscenity in the public square. Nothing short of taxpayer-supported smut. Something must be done.

In polite Midwestern form, the university leadership, State Board of Regents, a number of restless civic boosters, and one musty state senator became quickly and ineffectually involved, expressing concern and understanding, as well as, obviously, of course, tremendous appreciation for the arts. The mayor made a statement about the importance of public decency and something about our young people and free expression and all that. The university removed the paintings and photographs in question, replacing them with pastoral landscapes, many featuring livestock.

Everybody at the SVA hit the roof, including Dunbar, who found himself in the uncomfortable position of alignment with SVA administration, which upset him more than suppression of art. He devised corrective measures.

Ramona and I, along with several faculty representatives and a handful of otherwise interested parties, got together with university honchos to form the Nudity in the Arts Review Committee. The acronym, NARC, was bad enough, and then it was unofficially rebranded The Butthole Brigade by some clever adjunct. I remember very little about our initial meeting except Glory Hedgeman. Glory, a lovely printmaker a couple years behind me in grad school, was, and likely remains, a vocal Dunbar apologist. On the day of NARC's first meeting, she marched into the large brown conference room and, in a swoop of drama, whipped off a floor-length canvas duster to reveal a skin-toned bodysuit with oversized male sex organs affixed in the appropriate place. What I remember most, as poor Glory honked on about injustice and the First Amendment and the Miller standard and how there was nothing sexual or excretory about the paintings and photographs, is the calm. The attentive quiet. There were no gasps of horror, no outraged harrumphs, no calls to campus safety. Nobody interrupted. Nobody even stood. After a few minutes, in the face of unresponsiveness, Glory slowed, and the university provost said something courteous like, "I appreciate you coming in and sharing your thoughts with us. These are exactly the issues up for discussion, and you can rest assured everybody here intends to protect your creative freedom."

Glory wasn't an artist in that moment. She wasn't a courageous advocate, wasn't remotely helpful to the cause. She was a stooge, dazed and pitiful, naked in her body stocking, a misshapen penis safety-pinned to her crotch, her only service to Bert Dunbar and his outrageous ego. Modest and unsure, she picked up the canvas duster and covered her man parts. Addressing the carpet, she said, "Thank you for your time." As she left the room and we got on with the business of writing a perfectly reasonable, constitutionally sound nudity policy, I recalled the moments when I had been Dunbar's lackey, and I wondered who might have looked at me the way I looked at Glory Hedgeman that day.

I compose and "file" Mathias Daman's internal theft report then rush out of the office without checking on Ramona. I'm late for lunch with Ethan. At the back of the SVA building, I open both the door and my umbrella in concurrent motions and break into a trot toward my car, cursing to high waterlogged heaven because I forgot to take out my keys, so now I'll get soaked while I fumble with the umbrella to dig through my purse.

When I get to my car, I discover this will not be a problem; the engine is running. I look around to see if somebody is out there, if I'm about to become the butt of another sick joke. Seeing only a handful of hurrying students, I pull the door handle and am relieved to find the car is at least unlocked. I get in, toss my purse and umbrella on the passenger seat, buckle my seatbelt, step on the brake, and put the car in reverse. I do not move my foot to the gas, do not switch on the wipers. Instead, I watch rain curtain the windshield and consider the fact that I pulled into the SVA parking lot this morning, put my car in park, and went into my office, leaving the engine running. For four hours.

Inside the Red Herring Grill, Ethan stands next to the hostess, soggy and expectant. He is not wearing a raincoat and does not have an umbrella in his hand. His soft, grayish-brown curls are even more disordered than usual, sopped into ringlets and pressed to his forehead, neck, and ears. He's wearing a threadbare cotton sweater that was originally forest green, now olive from washings, my favorite of his worn out wardrobe. I have always found Ethan gorgeous. His face is all angles and chin, a classic middle-period Picasso, his cheekbones meeting in a plateau at his symmetrical, almost rectangular nose. He is wiry, boyish, his body mirroring the contours of his face. There is something about the way Ethan's pheromones mingle with mine that causes a braid of sugary excitement when I see him. After seven years of marriage I can still feel the chemicals at play, only now they're entwined with an ulceric ache, one that brings to mind the same disquiet and confusion I felt when, as a small child, I saw my mother crying for the first time.

"Hi," Ethan says and steps toward me.

"Hey." I pull my umbrella partly closed and shake it hard. He backs up to avoid the circumference of rain spray. "Cats and dogs out there," I say. "It's crazy."

"I know." He swats at his damp hair. "You ok? Everything all right?" Anytime I'm more than five minutes late Ethan indulges a loving impulse to presume I am burning alive in a fiery car crash rather than, for instance, pondering the fact that I left my car running in a parking lot for four hours. I should have called him, I know, and normally I would have, but, I don't know, I just didn't.

"Yeah, sorry, I must have left my phone in my office," I say and then pray that my cell phone, nestled somewhere in the depths of my purse, doesn't ring during lunch. I stop shaking the umbrella.

Ethan steps in and kisses me on the cheek. "Shall we?" he says, and gestures toward the hostess waiting with two menus.

We settle ourselves at the table and order iced teas. Ethan says, "How's work today?"

"Dunbar struck again."

"Oh shit." He laughs. "Did you catch him?"

"Not yet." There is no way I'm telling him about the gourd or my smashing it. He'd enjoy it too much. "How's your day?" I say.

"Good. I got another hog."

"A-ha." A tribe of groundhogs is digging holes under our front deck. Last weekend, Ethan rented a trap into which he placed apple slices as bait. He's been imprisoning vermin all week then painting orange stripes down their backs so we'll know if they return. At the end of each day, he takes the whole operation to the treeless, mansioned, gated development up the hill—a neighborhood that offends Ethan's sense of community and good taste—and lets the groundhogs go. His own vindictive catch-and-release program. It occurs to me that my husband is not, in this way, entirely unlike Dunbar.

Ethan is beaming at me like a child telling his mom he hit a homerun during recess tee ball. I reach up over the table and offer him my palm for a congratulatory high five, which he accepts. He leans back in his chair and says, "I actually wanted to talk to you about something."

"I figured," I say.

He takes a long slow breath. "The thing is, Nina, I want a baby."

"What do you mean?"

"A baby. You know, a tiny child." He makes a cradle gesture with his arms. "A baby."

So that's it. Ethan's next adventure. Human infant. Perhaps I should have known. He would probably say I did know, somewhere in my subconscious. He's a believer in the power of our psychic connectedness. Nevertheless, I feel genuinely dumbfounded and slightly horrified that he is going to try to have this conversation in earnest, in public, over the lunch hour.

"I've been thinking about it for a long time," he continues. "It's something I really want."

Ethan first brought up having a baby a few months ago, saying something like, "You know what I need? A mini-me. Think of all the time I could save. He could mow the lawn." He's made similar comments since, always in that casual, playful way, and I have responded accordingly: with the kind of twisted, tasteless jokes a woman can make only in the presence of her spouse. Ethan would say, "If I had a kid, I'd turn him into a child prodigy. I'd teach him all of the laws of thermodynamics by the age of six. Little Lanning genius." And then I'd say, "Not only do you not know the first thing about thermodynamics, but your kid would be a disaster. You'd use some hands-free New Age parenting technique, and then one day he'd mow down his classmates with a semi-automatic weapon and tell Oprah it was because his father didn't give him enough structure," and then Ethan would chuckle and throw something at me and we'd both wonder if the other was completely joking.

A waiter comes to the table wearing a cartoon smile. He's young, a college kid, a dark-haired, straight-toothed, body-centric frat guy. From the circles under his eyes and his too-tight grin it's clear he'd rather be in bed sleeping off the Jäger-meister seeping from his pores than here bringing us lunch. "I'm Lucas, I'll be your server today. I see we've got beverages already. Are we all set to order or are we going to need a couple of minutes?" Somehow he makes the first person plural sound like an insult.

"I think we can be ready," Ethan says. "Nina?"

"You first," I say.

"Mm-kay, I'll have the Cadillac chicken sandwich, no bacon." He smiles at me, indicating he is foregoing the bacon, his favorite pork product, for my sake. I find this irritating.

"Great. And for you ma'am?"

"I'm not sure what I feel like." I scan the menu. "What do you recommend?"

"Oh, ok, I like, um, the wings. And the chicken strips are pretty tasty too. They come with a side of ranch, which is super good here."

"I think I'll have the seared tuna salad."

"Perfect," Lucas says.

"And you know what, can I have a glass of wine too? This pinot grigio?"

"I would love to get you a glass of pinot." Lucas' smile is almost burlesque now. He walks away and we're quiet for a moment, Ethan waiting for me to say something.

"Nina?"

"Yes?" I respond brightly, as if I don't know what he's asking.

"I want to talk about this."

"About what?"

"About a baby. I want this. I want to be a father." In his tone I understand, like a beeline through the jokes and banter, Ethan is already devoted to his unborn, unconceived child. He has already taken a flying leap off the cliff of fatherhood and needs me to follow. I feel a surge of appreciation that Ethan would want to have a child with me, but it is fused to an equally strong sense of resentment—I can see that if I don't jump off this cliff it won't be like past dissentions, like the time he wanted to paint the house a neighborly *Beckoning Sea Blue* and had already bought ten gallons of paint when, as he ascended the ladder, brush in hand, I said I thought the house might be better a less chirpy *Collard Isle Green*.

For one split second, I follow Ethan's wind-blown expression into our future. I imagine I first refuse motherhood then pretend to agree but secretly keep taking birth control pills and then, equal parts relieved and devastated when I don't get pregnant, stand by as a sinkhole opens in our marriage and consumes the happiness we spent so many years trying to cultivate, leaving me childless and divorced, a circumstance I begin to understand and lament only after Ethan is long gone, starting a family with his new, more reasonable wife, while I am alone, ten years older and functionally barren with no romantic prospects of any kind. An image of Ramona buried in *The Ways She Was Wicked* flutters through my mind.

Lucas comes back with the glass of wine and sets it in front of me on the table.

"Thank you," I say, and he cracks that backhanded grin over his already turned shoulder. I take the stem between my first and middle fingers, slide the glass toward me, lift, and sip.

"What are you thinking?" my husband asks.

I sigh and replace the wineglass on the table. "Are you serious about this?" My tone is distended with exasperation, and Ethan looks like I've hurled a fork at his eye. Of course he's serious. He's painfully serious. He is so absolutely serious, so utterly heartfelt, it is beyond insulting I would ask this question.

Instead of being angry, he says, "All I'm saying is I want to talk about family. I'm at the point in my life where I'm ready to have kids. I want to talk about what that means for us." I hold steady and he continues, "I don't want to be that crotchety old dad at high school graduation."

"You really think we're ready? This morning I ironed your pants, while you were wearing them, with a hair straightener—how's that burn, by the way?" He doesn't say anything but looks annoyed so I reach out and cover one of his hands with both of mine. "I'm more than happy to discuss the idea. I just want to be sure we think it through, carefully, with all the lifelong implications, before deciding we're ready to have a child over a Cadillac chicken sandwich. I mean, we're not exactly the most tutelary couple." He squeezes his eyebrows into a pinch, dazed by this comment, not only because I'm talking to him like he's a kindergartner who doesn't understand big boy words, but because he considers himself the emotional custodian of our relationship, the lover, the healer. And I'm sure he is further offended at my implication that a haphazard lifestyle renders one unfit for parenthood. He grew up in a circus of a household and remembers it as a cheerful way to have been raised, though I know for a fact he and his siblings made every last one of their babysitters cry.

"That's unfair," he says. "What about the emu egg thing?"

"What about it?"

"I think it demonstrates I can be very nurturing." There is a strain of compunction in his voice, and he tries to make it sound like persuasiveness.

"You're really going to cite the emu egg thing as evidence in your favor?"

"It was an act of compassion."

"Yeah, if you ignore the reason we bought the emu egg in the first place." I raise my wineglass. "To make, I believe you called it, 'the world's most monstrous omelet.' Do you recall that bit of nurturing?" I take a pull of wine, looking at him over the rim of the glass, celebrating my point.

He looks a little hurt. "Are you ok today?"

"I'm fine, I'm just saying we weren't planning to care for the emu, we were planning to eat it. Or wait, it was the emu embryo we wanted to eat. We were going to fry it up with spinach and feta."

He swipes at imaginary crumbs on the table. "I tried to save it," he says. "You know I did." There is accusation in his tone, as if I'm perverse for reminding him what really happened.

"And how did that work out?" I'm being cruel now, a gesture of protest against Ethan's earnestness and revisionist memory; the emu egg thing actually upset him deeply. When we got it home, we couldn't crack it open, and since we couldn't eat it, Ethan didn't know what else to do but incubate. He went from chef to mother hen or, rather, mother emu, in a matter of moments. I thought it was another goofball misadventure, the kind he always used to be dreaming up and executing, but after eight weeks in a homemade incubator (three heat lamps, two pillows, one tea towel, and a roasting pan), the emu chick was ready to hatch. We found out later

Ethan hadn't applied enough moisture to the shell's exterior during the incubation period, causing it to harden beyond the chick's pecking capability. For a few horrific moments, the bird was alive, trapped inside the shell, struggling to get out, pecking madly from the inside, unable to make even a dent. In a panic, Ethan ran for his electric tools, hoping to drill through the shell and free the baby emu. When he finally cracked the steely chamber, the bird was dead, we assumed from a fear-induced heart attack caused by the screeching, whirring drill bit coming straight at its fluffy head. I can't imagine Ethan was planning to keep the bird—those things get huge—but he was nonetheless grief stricken when it died.

Lucas arrives with our food and places Ethan's sandwich in front of me and my tuna in front of Ethan. "All set?" he says.

"Looks great," Ethan says, and Lucas walks away. We trade plates and begin to eat. Even though I'm not pregnant, the nearly raw fish and wine feel like defiance, like I am spiting Ethan with each bite and sip while he nibbles his baconless chicken sandwich. After several minutes he says, "Nina, all joking aside, do you think you might be resistant to discussing this because, you know, of the abortion?"

The tuna turns to paste in my mouth. It's one thing to discuss having a child in public over lunch, but I'm disgusted he would mention the abortion. "That has nothing to do with it," I say.

When I was twenty-five, shortly before I met Ethan, I spent a weekend with a guy from my grad school class, just as we were graduating and he was leaving town. It wasn't serious; we both figured we'd never see the other again, so a month later when I found out I was pregnant, I went directly to Planned Parenthood, confirmed the pregnancy, and scheduled an abortion three weeks hence, the soonest the procedure could be done. I didn't think twice about my choice, didn't feel uncertain or conflicted, didn't even consider involving the father, a man I have, as suspected, never seen again.

I told Ethan the basics only after he asked me to marry him. I worried if I didn't he'd find out one day and feel I had withheld something important. He is the only person, aside from the doctor and some medical student, who knows, and we haven't spoken about it since the day I told him. What I never mentioned, though, is that I think of the abortion often and worry my experience exemplified, or perhaps formed, the limits of my maternal proclivity. I wonder about that now and consider if Ethan and I have, over our years together, established an intimacy so penetrating that through a kind of emotional osmosis he has understood my fears without my ever hinting at them.

"I'm sorry to bring it up," he says, "I just want to be able to talk about this."

"We *are* able to talk about it," I say. "I'm just choosing not to at this particular time and place."

He picks up a french fry and stabs it into a puddle of ketchup on his plate then lifts it toward his mouth and holds it there loosely between his thumb and forefinger, looking like he might say something. I watch as a blob of ketchup drops off the end of the fry and lands in his lap. He doesn't notice and I don't tell him.

Chapter 3

HE MIXTURE OF WINE and dreary weather is like a barnacle on the hull of my sinking mood, and I consider calling in sick for the afternoon, going home, retreating into a prolonged coma-nap. Normally I wouldn't think twice about doing just that, but I feel compelled to check on Ramona and find out if she has even begun the faculty memo the dean directed us to compose and distribute, addressing the potentiality of spring flooding and the university's risk management strategy. I, in my capacity as administrator, must ensure clear communication with SVA faculty, especially now that they're basically unsupervised. Art faculty are the sort of individuals so self-involved or entirely oblivious they could easily be unaware of crisis, even one right in front of them. Rising floodwaters, for instance, could be swirling around their ankles and they still might not recognize the danger.

Without sitting down, checking email or even logging in to my computer, I head back to Ramona's office. After knocking lightly and hearing nothing, I open the door and step inside. I am shocked to find Ramona not reading a romance novel but engrossed in something on her computer screen, something I hope, with optimism and relief, is a faculty memo. I also notice to the right of the doorway a new picture frame hanging on the office wall. Feeling reluctant to disturb her productivity, I say nothing and walk over to examine what's interned behind the picture frame glass. Ramona has trimmed and framed the cover of one of her romance novels, cutting away the title so that it looks, unconvincingly, like a photograph of a man—a half nude, long-haired, excessively tanned, airbrushed, dreamy-eyed man holding what appears to be a semiautomatic weapon. I suddenly feel sure Ramona is not composing a faculty memo.

"Ramona?" She doesn't respond, entranced by whatever is on her screen. "What are you looking at? Did you find the Q?" I am pathetic in my own oblique denial.

For as long as I have known her, Ramona has spent afterhours and Saturdays trawling local consignment shops. Artifacts on Market Street, Revival downtown, Ampersand on Holiday Road. She hunts for a Q. An uppercase Hamilton No. 24, 12-inch Q, circa 1905. The one piece that will complete her set of moveable wood type. As far as I know, she hasn't found it, but several years ago she came across *Men and Other Fools* a vintage romance novel written by Mae Goodwin, published in 1936, the title set in Ramona's coveted Hamilton No. 24. It was no uppercase Q, but to Ramona it was precious, a vestigial token of a better time, before the lifeless days of offset printing. Over the years, as she searched for her Q, Ramona collected Mae Goodwin novels, all printed with Hamilton No. 24. *My Wife's Secretary. Regional Nurse. Chorus Girls: A Story of Deep Corners.* She found dozens, arranged them chronologically on her office shelves alongside a plastic-sleeved copy of *Platen Press Operation* and a rare first edition of *American Wood Type 1828–1900.*

Then one night during this past winter break, alone in the building, the only person at work over the cold holiday season, she took down one of those classic romance novels, examined the typeface, I'm sure, admired the kerning, opened the cover, read a page or two, just for fun, just to see. Kept reading. Finished the whole book, all in one sitting. We laughed about it a few days later, when I was back at work, but something seemed off. She seemed affected, the book a salve, a surrogate, a twisted stand-in for what she really desired: companionship.

By Martin Luther King Jr. Day, Ramona had read all the Mae Goodwin on her shelf and was on to *Shameless Virtue* by *Noreen Smithson* and *Dawn's Desire* by Donna Langley. She no longer laughed about it, no longer claimed it was about wood type or vintage memorabilia or nostalgia. By spring break, she was up to a romance novel a day and had burned through Marguaex Marks' Slow Rider series, as well as everything April Nightbird ever wrote, *Drawn to You* twice. She lost focus at work, canceled meetings, ignored deadlines, stopped responding to emails, even from me. She stopped talking about relief printing. Stopped hunting for the Hamilton No. 24 uppercase Q. When she wasn't in her office, I could usually find her squirreled away in a bathroom stall, feasting upon the pages of some daring melodrama, overcome by delusions of reckless love.

"Ramona?" I feel badly interrupting, like I'm disturbing a sound sleep, and this frustrates me. Lately I find myself handling Ramona the way I might a maimed child, treating her like she's suffering rather than what she actually is: willfully unscrewed. Just totally bananas. Lovey-dove batshit crazy.

Ramona was only thirty-six when she took over as director, ten years ago, the same semester she became full professor. The dean of the College of Arts and Sciences wanted a fresh face, a working artist in touch with recent generations of students, but still administratively competent, that unicorn-rare breed among academics. Ramona was perfect. All her life she'd been so focused on her work and career she'd not found the time to accumulate any of the usual studio artist distractions: a drinking and/or drug problem, any number of untreatable personality disorders, strange and lucrative commissions from close friends in South American governments, voluntary or involuntary stays in state psychiatric wards, strings of illicit (or, in her case, even licit) love affairs. She jumped at the opportunity and has been, until this semester, a relatively beloved director, an even more impressive academic rarity. I look at her now, crammed into a cheap, low-cut black dress, so tight fitting I can't tell whether she is trying to squeeze into or bulge out of it, and wonder if anything can remedy her strange decline.

"Ramona?" I say again. She still doesn't acknowledge me, and I wave a hand above my head like I'm flagging down a cab. "Ramona," louder now.

She looks up. "Nina."

"How are you?" I say this the way I would to a loved one in a hospital bed and the honeyed sound of my voice annoys me.

"Come here, look at this." She flaps her hand in a come-hither motion. "Did you know about this?" She points to her computer screen.

"What's that?" I say, walking around the side of her desk.

"You've got to look at this."

I look. On her computer screen is an image of a woman's lacquered she-claws and meaty fingers, curled around a veiny, erect penis. In the search bar, I see Ramona has Googled *Lucky Savatos throbbing member.*

"I had no idea a phallus could look like *that.*" Ramona stabs an upturned hand toward the computer screen like it's an accomplishment, like it's the New York Times Sunday crossword puzzle and she's just completed it in pen. *How about that?!*

"Ramona, you can't look at this on your work computer. You could get in trouble." I feel sweat prick my waistband, my anxiety level climbing as if I'm about to get caught, well, looking at dirty pictures at work.

"You'd think the books would be clear about these things but I still have a lot of questions." I want to tell her that the answers she needs cannot be found in those books but I don't say that. I'm not sure what to say to her, my boss, Ramona Holme, director of the School of Visual Arts, accomplished fine printer, marathon runner, professional mentor, and friend. I feel like I'm dealing with a recently whetted pubescent boy who's maybe a few bricks shy of a load.

"Ramona, please. You can't be looking at this stuff." I reach across her and depress the monitor's power button. The screen goes black and I feel like I've diffused a bomb, just in the nick of time. Ramona doesn't look at me, doesn't say a word, she just reaches up, almost robotically, and clicks the monitor back on. She closes the picture of the she-claws and clicks on the next image, a fit young man, Lucky Savatos presumably, whoever that is, his pants around his ankles, a clear outline of his throbbing member through sky blue boxer briefs.

"Come on, Ramona, seriously. You can't have this on in your office. Someone could catch you."

"I need to find this one photo," Ramona says, almost in a whisper, mostly to herself. I don't think she remembers I'm standing there.

"Please," I say. "Turn it off."

She closes the picture of the man and scrolls down the page. She is clearly not going to heed my warnings, and, anyway, I'm not the ranking officer—who am I to say the director can't conduct a little personal research in her own office?—so I leave, twisting the doorknob lock on my way out, doing what I can to prevent anybody discovering Ramona and her search for answers.

Maybe I should have seen this coming. Ramona has always been fanatical. When I first started working at the SVA, she would keep me late, talking, expounding on the intricacies of her one-hundred-year-old 10×15 Chandler and Price printing press or the beauty of letterforms. She once spent what felt like hours describing the sound of her Chandler and Price in motion. The hum of the gears, the hiss of the rollers, the ka-klunk of the platen closing against the bed, the clank of the pawl advancing the ink disk, and all of it obedient to the rhythm of the treadle and the movements of the printer, one foot standing, one foot treadling, one hand feeding, one hand delivering, working in time with the press, playing it like an instrument. A one-woman symphony. Ramona was rapturous in veneration of what she called "oldfangled art." And she approached her job as director with the same intensity. Last year she decided to add one credit hour to School of Visual Arts courses—"They're worth more," she said—which meant petitioning the college, writing new curriculum, rearranging course schedules and adjusting major and minor tracts. Ramona didn't find it fun exactly, but gratifying. Fulfilling. Energizing. We stayed late every night for two weeks until it was done, not because Ramona insisted but because we were working hard, getting something done, and didn't want to stop.

———————

I'm digging through my desk drawers looking for batteries for the noise-canceling headphones when Suzanne comes crashing in. She flops into one of the armchairs in the corner, slings one leg over the side, and heaps her messenger bag onto the other chair, its innards flying onto the seat cushion and floor. I didn't notice this morning but I see now that under her red sundress she is wearing pale blue bloomers trimmed in white eyelet lace. Anybody else might look clownish in the getup but she pulls it off.

"Thanks for helping with Mathias this morning," she says, reworking her mane of wavy ash-blonde hair in an oversized claw clip atop her head. "He's a sullen little shit, but his work's pretty good."

"No problem." I'm distracted, manhandling the headphones, staring blankly.

"What's wrong?" Suzanne says. "Are you pissed at me because of Dunbar? I smelled the bacon this morning, that man is diabolical, though I will say the gourds lack his usual imaginative flair. Not in execution, no, they're completely impressive pieces, but in concept, I mean, what's he trying to prove? There's no *there* there, don't you think? Who said that? Wasn't it Gloria Steinem? No, no, not her, it was that wonderful lesbian, what's-her-name. You know who I'm talking about." She pauses long enough to blink. "I mean, generally, Dunbar has managed to maintain *some* artistic integrity through all the insanity, but the bacon frying, my god, it's just over the top. Is that what's got you looking like you're on the verge of a conniption fit? You're pissed at me, aren't you?" I've often thought Suzanne would be well served by an extra set of vocal cords, that way she could, as she so often tries to do anyway, speak more than one sentence at a time.

I'm not about to tell her what's going on with Ramona, so instead I say, "Ethan wants to have a baby."

She squeals, jumps out of her chair, and stomps in place. "Neens, *finally!*" She does a jumping jack then stands before me twittering, giddy, her face a gaping red grape. Suzanne, esteemed university professor and gifted artist, has long dreamt of adding *mother* to her list of accomplishments but has found neither the willing partner nor the self-sacrifice required for motherhood. I've heard her say, "I cannot imagine the degree of mutation I've inflicted upon my eggs, I'd have flipper babies, fins instead of hands."

"It's complicated," I say.

"People still make babies the usual way, don't they?" With her thumb and forefinger she makes a circle and, with the forefinger on her other hand, pantomimes intercourse.

"I don't know if we're ready. I mean, you know Ethan. He has the foresight of a second grader. Does he seem to you like the kind of guy who should become a father?" I'm in search of female alignment here, for my closest friend to seize upon the tremors of doubt in my voice and affirm for me that my mate is not, by any stretch of the imagination, ready to have a child. To relieve me of having to explain that *I* am the terrified one, that I fear we'll have a child, and, after it's born and named, after all exit doors to other futures are slammed shut, I won't love it, won't know how to care for it, won't know how to be generous with it.

But Suzanne looks at me like I'm speaking in tongues. "Are you out of your mind?" she says. "Ethan'll be a phe*nom*enal father. He's the most self-actualized person I know." Suzanne is big on self-actualization. In her mind there is no greater human accomplishment as it indicates overall life balance, an equanimity of which, in her place and line of work, there is next to none.

"We'll see. We're going to talk about it more."

"For fuck's sake, Neens, what's there to talk about? Go home, spread your legs, and let that man knock you up. Maybe you'll finally grow some jugs." She cups her own sizable breasts and springs them up-down, up-down.

I twist the headphones in my hands and feel Suzanne watching me, catching on that something is not right, that I'm not telling her the whole story.

"Ok, listen, we'll talk later. I need to go addle some young minds." She stands, scoops papers and various other paraphernalia back into her messenger bag. "I'll swing by after class, and if you're still here we'll go for margaritas. Your last hurrah before the bun's in the oven."

"You got it."

"Ciao," she says and blows me a kiss.

At a little after seven o'clock, more than two hours past the official end of my workday, I stand at the building's back doors and watch rain pummel the roof of my car. The drops ricochet with force, and I squint to see if it's actually hailing now.

I spent the afternoon researching and drafting the faculty memo Ramona is supposed to send out by tomorrow morning. Even if I finish it, I can't send it without her signature, and there's no way to know if that'll happen. Around five-fifteen I saw her wander out of her office and scoot down the back hallway, skin-tight black dress riding up her thighs, sneakers squeaking on the polished cement floor, not a thing (purse, book, papers, umbrella) in her hands.

I saved and closed the memo and pulled out my Dunbar map. Last week I marked a green X at the locations where the gourds have been found, and I spent an hour or so trying to decipher any pattern or tactical scheme, thinking maybe I'd be able to anticipate the location of his next attack. Finding, unsurprisingly, nothing logical in his moves, I rolled up the map and put it on the bookshelf with the gourds.

Now, standing at the back doors, dreading going out into the rain, I worry about Ethan. He is a man of momentum. It is his defining characteristic, one that has brought him great success, personally and professionally; he has no capacity for self-doubt, even when intentions, plans, and outcomes are fuzzy. I'm brainstorming what I might say to get him to change his mind about our offspring when somebody gooses me.

"Ouch." I drop my umbrella and whirl around, placing my hands on my butt to rub the sore spot. Standing behind me is James Brenton, assistant professor of Graphic Design, once my grad school classmate and friend, later my colleague, most recently the object of my semi-infatuation, and, in certain moods, my imaginary paramour. He is also Suzanne's real-life lover of several months, though he doesn't know I know this last bit. He's under the impression he's been discreet about the affair, which he has, the ambitious, talented young professor sleeping with the ten-years-older master sculptress and head of his tenure review committee. Suzanne, however, believes that in order to have internal harmony she must "give it all up to the universe," by which she means she doesn't keep secrets, even delicate ones. She's blabbed to any number of people, myself included. When she told me I wondered, with low feminine jealousy, if James wasn't sleeping with her as a career move.

"I don't think it's going to let up," James says. He points out to the parking lot and I follow his hand. Something about the extreme flexibility of his hitchhiker's thumb strikes me as erotic.

"That hurt," I say, still rubbing my butt, bending down to pick up the umbrella.

"Shouldn't you be home by now?" James is an involuntary flirt, evoking intimacy through unbroken eye contact and self-possession, though he rarely says or does anything actually intimate, which makes him all the more alluring. I have this recurring dream where I make him a sandwich, not some obvious meatball on baguette, but smoked turkey on thick-cut white bread. Half-moon tomato slices that look just like his fat lower lip. Iceberg lettuce. Extra mayo.

"I had some work to do," I tell him. "Stuff for Ramona."

"What's going on with her? I don't think I've seen her since spring break."

"She's been really busy." And then, with barely a moment's hesitation, I say, "I caught her watching porn today," which is not really true. I become a liar and a tattletale with one sentence. Worse, I recognize a junior high desire to impress James with the mention of pornography, and this causes me to picture him naked. For some reason I imagine him flaccid, his wide, dimpled smile welcoming, that bulging lower lip, scarred from a childhood accident, making him vulnerable but not shy. I drop my umbrella and bend to pick it up again.

"Where, here?" he asks. "In her office?" He looks confused, or perhaps conspiratorial, and I get the idea he may be chewing over how best to use this information to his advantage. For a regular faculty member I'm not sure office porn would be any big deal, but for a director already under fire, it's solid ammunition. Ramona could lose her administrative appointment, perhaps her job. I think about how James is close friends with half the painting faculty and drinking buddies with Dan Holdt, our Montana cowboy ceramicist. I recall that when we were in graduate school he was, like me, a Dunbar follower, and how he has commented, admiringly, I would say, on the gourd collection in my office. He has no allegiance to me, whatever I may fantasize about him. With my free hand, the one not gripping the umbrella, I take him by the upper arm.

"You can't say anything." No matter how much Ramona's hobbies may confuse and trouble me, it's my duty to protect her.

"I won't," he says. "I like Ramona. Besides, there's nothing wrong with a little porn."

"Not even to Suzanne, James."

He shifts his weight. "Why would I say anything to Suzanne?" He's uncomfortable and I realize I've stumbled into a workable, if unfriendly, play, apparently my modus operandi these days. James thinks I'm blackmailing him. He tells anybody about Ramona, I tell about him and Suzanne.

"Just don't say anything, ok? To anybody."

"My lips are sealed." He forces a smile and I can tell he wants to leave but seems to think it would be worse than staying. He looks down the hall in the direction opposite the back doors and I realize this transaction will be there between us now.

When James doesn't turn back for several moments, it becomes clear he's watching for somebody. Suzanne never came by for margaritas—he must be here this late waiting for her or perhaps sent on an errand to usher me out the door so they can leave together.

When he finally turns back, I make a show of looking at my watch. "I'm sure Ethan's worrying," I say and open my umbrella. "I'll see you tomorrow morning at the faculty meeting."

"We have a faculty meeting tomorrow?"

"First Friday of the month. Ten-thirty." I put a hand on the door and lean into it.

"I don't think anybody remembers," James says.

"I'll send an email," I say and push out into the rain.

Chapter 4

I LOVE OUR HOUSE. IT'S a craftsman bungalow, built in 1912, set back from the street, squat and wide with a low-slung front porch and an attic window perched top center, the trim bright white against the seasick-green siding. Sitting in my car I can see, through sheets of rain, that the storm door is closed but the inner front door is wide open. Ethan likes the sound, smell, and warm dampness of a summer storm, especially in the evening. "Let the weather in," he says. From outside it looks like a house with a rich inner life—door ajar, windows lit, the whole place abuzz with activity, a home where affection, merriment, and probably unselfconscious dancing are likely to be found, maybe even right at this very moment.

We bought the place six years ago, shortly after we were married. It was the first property we looked at—thirteen hundred square feet, two bedrooms, one-and-a-half baths—and though we saw at least a dozen more, I knew it was the one we'd buy. The original end-grain cherry floors, glass-paned pocket doors dividing the rooms on the main floor, a wood-burning fireplace, eat-in kitchen, and built-in bookshelves—I loved it all. Love the way it moved and felt, loved the nighttime water hammers and creaking floors, banisters worn soft, the whole place broken in, kneaded over a century into a real home. It seemed like exactly the kind of place a happy couple like us should live. The kind of place we could start a life together. I was never sure whether or not that life would include children.

When I went in for my abortion all those years ago, the doctor asked if I'd mind having a medical student in with us, observing. I remember thinking, *sure, fine, the more physicians who are trained to do this, the more women will have it available to them.*

I lay back on the surgical table in the procedure room and saw a beach taped to the ceiling above me, two pages ripped from a travel magazine. The tape was peeling away from the ceiling, the edges of the magazine pages dingy from repasting and time. I remember wondering if the doctor had climbed up on the surgical table himself to hang it, standing on tiptoe right where I was laying, reaching overhead to stick the beach up there. I suppose he meant it to be a pleasant distraction, a better scene than the one actually taking place, but it struck me as vulgar—a pathetic attempt to mitigate such a troubling, intimate occasion.

Instead of staring at the beach, I focused on the medical student, centered in a frame of my open legs, just beyond the stirrups where I dug in my heels, lifting my pelvis to relieve pressure from the suction. He was some guy about my age, watching the doctor's movements, listening to him explain how the vacuum expels the embryo from the uterus. He would observe more abortions during his rotation at the clinic but, the doctor told me, mine was his first. I remember wondering what the experience was like from his perspective. What he would say about it to his girlfriend over dinner that night? I don't remember if he ever looked at me, at my face, I mean, but I watched him for the duration of the procedure.

I've seen him around town since then, at the Crowing Goat restaurant, at O'Connor's Pub once on St. Patrick's Day, in the crowd at a university football game, once at Target buying greeting cards and laundry detergent. He seems like a nice man. Friendly. Polite. I worry he'll recognize me, smile, say hello, ask my name. Ask where he knows me from.

When the abortion was over, I sat in the recovery room, a row of five recliners at the back of the clinic, curtained off from the exam rooms and operation suite by thick oatmeal-colored canvas. I was in the second-to-last chair, brown corduroy, well-worn, a heating pad on my abdomen and a blanket over my legs. The chairs on both sides of me were empty but two recliners down, a woman sat bawling. I automatically looked for her left ring finger and saw an enormous diamond and a thick gold band. There was a man with her, holding her hand as she cried, and I wondered who he was to her, whether he was her husband or her lover or her friend or her brother or what, and how it could be that a married woman ended up in that recliner. *She's got it right*, I thought. *Hysteria is the only appropriate response.* I worried the curtain would be pulled back and the young medical student would see me there, tearless. It was one thing for him to witness the procedure, to know of the choice I'd made. That, I was ready to own. But I could not bear to be seen unmoved, reclining as if I were at home watching television.

But I didn't feel hysterical. I felt relieved. The only thing I found upsetting was *not* feeling guilty, not having a drop, not a flash, not one second of hesitation or sorrow. I felt cold and detached, verifying all the more that I'd made the right choice.

My cell phone rings and I assume it's my husband, calling to find out which emergency room I'm in. When I dig the phone out of my purse, I see on the caller ID it's my mother. I push *ignore* and wonder why Ethan hasn't called; I'm over two hours late. I begin to worry again about what he might be up to and dash out into the rain, not bothering with my umbrella. What I first notice upon stepping, soaked, into the house are two giant duffle bags on the floor in the center of the living room. Then I hear the music.

In our dining room, beneath the polished brass chandelier, where a table and chairs should be, sits an old, scarred, walnut-finished Kimball baby grand. Ethan found the piano on eBay five years ago, locally listed for two thousand dollars, and thought it would be better in our house than a dining room table and chairs. We'd never have to host holidays, he argued. We'd never have to buy tablecloths or place settings or stemware or flatware. It'd be so much fun! A piano! In the dining room!

We used to sit side-by-side on the bench, dinner plates balanced on our laps or on top of the piano where sheet music would have been if either of us could read sheet music, and he would plunk out *Great Balls of Fire* or *One for My Baby* or *Rudolph the Red-Nosed Reindeer*. Tonight I hear *Pachelbel's Canon*, played slowly by a beginner with great affection for the sustain pedal. Maybe Ethan spent the evening learning the matrimonial tune as a romantic gesture after our tense lunch. I close the front door behind me and shake some of the rain from my hair, swipe at the water on my shoulders and sleeves, and see Ethan walk past the doorway to the kitchen at the back of the house. He feels me looking at him, stops, turns his head, smiles.

"Hi," he says, and comes toward me through the living room, his cheeks a medium-rare pink. He seems to have no sense of what time it is or how late I am. In one hand he holds a Sierra Nevada and, with the other, takes my purse from my shoulder and drops it on the entryway table. He's still wearing work pants but is shirtless and has on what looks like a fanny pack, his lean torso rippling like a wave pool, his slight chest bobbing on the wake.

"You dug out the belly shocker," I say, and poke at his pulsating middle. He ordered the device years ago, not because he thought it'd yield six-pack abs, not because he gives two shits about six-pack abs, but because he wanted to see it for himself, wanted to play with the thing, test it out. At the time I found it funny, making a game of an infomercial, seeing what we could wrap it around and make vibrate, Ethan threatening to wear it to a faculty meeting. Tonight it seems childish.

"The Contour Core Sculpting Belt," he says.

"I remember."

"Pretty amazing we could even find it, huh?"

"Incredible," I say. I take the beer from him and sip. "Who's playing the piano?"

"Come in," he says, his rosy grin widening. He takes back his beer, puts his other arm around my shoulder, and starts to pull me into the house. "I'll introduce you."

It's hard to guess who could merit a personal demonstration of the Contour Core Sculpting Belt. One of Ethan's old grad school buddies? Surely not a visiting faculty member. "I'm going to run upstairs and change quick," I say.

"Really?"

"I'm soaked. I'll be two seconds."

I duck out from under his arm and trot up the stairs. He walks back into the kitchen, and I hear him move a pot or pan on the stove. *Pachelbel's Canon* stops and Ethan is talking.

In the upstairs bathroom I close and lock the door. A couple of years ago Ethan offered to turn the detached garage into a studio for me so I could start making artwork again. Instead, I asked him to redo this bathroom. He knocked down a wall, combining the bathroom with what used to be a huge hallway linen closet, laid black and white checked tile, painted the walls *Summer Marigold*, installed a white claw-foot bathtub and a china pedestal sink, and found a gold-on-burgundy paisley armchair just small enough to squeeze into the corner. Last year I started spending more time in here, eventually moving in my dresser and, a few months after that, a small writing table. It's the only room in the house where Ethan respects the boundary of a closed door.

I flip down the toilet seat, letting it slam, and do the same with the lid. My blouse is soaked through, and when I peel out of it and toss it over the shower curtain rod, I notice the smell of second-hand bacon. I unzip my skirt and, kicking off my clunky work loafers, pull it up over my head, and hang it next to the soggy blouse. Sitting in the armchair, I reach around my back with both hands, unhook my bra, slip the straps down my arms, then hold the bra to my nose and sniff.

I'm both annoyed and relieved Ethan has a dinner guest. I'll be able to delay further baby talk but instead have to make conversation with a stranger over whatever entrée Ethan is cooking up, sitting elbow-to-elbow on the couch, the only site for dinner parties of more than two at our house. I drop the bra and interlace my fingers in front of me, stretch up overhead, back arched. I rub beneath my breasts where the underwire was all day, run my fingertips up and down over my nipples causing them to harden. *Pachelbel's Canon* resumes downstairs. I dig through a basket of clean laundry for jeans and a t-shirt.

Downstairs in the kitchen it is bright and warm and smells like bologna and onion. The faucet is running even though Ethan is standing at the far counter, next to the stove, slicing a green pepper, still wearing the Contour Core Sculpting Belt, belly and breasts still quivering. Spread around the kitchen are a block of cheddar, a red pepper, a head of lettuce, several empty beer bottles, a container of black bean salsa, an emptied box of Spanish rice, an open bag of tortilla chips, and, on the breakfast table, a plate of uncooked boneless skinless chicken breasts and a package of large flour tortillas. There are a couple of pans going on the stove and the Griddler is plugged in and sizzling on the other side of the sink.

"Quite the operation," I say.

Ethan looks up, smiles, doesn't stop slicing. "Feel better?"

I walk to the sink and turn off the faucet. "What are you making?"

"Fajitas." He gestures to the Griddler. "It was Gary's idea to add hotdog."

"Hotdog fajitas?" I walk over to where my husband is slicing. "That's disgusting," I say, and pick up a sliver of green pepper, snap it in half, put one piece in my mouth.

"I know." Ethan laughs.

"Who's Gary?"

"Come." Ethan puts down the knife. "Meet him."

I pop the other piece of green pepper into my mouth. Ethan takes me by the elbow and guides me through the second doorway in the kitchen to the adjacent dining room and the baby grand. An Asian kid at the piano stops playing when we come into the room.

"Nina, this is Gary."

He stands, pushes back the bench. "Hi," he says and nods. He has days-old stubble on his face, which seems maliciously impolite, and large hands that he rests awkwardly on narrow hips. His long, impeccable fingers suggest better piano skills and a standing manicure appointment. *Time for a manicure but not a shave. Real nice.*

"Hi," I say.

"Gary's in my physical mechanics class," Ethan says. "Best student I've got. From China?"

"Guangzhou," Gary says.

"You're a very talented piano player," I say.

Ethan puts a hand on the small of my back, leans toward me until his lips are against my ear. "I'm not sure how advanced his conversational English is."

"I hope you'll join us for hotdog fajitas," I say. Gary looks to Ethan for explanation but my husband is looking at me, giving me a dirty look. I elbow him and gesture to Gary.

"We'll eat soon," Ethan says. Gary nods, sits down at the piano, steps on the sustain pedal, and reprises *Pachelbel's Canon.*

I turn and walk back to the kitchen and Ethan follows. "Doesn't he know how to play anything else?" I open the fridge and take out a beer.

"I think he's putting on a concert for us."

"Hmm."

He takes the beer out of my hands, opens it with the magnetic opener from the side of the fridge, drops the cap on the kitchen table, and hands the bottle back to me. "So, what do you think?"

"I think *Pachelbel's Canon* is kind of annoying. I was just being polite."

"He's nice, right?"

"He barely said anything."

"He's shy. He's a great kid, excellent student. Smart."

"I have no doubt." I take a drink of the beer.

"Nina, listen, I'm sorry about lunch today."

"Oh god, Ethan, come on, you don't want to talk about this now, do you?"

"It's just, it didn't go the way I planned."

"I really don't want to do this." I turn away from my husband and the fridge, walk over to where the green pepper sits, half chopped, and turn to lean against the counter, crossing my arms over my chest, beer bottle dangling from one hand.

"Nina, please, this is important to me."

"I know it is. And we can talk about it tomorrow or this weekend or whenever. Anytime other than right now."

"Can I just say one thing?"

I raise my beer to him, shrug a shoulder. "Go ahead."

"I just really need you to understand how much this matters to me, that I want to be a father, that I'm serious..."

"Ethan..."

"...which is why I invited Gary to stay."

"What, stay the night?"

He shoots me a grin I haven't seen in a while, one part anticipation, two parts mischief, then hooks his thumbs into the top of the Contour Core Sculpting Belt and tugs it away from his body. His stomach stops convulsing, his breasts stop bouncing. "For the summer," he says, and lets the belt snap back against his skin.

I put the beer bottle down too hard. Foam crawls out the top and snakes down the side to the countertop where it pools. "That's not funny."

"He showed up in class this afternoon, distraught, I mean literally in tears. He'd just figured out they're closing his dorm for the summer. He hadn't been able to understand the email notifications or fliers. He had no idea. Nobody told him. Can you believe that? Nobody checked that he had made arrangements. He can't go home because his visa is for one entry per year, so if he leaves he won't be able to get back in time for fall semester. He has nowhere to go."

"You've got to be kidding me."

"I want to look after him." He searches. "Practice."

"Practice what? Feeding and sheltering a non-English speaking Chinese national? I'm not sure you need help in that area. What is he, twenty years old?"

"Nineteen."

"He doesn't need a father figure, Ethan. He needs friends, roommates, a summer job, a girlfriend."

"He's taking summer classes but he can't drive, he has no idea how to sublet an apartment, doesn't have any close friends. What was I supposed to do, leave him on the street?"

"That would have been one option."

"I'm ready. I want this." He claps his hands hard, rubs his palms together with vaguely combative enthusiasm, like he's challenging me.

I suppress a derisive grunt. "You're ready?" I say.

"I am."

"So—and correct me if I've misunderstood—you've invited Gary the Chinese, who can't speak English or get around on his own or take care of himself, to live with us, in this tiny house, for four months, without talking to me about it first, because you're 'ready,'" I make exaggerated air quotes, "because you want to demonstrate that you're a responsible adult who's prepared to start a family? That's what you're saying? Really?"

Aghast. That's the word that comes to mind as I watch my husband react, and I think how I've never seen a person truly aghast before. In this case, it could be over any number of things. My flippancy. My complete disregard for Gary's plight. My questioning Ethan's maturity. The suggestion that my husband needs my permission for acts of kindness.

"You can't call him that, Nina."

My racism. That makes sense too. I struggle to keep myself from apologizing. "You think that's the problem? What I call him?"

"Don't do this," he says.

"Do what? React like a normal human being?"

He looks down at the kitchen table, picks up a package of tortillas, pinches the corner of the resealable closure, drags his fingers along the opening, tosses the package back to the table. "You're so angry all the time."

"I'm not angry, I'm baffled. You're a smart man. How could this have seemed like a good idea?"

"I can't believe you." He shakes his head at my rancor, my heartlessness, probably my racism still. "When was the last time we did something adventurous? Something good for someone else?" He looks up to the ceiling like he's really trying to remember. "I thought you'd be glad to help him."

"Sure, help him find appropriate accommodations or get him a bus pass or whatever. But what could have possibly made you think I'd want to live with some strange Chinese kid for four months?"

"Stop saying 'Chinese' like that."

"No, really, I want to know. Please. Explain it to me. How could this have made sense to you?"

"What should I have said? 'Sorry, Gary, I'd love to help you so you aren't homeless in a strange country for the entire summer but my wife would really rather not share her bathroom.'"

"That would have been fine, yes."

His shoulders sag and he drops his gaze to the floor, disappointed at my selfishness. I feel exactly the same toward him.

He's right that I used to find his exploits exciting, used to be up for anything. A few years ago I'd have gladly made up a guest bed and shared my bathroom with Gary and laughed as Ethan taught him English curse words. But right now I can't handle any more need in my life, in my home. I don't want the intrusion. I just don't want it. Not all summer long. Not tonight. "Who's going to drive him around, Ethan? Who's going to make him dinner? Wash his dirty underwear?"

"Will you please keep your voice down?"

"He doesn't speak English. He can't understand me."

"I think he'll get the message from your tone."

"As if he could possibly hear my tone over that bridal march."

"I think it sounds alright."

"Are you kidding me? Listen to that sustain pedal."

"Nina, please, he's going to hear you."

"I don't really give a damn if he hears me." *Pachelbel's Canon* stops. Hotdogs pop and burn on the Griddler. I pick up my beer, swipe at the foamy puddle on the counter, look at my husband, his upper body still fluttering. I feel embarrassed, for him, for me, for Gary, for Johann Pachelbel. "Will you please take off that stupid belt?"

He opens his mouth like he's going to say something but instead flips a toggle on the belt. It stops vibrating. He unfastens it and gently lays it on the kitchen table. "He needed help, Nina. And I thought it would be nice to have somebody else in the house, so it's not just the two of us around here all summer."

I stare at my husband, the man I've lived with for seven years, who has apparently come to need a buffer guest in our home to better tolerate my company over the long summer holiday. I can't help but wonder if his desire to have a child isn't motivated by a similar sentiment.

"If you really want me to, I'll tell him he can't stay."

"No." I walk to the sink, pour out my beer. "You already invited him. You can't ask him to leave now."

"I should have talked to you about it first, but don't worry, I'll be in charge of him. You won't have to do a thing."

"I'm going to the gym," I say. "There's a yoga class tonight."

"What about dinner?"

"I'll eat something later."

"No, come on, stay. We can talk more, figure this out."

"I'll be back in a couple hours."

———————

The lights are dimmed in the "Find Your Inner Warrior" yoga classroom. Women of all ages and shapes are unrolling mats, chatting, stretching, sipping from water bottles. I'm glad it's crowded—I can blend in, unnoticed in the back row, and have an hour to myself. I stand on my mat and, with hands on hips, bend to the right into a lateral stretch, trying to unwind, trying not to think of Ethan and Gary sitting side-by-side on the piano bench eating hotdog fajitas. Because of course it was terrific of Ethan to help. Few people are so genuinely, guilelessly kind. And it's that kindness, not the prospect of sharing my bathroom, that upsets me. It's irrational, I know, but I can't help taking personally Ethan's largesse, his goodness, his impulsiveness. His fearlessness. His happiness. These wonderful qualities that leave me feeling small and stingy and rotten.

I exhale, bend deeper into the stretch, and begin to sweat, feeling the stress start to seep out. The woman to my left, middle-aged, gray, and round, leans over in my direction. She sniffs the air and looks at me. "Do you smell that?" she says.

I right myself. "What?"

She sniffs again. "I swear I smell bacon."

"I don't smell it."

"Yuck," the woman says.

On the other side of me a tall blonde college girl looks up at us from the depths of an impossibly deep lunge. "I smell it," she says. "It reeks like an IHOP in here."

"I don't smell anything," I say, sinking to the floor. I bend my knees, close my eyes, drop my chin to my chest, and pretend to concentrate on my lotus position.

Chapter 5

*I*T RAINS ALL NIGHT and does not stop in the morning. On my drive to work, the local NPR affiliate interrupts its regularly scheduled programming to warn of possible flooding throughout the river basin. It's been months since I've felt much enthusiasm walking into the School of Visual Arts Building, but this morning I'm happy to be here. Or at least I'm happy to be out of the house, where the flinty current of my disagreement with Ethan lingers.

It's before eight o'clock and, apart from the deep thrum of rain, the building is quiet. Ramona won't be in for at least a couple hours, and there won't be many students around today since SVA classes don't meet on Fridays. The justification being that students need time to work on their art; the real reason being that faculty consider even four half-days per week professional abuse. Since there isn't much of an audience, Dunbar usually ceases and desists on Fridays.

My office alights as my computer fires up and my email opens with thirty-eight new messages, a few of which are junk, most from faculty and graduate students with routine end-of-term questions, requests, and complaints. At the top of my inbox, a message, sent today at 6:18 A.M., catches my attention:

From: President Ronald Havercamp
To: All Members of the University Community
Subject: Impending Flood

Dear Members of the University Community:

As you should be aware, the United States Army Corps of Engineers has predicted there will be spring flooding this year. In the month of April alone, our county had twenty-two inches of rainfall, more than ten inches above average. With excess groundwater and continued heavy rains in the forecast, we have been told to prepare for flooding far sooner, and far more seriously, than originally expected.

The current prediction is that the spillway will overflow sometime in the next three days, followed shortly thereafter by the river cresting at anywhere from twenty-five to forty feet, meaning we may well reach five-hundred-year flood levels, perhaps as soon as next week. This means many of our riverside buildings could take on twelve to fifteen feet of water.

Those of you stationed along the river will need to begin preparations for worst-case scenario evacuation immediately. Please consult your University Disaster Preparedness Handbooks.

A group of risk management and US Army Corps of Engineer officials will be sending further information and instructions as these become available.

Best Regards,
President Ronald Havercamp

I look out to the cold, quiet atrium. ...*riverside buildings could take on twelve to fifteen feet of water.* As with most things these days, I have a love-hate relationship with the School of Visual

Arts building. It went up during Provost Fontane's heyday, a man who retired last year with the admiration of the community at large and the disdain of faculty and students. Fifteen years ago he spearheaded an initiative to re-energize the university's long-forgotten strategic plan, *Reviving the Promise: Great Opportunities, Bold Expectations.* He requisitioned a faculty/staff task force and gave them instructions to devise policies and procedures that would achieve such definitive goals as undergraduate sobriety and success; academic excellence; faculty productivity; campus superiority. Nobody had a clue what any of it meant, or what the campus was supposed to be superior to, but somewhere along the line a member of the task force dug up a statistic claiming 91% of prospective graduate and undergraduate students make matriculation decisions based on facilities: buildings, landscaping, equipment, and computers. Whether or not this information was true, whether it was even verifiable, it became Fontane's guiding principle.

Over the course of the next decade, he spent more than one billion dollars on what he called "campus enhancement." The university purchased land like it was Oklahoma 1889. They lit out with their money and mission and snatched up any plot, home, or business anywhere near the university. Properties were rented out for profit or demolished for something striking and impractical like the SVA building. Meanwhile, tuition went up and faculty salaries and hires went down to cover the expenses of acquisition and construction. Boy, did the campus look sharp, though.

The SVA building, completed the year before I began grad school, is a special favorite of Provost Fontane's. An über-contemporary three-story steel cylinder with polished cement floors, glass and cork walls, custom-made ergonomic light switches and bionically contoured door handles. It is the harvest of the most protracted and lucrative fundraising effort in university history; after seven years and fifty-six million dollars, it is the campus' crown jewel. The building was designed by world-renowned German architect Karl Stahl, who worked closely, almost giddily, with SVA faculty to create something in the artistic spirit of the school. After moderating a series of charrettes and area-by-area craft colloquia, Stahl concluded the building should be more implied than actual, more formless mechanism than physical object, the architectural features capturing theoretical ideas rather than physical properties, the most foundational being, porosity. This approach, Stahl said, would transport the Artist to a necessarily generative level of existence. The third-floor painting loft, for instance, would not be a room so much as a notion, specifically, "stirring tonality." The second story art library would house not books but rather a concept, "lancing tentativeness."

When I arrived here as a student, I loved this building. Everybody did. Not only was it a feat of architectural glory, amassing one acronymed award after another, it provided validation, even prestige. We artists deserved this, a building, an *idea*, so particular, so extraordinary, it could not be described in physical terms. It was our sanctum, the cradle of our imaginations. And what went on inside could not be diminished by physicality either; yes, we made sculptures and paintings and video art, but the work was so much more than that, so much more than tactility. It was supernatural. Megan Malone's "process program," road kill carcasses she scooped, froze, and arranged around the building, where they'd thaw and decompose, exemplifying the foulest corners of societal decay; Ricky Step's "Corncob in the Cornhole" performance piece, something about processed foods and where Monsanto could shove it; the only slightly less obvious "action sculpture" by, as only she called herself, Massive Michelle: a man's three-piece suit made entirely of unwashed clamshells. It was sacred work, done in sacred space. Capital-A Art. It seems unbelievably silly now but I actually believed that.

These days, walking around the SVA, I rarely find myself pondering the ontological implications of this classroom or that stairway or thinking about the transcendentality that might be underway right at this very moment. Instead, I wonder what metaphysical dilemma prevented Karl Stahl from frosting the floor-to-ceiling windows in the women's bathroom, or how we might mystically remove the mountains of bird shit from the overlapping planarity of our steel exterior.

The building, it turns out, is entirely tangible and stationed alongside the Iowa River. Because of Stahl's focus on porosity and his concern for the Artist's engagement with her surroundings, the physical site was deemed central to the project. Stahl torpedoed the original hilltop city-center location in favor of the riverside lowland, cantilevering the building's second and third floors out over the river itself. It was essential, he said, to integrate the building with environment, making the interior walls, floors and ceilings transparent and permeable, semiporous and glass within the steel chamber, never discontinuous from natural habitat.

The dean of Arts and Sciences, Oscar Reyes, was all too happy to stick the School of Visual Arts Building in the river bog. Not only did its position there improve an otherwise swampy part of campus, it relegated the art faculty to the distant west side of the river, keeping them contained and far away from the administrative center of city and campus.

In spite of the distinction of the building, the SVA maintains its position as university embarrassment, the faculty generally considered a bunch of clowns running loose on the arts campus, their "research" nothing more than the public exhibition of lunacy. It took decades of debate and revision to settle on tenure criteria for art faculty. At one point Dean Reyes, himself a professor of mathematics with a specialization in multivariable operator theory, actually fought to revoke art tenure altogether, arguing that because visual artists don't lecture, publish, present papers, or, really, produce substantive material that might pass even the most basic academic muster, they should not be awarded the honors of tenure. "Where is the text?" he argued. "I see no text whatsoever. It degrades the measurable accomplishments of the serious professors."

The compromise was converting Visual Arts from a department under the College of Arts and Sciences, and Dean Reyes' direct rule, to a school of its own, complete with technical, if not actual, autonomy, and a directorship. It is generally accepted that we continue to exist only because there is an unending supply of eighteen-year-olds disinterested in pursuing more scholastic subjects but with parents willing to pay full tuition, even for a studio art major. It's still technically a bachelor's degree, after all.

Some faculty (Dunbar) consider SVA banishment an act of war while others take it as a badge of honor, a testament to creative indomitability—*you can move us but you'll never stop us.* Suzanne is one of these. She feels the SVA's position corroborates what she believes art must be: ruthless and unapologetic.

On the first day of the first course I took with Suzanne, an upper level sculpture seminar, she distributed syllabi and said, "I expect you to do these projects and have them ready for critiques on the dates listed but you should know," and I swear she looked right at me, "nobody really gives a shit. I'm sure each of you was the best artist in your undergraduate program, and you got all kinds of attention and flattery from your faculty, and all kinds of superior, competitive satisfaction from being better than your classmates, and I'm sure you all have glowing letters of recommendation and scholarships and a sweet portfolio but the truth is, nobody cares. There are many artists better than you, much better, than all of you, and they're out there already, making art, showing art, trying to scrape together lives as artists, and you know what, even they can't do it. They're waiting tables and tending bar and babysitting, *babysitting.* That's what you have to look forward to, and that's if you're lucky, if you're the absolute best and you work the hardest, and if you don't bail out and take a job as a mortgage banker or a high school counselor or a florist, then maybe, *maybe* you'll get to be an artist/babysitter, and still, even then, nobody is going to pay attention to you or your work or your scholarship awards or your portfolio and, sure as shit, nobody is going to give you money for any of it. Except the babysitting. For that, you'll get eight dollars an hour. Congratulations." We were silent. Stunned, furious, heartbroken. Mentally listing the ways and reasons she was wrong. But then Suzanne said, "But you're going to do it anyway. Day in and day out, knowing nobody gives a shit, knowing it won't lead to anything that even resembles a decent standard of living, knowing there is not always going to be a target or even necessarily a clear direction, you are going to make your art anyway because you have to, and you have to do a fucking great job of it, without knowing how you're going to pay your rent or get health insurance or explain it to your father. That's why we're here, all of us, together, me included. Because we're going to do it anyway." And then we loved her. I think some of my classmates actually gaped. Because she was the first person to do us the courtesy of being sincere and because she made us feel serious in our pursuits and capable in our failings. That's Suzanne's power. She has the sort of magic that makes the people around her feel they can be magical too. She makes you think you really are the person you want to be: mighty, original, creative. Able. Free. I still don't know if her speech was inspirational gimmick or personal gospel but I loved her for saying those things. For convincing me, at least at the time, that they were the truth.

When Suzanne asks about my work these days, I lie. "It's going well," I say, "I'm working on a lot of new ideas, stuff I'm really excited about." I tell her I work at home, a few hours here and there, when Ethan is at a late meeting or out with friends. At some point, she stopped asking to actually see this exciting new work, stopped asking if I wanted her help sending my portfolio to galleries. I know she believes I'm still in the fight, but I imagine she thinks I'm on the wrong side now, playing by the establishment's rules instead of resisting them, inventing my own.

The spillway will overflow sometime in the next three days. Begin preparations for worst-case scenario.

I reread President Havercamp's email, verifying my initial understanding. The School of Visual Arts is about to flood. Biblically.

My immediate reaction is to grab my purse and leave, pack it in, abandon my post, let the place go under, not because I want to see the SVA flood but because my fight-or-flight instinct screams, *run for your life!* But Ramona isn't equipped to navigate the school through a natural disaster. And there's no way I'm going home to batten the hatches with Ethan and Gary. For a moment I consider what it means that I prefer a flooding steel silo to my home and husband. I think of Karl Stahl and how his notions of porosity and environmental integration are about to become a lot more than architectural metaphor. I wonder what tips he might have for philosophically dematerializing twelve feet of water.

I open the faculty flood memo I prepared last night and begin making revisions.

Chapter 6

*A*RE WE MEETING OR no?"

It is 10:28 A.M. and, of twelve tenured and tenure-track faculty members, only Hans Mueller, professor of painting and resident prima donna, is in the SVA conference room, sitting at the head of the table, bent over a piece of paper, scribbling. The poor turnout concerns me, not because faculty absenteeism is unusual or especially problematic—what are we going to do if they don't attend meetings, revoke the ill-gotten tenure we fought so hard for?—but because this is one of the few times we actually have something to discuss. Plus I forgot to remind people. The truth is, I suspect everybody is aware of the meeting but when they didn't receive a red-type all CAPS reminder email from me, they took it as a free pass.

"I'm sure everyone's on their way," I say to Hans

He grunts and returns to his scribbles.

What Suzanne told me is that a decade ago Hans Mueller was next in line for directorship and when Ramona was installed instead, he became enraged. He began campaigning to convert the School of Visual Arts into a painting institute and to revert the other areas (ceramics, sculpture, printmaking, graphic design, and photography) back to departments within the College of Liberal Arts. "It's a school of art, not a school of arts and *crafts*," became his catchphrase, but his real argument was basically, "I called it first."

Then, four years ago, Astrologie, a national high-end women's clothing store, selected one of his more colorful, angular paintings to adorn its holiday shopping bags and Hans felt vindicated, his larger point made by big city housewives schlepping Christmas presents home to teenage daughters. He threatened to leave if he wasn't given a raise (he was given no raise) and the promise of directorship (he received no such promise). He insisted his Astrologie painting be hung in the School of Visual Arts atrium, replacing the Jackson Pollock that was there at the time and remains there now.

Though his moment in the spotlight emboldened him, his boorishness obliterated all legitimacy with his colleagues, and he was forced to reverse tactics, from pro-Hans Mueller to anti-Ramona Holme. This position has made him Dunbar's primary ally, despite their being intellectually and sartorially inversed, and together they document her every move—each personnel, budgetary, and disciplinary decision, every out-of-town conference, each administrative meeting, and, worst of all, her SVA arrival and departure times. Lately Hans has observed weakness, and Suzanne told me he's been trying to recruit faculty support for a coup, which, she said, he hopes to execute at the end of this semester, one week from now. He wants Ramona out.

"I saw no reminder email," Hans says. To him, I am Ramona's proxy, and my failures are her failures.

"I guess I thought after nine years of reminder emails, people might be able to remember all on their own."

He grunts and licks at his mustache.

Vanity is part and parcel of Hans' station as luminary artist—the biggest asshole in the room must be the most important. Whimpery bravado, victimized superiority, incessant complaining, general astringency. All the usual delights of any self-respecting pedagogue. But still, these are not the reasons I can't take him seriously. No, that's because of his mustache.

It's really more of a lip tuft than actual facial hair, a feathery fringe that looks like it'd be silky to the touch, like luxuriously conditioned head hair, growing out of his face. It's as if his nose is wearing bangs. Something about the combination of Hans' overerect posture and his globular philtrum causes the shortest of these wisps, the ones just above his lip, to stand at an angle. He curls up his tongue and pokes at the bottom of these barbs, toggles them back and forth like loose teeth. When he's not tonguing his face hairs, he's touching them, and not the classic two-finger mustachio stroke, more like gentle petting. It's prissy and tender and does not at all suggest leadership.

The door opens and James comes into the conference room with Dan Holdt, cowboy ceramicist, one step behind. Ever conscientious in their pursuit of tenure, junior faculty are always attendant and punctual, with or without a reminder email. James sits next to me, looking desperate, and I wonder if he's still upset about my accidentally blackmailing him last night or if perhaps he and Suzanne had a tiff that led to the dissolution of their arrangement. I have an urge to tell him about Ethan bringing home Gary with the hope he, James, might say something like, 'He didn't even *ask* you?' and then maybe lay a hand on my forearm in consolation, rub that hitchhiker thumb back and forth on the inside of my elbow.

Instead he says, "Are we about to be under ten feet of water?"

"Possibly," I say.

"Holdt told me about President Havercamp's email this morning, but I haven't seen it. My phone's dead." He holds up the dead phone as proof.

Maybe you should have gone home last night and plugged it in. "We're going to talk about evacuation," I say.

"Shit," he says. "So this is serious."

"It's just the first floor." I look back at Hans sipping gas station coffee through a brown stir straw and consider the logistical nightmare of evacuating the first floor of the SVA building, ticking off in my mind what we'll have to move: 115,000 slides, a virtually unused archival collection worth over a million dollars, stored in several tons of metal flat files (not on wheels); the ceramics studio, including dozens of barrels of clay, three basically immobile wood-burning kilns, hundreds of lopsided bowls the undergrads made for final critiques; the woodshop, which has a table saw, band saw, and two double-compound miter saws, all of industrial size and strength, an enormous belt sander, and one mean-looking plasma cutter; dozens of computers, desks, and chairs; two photocopiers; three refrigerators that I know of; one commercial-grade espresso machine; five iron sculptures adorning the front and back lawns. And that's just the big stuff. There are closets overflowing with accounting and personnel files, miscellaneous decades-old archives, every manner of art and office supply. It'll all need to be boxed up and hauled out.

It occurs to me this will not be possible. We will be unable to evacuate everything in time for the river cresting. Things will be lost. Equipment. Furniture. Art. We'll have to prioritize, decide what to save and what to sacrifice, designations over which there will no doubt be disagreement. Panic sets in, and I feel my chest constrict. I look around for help, for Ramona.

My growing dismay is interrupted by commotion in the hallway—somebody is pushing at the door handle, struggling to get into the room. The door opens partially and the corner of a cardboard box appears, then retreats, then comes crashing all the way into the conference room. Pete Mustard, a member of Dunbar's current grad claque, stands next to Hans at the head of the table, a refrigerator box strapped over his bare shoulders with twine, hanging on him like a muumuu, his forearms sticking out from the sides through round holes in the cardboard. The box is pasted over with newspaper and magazine clippings, photographs, ribbons, and small toys that look like they came from McDonald's Happy Meals, all of which is covered in colorful scrawlings, doodles, lettering and symbols. Front and center, right at heart level, is a green gourd in the shape of a palm branch, affixed to the box with one nail. I scan the hallway through the glass wall, as if Dunbar might be out there, frying pan in hand.

"I am here!" Pete lifts his arms overhead like a preacher, the refrigerator box rising to expose bare shins that, for some reason, seem to indicate he's naked underneath, calling to mind poor Glory Hedgeman. Why must art-as-statement so often involve nudity?

"I am emissary for Dunbar the Persecuted and ye shall hear me speak." Pete beats twice on his refrigerator box chest. The palm frond quivers.

"Nobody cares." Hans' alliance with Dunbar does not extend beyond Ramona's undoing and most certainly does not include graduate student exhibitionism.

Pete drops his arms like dead weights. "Shoot. Isn't this the faculty meeting? Where is everybody?"

"Hans forgot to send a reminder email," I say.

Hans sucks loudly on the stir straw.

"Will more people be coming? Will Professor Holme be here? I have a whole speech I'm supposed to deliver." I have sympathy for Pete. I do. He's a patsy, but I think of Dunbar and my sympathy curdles.

"Everyone's always late," I say. "They'll get here."

Pete presses his hands flat against the sides of the box and lifts, releasing the weight from his shoulders, which I see have deep red divots from the twine.

"Okay," he says, "I'll be back in ten minutes. Act like you never saw me." He shuffles to the door but, inhibited by the box's girth, can't quite reach the handle. He tries turning sideways and reaching out his hand, but Hans' chair in his way and Pete can't get the angle right. James gets up, walks over, opens the door, and holds it ajar as Pete struggles to maneuver out. He doesn't fit through straight on, so he tries turning on a diagonal, standing on tiptoe and lifting his left shoulder. "How'd I get in here?" he mumbles. He tries forcing the refrigerator box through and bumps one of the McDonald's toys against the doorframe causing it to rip off the box and fall to the floor. "Shoot," he says, and backs up. He attempts bending to retrieve the toy but can't get anywhere near the ground. "Oh forget it." He turns back into the room. "I bet I can fit in that closet."

Nobody objects when Pete opens the door to the storage closet in the corner of the conference room and shuts himself in. And nobody objects when James walks over and clicks the button lock on the closet doorknob.

A few more faculty members trickle in and people are chatting and grumbling. I see Suzanne through the glass conference room wall, scooting down the hall, arms overflowing with papers, a pile of books, her messenger bag, which dangles from one forearm, and what looks like an oversized fuchsia crucifix balanced on top of it all. She sees me watching her and shuffles her load in order to hold up a forefinger signaling, *just one minute*, then disappears into the women's bathroom.

"I wonder if we'll even be able to have fall classes," James says to Dan Holdt.

"I guess it'll depend on how bad it is," Dan says.

Bunny O'Brien walks into the conference room, acknowledging everybody individually with a smile, nod, or wave, then comes to sit on the other side of me.

"Hey kiddo," he says. "How we doing?"

"We're hanging in there, Bunny."

If Hans is resident prima donna, Bunny is resident buttercup. He is professor emeritus of drawing and Ramona's predecessor as director, a post he held for five terms, twenty-five years, through the 70s, 80s, and 90s. Bunny has the precise mien of his namesake, wide-eyed and gray coiffed seemingly since birth, so soft-spoken I used to think he had a speech or hearing impairment. In his older age, he's even got the long, narrow ears. He is the dearest man I have ever known. As leader of the school, Bunny was an asset to the faculty on account of his suggestibility and craving for professional comity. He's everyone's pal, even Hans and Dunbar, and he happily served as decoy and diversion, always taking so much heat from university admins for his incompetence that the faculty could perform Wiccan initiation rituals and it seemed like proficiency in comparison.

At that time, as I understand it, the SVA wasn't the fight-to-the-death free-for-all it is now but more of a commune. People did what they wanted and stayed out of each other's way and always, en masse, out of sight of deans, provosts, and especially, ombudspeople. They settled disputes amongst themselves and, so the legend goes, even collaborated on projects and curriculum now and then. It was when Provost Fontane started in about the fancy new building that the higher-ups began to figure out Bunny wasn't the only monkey in the nuthouse. They cracked down. No more nude drawings strung from the ceiling with human hair; no more twenty-foot towers constructed of railroad ties, erected in the parking lot for "Art happenings only!"; no more students marrying one another for their graduate theses. Personally, I can't understand why it surprised Fontane that Bunny had no aptitude for management, that he could not for the life of him responsibly disperse departmental funds, resolve personnel conflicts, or conduct faculty searches. Why it is assumed that any academic, let alone academic artist, might be capable of these tasks is beyond me.

Nevertheless, Bunny was out, Ramona was in. Poor Bunny, a man devoted, has been lost ever since. As professor emeritus he isn't supposed to attend faculty meetings, but nobody has the heart to tell him he must stop coming. Instead, in its last act of solidarity, the SVA community banded together to indulge Bunny's once and only fantasy: to be part of the group.

"Are we a little behind schedule today?" he asks.

"As usual," I say. I cannot imagine how he'll take news of the flood.

Through the glass wall I see Suzanne exit the bathroom, arms still overfull. She's wearing a loose black off-the-shoulder sweater atop a deep purple pencil skirt and black motorcycle boots, an outfit that complements her strong, curvaceous body. When she moves toward the conference room, she missteps. The crucifix slips from her pile and falls to the ground, bouncing a few feet away from her. The conference room becomes quiet, and all of us watch as she walks over and carefully bends to pick it up.

Suzanne has clout at the School of Visual Arts, not only because she was awarded a Guggenheim three years ago but also because her virtues demand it. She is outspoken and righteous but her countenance is warm and accepting. And she's deft with the CNC plasma cutter, which many people, myself included, find imposing. I watch her through the glass wall and experience a booming echo of envy. I used to want to be just like Suzanne, wanted what she had, wanted, in my dreamiest moments, to *be* her. Now I can only recall that lusty feeling, not actually experience it. Sometimes I wish I did. Sometimes I wish I was still the woman who wanted to be Suzanne Betts.

She snatches up the fuchsia crucifix, rights herself, and knowing she's being watched, bows her head and dips into a curtsy. The conference room breaks into applause, and for a moment I think maybe everything is going to be all right.

Once Suzanne has settled herself and her possessions at the table, the room takes on a new, more impatient air. *We're ready to start.* Hans says, "Suzanne, did you have those papers in the bathroom?"

"Thank you for asking, yes, I did, but I only went number one, and I while I tried to avoid putting down the minutes from the last faculty meeting," she holds up a pile of copy paper and flops it back and forth, "in a colony of fecal bacteria, there is really no way to know for sure." She slaps the pile of papers down on the table, locks eyes with Hans, and licks the pad of her thumb with obscene enthusiasm. "And I didn't have time to wash my hands," she says, "but I'm pretty sure I didn't get any pee on them." She distributes copies of the minutes, and I notice James grin slightly to himself.

I watch James watch Suzanne and sense intimacy. It's different than the last time I was with the two of them. Warmer. More familiar. More assured. Suzanne notices me watching.

"Neens, are we getting this thing going or what?" she asks.

I look at the wall clock. 10:43 A.M. Before I can say anything the closet door rattles, and Pete starts knocking and pushing from the inside. A muffled, "Hello?" comes from behind the closed door. "I think I'm stuck." James, sitting to my left, elbows me gently in the ribs and my neck warms.

Bunny looks at me with concern and walks over to the closet. "What on earth," he says, and turns the doorknob. Pete must have been pushing against the door from the inside because it flies open and he comes hurtling forward, colliding first with Bunny, then Hans' shoulder, then the floor.

He lolls around moaning for a moment then braces himself against the ground to try to stand. "Hang on a minute," he says. "Just a second." He pushes himself up on the side of the refrigerator box and looks at Bunny. "A little help?" Bunny reaches down and offers his hand. "Thanks," Pete says, and hoists himself up. "I'm here, emissary for Dunbar the Persecuted, and ye shall hear me speak."

"Pete, you can't be in here during a faculty meeting," Suzanne says and raises her rubber crucifix at him like a sword. "We," she stabs in his direction, "are" (stab) "conducting" (stab) "business" (stab).

After his second-year exhibition last spring, Suzanne voted to deny Pete's advancement to his third year and completion of his MFA. His show, entitled, *Citizens in Flight: Birds Are People Too*, was an installation of several six-foot-tall papier-mâché pigeons wearing top hats and tuxedos, drinking martinis and champagne. A pigeon cocktail party in the third floor gallery. His artist statement began: *My objective is to take a commonly held presumption and turn it on its head, forcing people to consider their prejudices and assumptions and then rethink their positions based on that fresh perspective.* Suzanne objected not on the grounds that it was an absurd display of meaninglessness, or that it was clearly a Dunbar puppet show, but because there were no girl birds. "So, what, birds are people but females aren't?" Suzanne said. Pete responded with a performance piece wherein he stood before an audience and, one-by-one, lit and blew out a book of matches. He is currently on course to complete his MFA with honors.

Suzanne turns to me. "Nina? A little intervention?"

"I shall not be silenced," Pete says.

"Oh come on, we're not talking about anything important," Dan Holdt says. Suzanne shoots him a disapproving look. "What? I say let the refrigerator box stay."

"Pete. Leave," Suzanne says and jabs the crucifix toward him again.

"Where is the director, Nina?" Hans says.

"I'm sure she'll be here momentarily." I rise from my seat. "She's in discussion with the president, which brings me to our first agenda item."

"Demand number one," Pete says.

"Oh for fuck's sake," Suzanne says.

"Don Dunbar intends to participate in the summer faculty show, but he has conditions, the first of which is that he will be addressed with the title *Don* from now on."

"Alright, Pete, sorry, but you probably should go," I say. "You can tell Dunbar we ganged up on you and forced you out."

"Ok, fine." Pete looks relieved and turns to the conference room door, pulling at the twine on his shoulders. "But can I wait here until after the meeting? I can't get out that door with this box on and, you know, I can't exactly take it off at the moment." He goes to the corner where he stands, still and quiet.

"Fine," I say, and distribute copies of the flood memo. "There was an email this morning from President Havercamp, if you haven't already seen it. There's going to be a flood. The US Army Corps of Engineers expects buildings along the river to take on water."

Suzanne looks up at me. "What does this mean for us?"

I can think of no way to dodge the truth. "We have to evacuate," I say.

"I refuse," Hans says, but stares at me. Everybody does. They're expecting answers. Rescue. A grand plan for diverting floodwaters and protecting the School of Visual Arts. The reversal of disaster. But I have no plan. No rescue. No answers. No energy. I think of Ethan and wish he was here, then consider if there is a way to somehow blame him for this moment of helplessness, him and his optimistic mantra and his desire to have a child and his invitation to Gary. Heat crawls up my spine, and I drop to my chair. *Where is Ramona?*

"Nina?" Suzanne says, imploring.

"We'll be under water in the next day or two, and the best we can do is try to get our stuff out." I speak with what feels like defeat but sounds like gall and then watch as whatever semblance of a meeting we had dissolves into confusion.

Bunny shakes his head and stares at his hands, flat on the table. Hans furiously tongues his mustache. Pete Mustard pulls out an iPhone from god-knows-where and starts, I imagine, tweeting.

"I'm going to find Ramona," I say to nobody, and leave the room.

———————

I can see from the corridor that Ramona's office door is ajar. When I enter, she is there, sitting behind the computer, smiling like a comic book villain. I do not imagine for one second she is engaged in something productive.

"Ramona, I could really use your help. Did you get the president's email?"

"I saw it," she says, and then, "I found him." Her ears are a preposterous shade of crimson.

"Who? President Havercamp?"

"Look." She points to her computer screen.

"I don't want to see any more photos."

"I'm saying, I found him."

"Found who, Ramona? Who did you find?" I am not tender. I'm tired of seeing her like this, unglued and useless, particularly on this day, with a flood coming. It makes me angry. Not angry. Aggrieved. The SVA no longer merits her attention, let alone urgency. Let alone affection.

"Come here," Ramona says. "Look." I turn the corner of her desk, and she presses the space bar on her keyboard. A YouTube video starts, something vaguely familiar. The quality is poor, pre-digital, pre-HD. Women with fluffy hair and large glasses rush around an office noting the time. "11:30," one says. Then, "Soda break," "Soda break," and the women run to the window. Etta James starts singing about making love.

"Yeah," I say, "I remember this commercial." We watch a gorgeous, dark-haired construction worker peel out of a sweaty red t-shirt, open a can of soda, and dip his head back to drink.

"That's him," Ramona says, her voice almost a squeak. "*That's* Lucky."

My confusion must be evident in my expression because, as elaboration, Ramona gestures to the cut-up paperback hanging on her wall. I squint at the framed book cover and recognize the construction worker then wonder what it says about Ramona that, of all the scenarios she could have nailed to the wall, she chose the one that includes a semi-automatic weapon. It's the one choice of hers I can relate to.

"Look at him," she says, minimizing YouTube and bringing up a website headed, *Lovely Bitches, Trampy Books.* "Before he became famous from that commercial, he was a romance hero." She clicks through a series of novel covers—it's no small feat, her ability to distinguish this particular rugged hunk from all the other rugged hunks.

"What's so great about this guy?" I say, more accusatory than wondering.

Ramona clicks over to another tab in her browser, another website. Across the top it reads, One Lucky Devil, beneath which is an image of the interior of a restaurant. "He's a restaurateur in Los Angeles." She drags an open hand through the air and says, "Hollywood," as if it were some magical land.

"Is that better than naked cover model?" I'm seriously asking.

She clicks over to the "Meet Lucky" page. "Look at him." Her gaze drifts momentarily to the picture frame on her wall then back to the handsome fifty-something gentleman in the chef's hat on her computer screen. "He's so happy now."

And there it is. This gorgeous man has moved on from the art of cover modeling and found happiness. Within her dissociative swoon, Ramona has conflated throbbing members and quivering mounds with middle-life contentment. Or at least a path in that direction. Something in my chest cavity crumples.

"You don't know that he's really happy," I say. "He could be faking it for the camera, like he did when he was a model." She looks more hurt than angry, sorry for me, for my distrust. "Can we just talk about the flood?" I say, discomfited. "Did you actually read the president's email?"

"I did," she says, looking a little bothered. But just as I think I might be able to reel her back to reality with the lure of natural disaster, she grins.

"What?" I say.

She turns back to her computer and navigates to One Lucky Devil's "Contact Us" page. Along the right side of the screen, I see a phone number, street address, and email address. I know what she's going to say.

"I wrote to him last night, and I got a message back saying he's glad I emailed and that I should come see him at his restaurant." Her eyes widen, if that's possible. It's the raving look of infatuation, that terrible prelove, more fixation than affection. She is flushed and beautiful. "He wrote me back," she says.

"Was it an autoreply?"

She looks at me like I've just said the most muttonheaded thing she's ever heard, like the "auto" part of autoreply is not the bit to focus on. "I'm just saying, they probably have a standard message that goes out in response to inquiries." She minimizes the One Lucky Devil webpage. "I'm not trying to upset you, I'm just saying…" I drift off. I don't know what I'm saying, I just know I don't feel like indulging her. "I'm sorry, Ramona. I'm a little distracted by everything going on around here." I feel ridiculous and sincere apologizing.

"Read his email."

"Fine, but then will you come to the faculty meeting and help me figure out what to do?"

She stares at me for a few moments. "Ok," she says, like I'm overreaching by asking her to do her job.

She opens her email and double-clicks.

Thanks for writing, and thanks for taking the time to check out One Lucky Devil! I try to respond to email right away, but please don't hesitate to come to the restaurant and visit me in person! I'll be here waiting, ready to make you my famous Pizza Diablo. Hope to see you soon!

Best,
Lucky

Beneath the autoreply is Ramona's message to Lucky. I feel like a creeper, peeking at her private thoughts, but read it anyway.

Dear Lucky,

I can't believe I found you. Let me get the gushing out of the way first: I'm a huge fan. I've looked at all your photos online and have read all the books in which you are the hero. My favorite has to be your depiction of Alec Rodman on the cover of *Inconveniently Wedded*.

I have never written a letter like this, certainly not to someone I've never met. But there are certain things a person knows without explanation or evidence— my feelings for you qualify. I realize you're probably used to gorgeous, buxom women like Carlotta from *Bitter Temptation* or Traci from *Bad Girls Do It Right*. I'm not especially tall and my bosoms are smallish as a consequence of the long-distance running, but I have other qualities. Like you, I'm an artist, an explorer, a woman of expression, and I must tell you: I feel a connection to you, Lucky, as if by some magic. This affection and kinship, even from afar, feel so real. Without even knowing it, you've become a part of my life. I think I could be a good friend to you (Hollywood seems so exciting!), and I know you could show me what passion is all about. I don't think I'm overstating when I say that I'm certain our futures are entwined.

Entwined. Entwined. Entwined.

Yours,
Ramona Holme

The repetition of "entwined" feels menacing, but when I look at Ramona, her smile is kittenish. Against my better judgment, compassion swells in me. For a moment I suspend my disbelief and slip into Ramona's delusion where I enjoy perfect respite—there is no flood in the Lucky fantasy, no Dunbar, no Ethan and Gary, no James and Suzanne, no petulant woe of any kind. I can halfway understand Ramona's choice to stay holed up here.

"See?" she says, thinking the wrung, gauzy look on my face is, like hers, a reaction to Lucky's message. "I think I should go to Los Angeles."

I can't bear to say anything so I just nod and wonder how the federal statute defines cyberstalking. I doubt there are exceptions for earnestness.

"I want to write to him again, but I haven't figured out what to say." She opens a desk drawer and pulls out a pad of paper, flips to a page in the middle of the notepad. "I've got a couple drafts started, but they're not quite right." Her voice is thin, almost falsetto.

A few years ago I set Ramona up on a date. Or, at least I tried to. I was giving her a ride home from the MFA graduation reception, and I remember she was dressed in a peach knee-length A-lined skirt with a rose-colored blouse and, in place of her usual foot-wear—last season's road-worn Nikes—she wore blood red Oxford lace-ups with wingtip broguing and a stacked heel. Those cardinal shoes summoned visions of courtship.

I'd been working at the SVA five years by then, but it was the first time I'd been to Ramona's house. I was shocked at how unremarkable it was. I don't know what I was expecting. Ascetic-sparse. Postwar-démodé, maybe, with endless wood paneling, an avocado-colored push-button stove, wall-to-wall Saxony in some hideous jewel tone. Instead, it was a humdrum ranch done in dispirited suburban-traditional.

Ramona poured me a glass of wine, then led me out to her studio, which was, in staggering opposition to the house, entirely remarkable. This was where her time went, her money, her style, her ardor. Six hundred pristine square feet of cement floors, tool cases, type cabinets with all their teeny drawers, tall triangular cabinets filled with printing furniture, flat files for paper, refinished steel-top imposing tables, a guillotine paper trimmer. Three beloved printing presses.

She showed me around, and I said, "So there's this guy on Ethan's bocce ball team I think you might like."

She pouted in disinclination.

"Mitch. He's cute. He wears cowboy boots." She frowned; it felt weird to me too, vicarious cajolery on Mitch's unaware behalf. "He's a great guy," I said, a little too breezy. "I could give him your number."

She gave an ambiguous shrug, grabbed a lever on the 10×15 Chandler and Price, fidgeted with the handle. "It would have been fun to have had you in my printmaking class when you were in grad school."

I drank some wine. "Mitch owns Greener Grass. Do you know it? It's a landscaping company?"

"How was Whiting? Did she cover letterpress the semester you had her?"

"Not really. Not in any depth."

"If you misfeed the paper, you just use the throw off lever to avoid printing on the tympan."

"He's funny, Ramona. Sweet-funny, not mean-funny. But still."

"See," Ramona said. "It rotates the back shaft and allows the chase bed to close against the platen. That's how the impression is made." She pulled the long handle in demonstration, distraction, avoidance. "What the…" She pulled again. "It's catching." Without taking her eyes from the press, she handed me her glass of wine and reached for an oil can. Along the left side of the press, by the curve-spoked flywheel, she bent down, oiled here, oiled there, tried the lever again.

"He's single, never married. I think he's probably forty, forty-five, but very active. He does RAGBRAI every summer."

"Maybe one of the bolts is overtightened or gunked up." Ramona went to her tool chest, found a socket wrench and a filthy rag, climbed around the side of the press again, hitched up the peach skirt, and knelt down.

I think at that point I made a joke, something flip about her ignoring Mitch completely and he wasn't even in the room. I don't remember exactly. But I do recall Ramona's expression, the care and concern on her face, the tinge of carnality, the perfect absence of self-awareness. I remember thinking, *How can I set her up on a date? She's already in a committed relationship.*

Ramona stood, came out from behind the press, her knees red, a swipe of grease on her hip that looked like the state of Tennessee. "Something's binding. It must be the throw-off saddle."

"I guess I should get going."

"You don't want another drink." It wasn't a question, just rote courtesy. The easy desire in her voice told me she longed to get her hands back on the press.

"Ethan's probably waiting," I said.

"Okay." She took a denim printer's apron from a hook on the wall, draped it over her neck, and stepped behind the press. "Let's see here …" She squatted down, her skirt up at her hips, the apron across her knees, both hands inside the back of the press. She didn't notice when I left her studio, got in the Subaru, and drove away.

Suzanne told me once that inertia is the quickest form of sabotage. If you really want to ruin things, do nothing. I think about evacuating the SVA building, about Ethan at home with Gary, probably trying to get the Contour Core Sculpting Belt on the neighbor's German shepherd. If he was here, he'd tell me to help Ramona with her email, to encourage her. He'd say, "Why do you get to decide Lucky isn't going to fall in love with her? Maybe he will. Maybe she's right. Maybe their futures *are* entwined." I imagine Ethan bent over Ramona's shoulder in composition, the two of them penning the gooiest of love notes then together clicking *send* just as the tidal wave comes crashing through the office window. I look down at Ramona, flipping through her notepad then turn and leave without saying anything at all.

Back across the atrium, the conference room is empty. It's been ten minutes since I left and the faculty have disbanded. I go to my office, shut the door, sit at my desk, close my eyes, and listen to the hammering rain against the steel building. The sound is ruthless, not so much severe weather as the din of carpet-bombing, intended as much to demoralize as destroy.

I compose a quick email to SVA faculty, grads, and undergrads, informing them that classes are canceled, personal possessions on the first floor of the building are about to be drenched, and general evacuation is underway. I implore them to help. I beg. I tell them the future of the school depends on their moving slides, easels, desks, chairs. I tell them they are needed.

Down the back hallway I pass the ceramics studio and see Dan Holdt and a bunch of undergrads sealing barrels of clay, Dan calm but commanding, issuing instructions. The next room is the woodshop, and Suzanne and James and a pack of students are working to organize tools and table saws, debating, I assume, what can be moved and what will be left behind. There are footsteps up and down the building's central staircase. Voices curl down through the open atrium. The hollow sucking sound of the heavy gallery doors being pulled open, the elevator chiming off the floors. The commotion of activity competes with the pounding of the rain.

"Hey." Suzanne is looking up at me from the floor where she sits, legs splayed, hand tools, nails, screws, and god-knows-what spread around, an open box at her side.

"I see you got things going," I say.

"The plan is to move as much as possible up to the second and third floors, just jam the galleries full, and get personal stuff out of the building—computers, works-in-progress, anything people want in the immediate future, any illegal contraband they don't want to be caught with," she winks, "anything that shouldn't be in a building full of toxic floodwater, or, more like it, anything that'll add to the toxicity."

I think of the logistical nightmare of inventorying and tracking all that university property, which is probably what I should be doing as others pack and haul. I comfort myself with the fact that even if I was my usual diligent administrating self, I'd be unable to record everything or stop a certain amount of pilfering.

"James told me people upriver have lost animals, their pets, cats, dogs, you know, rabbits, but also livestock, cattle, thousands of chickens they couldn't evacuate in time, washed away, dead, drowned." She turns a stone hammer over and over in her hands. "Can you imagine, your pet, your dog, or whatever, washed away in a flood? And now their losses will literally be poison to us because all those poor animals are in the water and there's a terrible risk of infection, like, from the debris and garbage and dead bodies, I guess, and, I mean, here we are, suddenly at risk for dysentery and all those poor people are mourning their pets." She puts the stone hammer in a box and picks up an oval scraper.

It seems preposterous to worry about stone hammers and personnel files. Unseemly. The thought of rescuing all that stuff leaves me exhausted—the physical labor, sure, but mostly the implication of hope.

Suzanne is waiting for me to respond, and when I don't she says, "So I assume it's cool if we put everything upstairs. I had to wing it in there."

"I know. I'm sorry," I say. "That's fine, everything upstairs." There is a low rumbling in the hallway. Two girls stagger toward me lugging a handcart loaded with flat files. Even together they struggle under the weight of their haul but their faces show resolve. I watch them lurch along but say nothing. Do nothing. I do nothing. I am going to do nothing. I am going to let this happen. This flood. This ruin.

I turn back to Suzanne. "I need to run out," I say. "Going to grab some supplies from home."

"Hurry," she says, her focus already back on the tools. "We need you here."

Chapter 7

 T THE START OF the fall semester three years ago, a group of four or five students—graduates and undergraduates, all disciplines—came to my office with a request: administrative support for a city permit application. They wanted to have a ceremonial fire outside the SVA. To burn us in effigy. Ramona, me, a few no-good faculty members, one or two distastefully generous donors.

The student group, Retinal Waggery, was led by Robert Blitstein. Bobby, he was called until grad school when he started going by the monogram, Blitz. According to Blitz' permit application, the Wags, as he called his membership, wanted to parade from the painting studios and down the hill to the SVA building where they would hold some kind of protest and then, on a pyre of "hysterically inferior figure paintings," burn their larger-than-scale papier-mâché effigies.

Blitz laid out their basic plan and then presented their decree, *Institutional Wagification*, a nonsensical mash-up of Dadaism, anti-art ethos, ecstatic confrontation, the cerebral arts, a rejection of postmodernism along with an ironic embrace of conformism, all executed through the disruptive betterment of society and culture, with one eye toward clownery and witticism. Their artistic philosophy. Or, as I joked with Ramona at the time, their artistic pathology. Normally, I would have suspected Dunbar of masterminding something so zonkers, but he was on leave that semester. Plus, buried amid the confused claptrap were valid criticisms—pervasive grade inflation, unfair admission processes, systematic favoritism. Dunbar would never be party to something even secondarily sensible. Suzanne signed the permit application as faculty sponsor, which was the only reason I didn't shut them down right away. Instead, I passed it on to Ramona—let her be the party pooper.

Later that week, Ramona met with Blitz, Suzanne, and a city fire marshal. I wasn't in attendance, but after the meeting, I went back to her office, curious to hear how Blitz took refusal. I was sure Ramona would deny the request—they wanted to torch her likeness, after all—but she didn't. She not only approved their plan, she persuaded the fire marshal to go along by agreeing to submit the permit application in her own name. A week later, she presented it to the city council in person, insisting Blitz and his group be allowed to proceed.

It was advertised as The Ravishing Riot and Other High Heights of Hypocrisy. The tagline was, *What kind of artist are you if you haven't learned to hate yourself?*

To my annoyance, Blitz came around almost daily for several weeks, hammering out the niceties of his program. Variety acts, displays, demonstrations, and refreshments but also safety procedures, university liability coverage, bad weather contingency plans, arrangements for fire, medical, and hazardous materials emergency professionals. Blitz had a talent for detail, and when the big day came, he had school-wide momentum as well.

It was a Friday, the vernal equinox, when Ramona, the fire marshal, the rescue crew, and I gathered in the parking lot. What I remember is creeping suspense; it was going to be embarrassing and probably moronic, but eventful. There would be marching. There would be fire. After a few minutes, the opposition arrived, most of them painters, the anti-anti-art group, themselves protesting Blitz' conceptual art drivel. But there was nothing to resist. No Suzanne. No Blitz. No pyre, no effigies. No witticisms of any kind. We waited two hours, me calling Suzanne every twenty minutes. No answer. Nothing.

In the tradition of World Art Hate Day, Blitz' Ravishing Riot and Other High Heights of Hypocrisy was an unevent. Imaginary expression. Mental art. A happening in theory only. Rather than attend, Blitz asked nonparticipants to spend 5–8 P.M. actively loathing populist art. They were encouraged to visit university galleries and abhor the work, violently and with prejudice. To be outspoken about their own boring, hateful work, work deemed interesting and relevant by School of Visual Arts curators—Ramona, me, a handful of faculty members. Those of us abstractly effigized.

What I didn't find out until much later was that Ramona knew all along. She knew nobody was going to show up. She not only let it go forward, she kept Blitz' secret. She let him publicize and plan, let the Wags provoke the painters. She thought it was silly— "Does Blitz actually think he's the first person to stage a conceptual unevent? Does he think this is *originality*?"—but she believed unequivocally in his right to expressive exploration, however ridiculous. It wasn't about her or her time or the waste of her time. It was about the students. About amateurs becoming artists.

The SVA is situated on the east side of River Street, which I can see from my position in the parking lot, is halfway underwater, the low parts, the dips, little lagoons. The main SVA entrance is still high and dry, but a soft wake laps at the back steps, and I wonder if we'll have even twenty-four hours before we're displaced.

I follow a detour for a few blocks, winding through the fancy neighborhoods around the park rather than my usual straight shot away from the school, along the water. I drive north half a block, then take my first left into Manford Heights. College Street Bridge is closed; the churning river has reached the bridge deck and will, in a matter of hours, minutes, seconds, overtake the bridge completely. Through the downpour, I squint to see if there are any animals trapped there. For some reason, I imagine a small pink pig treading water, gargling mouthfuls of contaminated river water, squealing for help. That is not what I see. Instead, it looks like a garbage truck dumped its entire load into the river. What appears to be an oven is lodged where the roiling water meets the bottom of the bridge, debris swirling around it. When the river does overtake the deck, when it finally breaches the confines of its banks, that oven will end up somewhere in town, perhaps in the SVA building, perhaps where my desk now sits.

This is a failure on someone's part. It has to be. If a large kitchen appliance has floated downriver and become stuck on College Street Bridge, surely someone must have known this flood was coming days, maybe even weeks ago. Why are we only finding out this morning? Why is it not until disaster is upon us, consuming us, that we become aware of the peril?

Maybe this is just the way crises come. Abruptly. A biblical flood in your email inbox. An emergency evacuation on your faculty meeting agenda. A long-term houseguest upon your piano bench. A newborn baby with your salad niçoise, crudely dressed with talk of a bygone abortion. Bon appetite.

I brake, slowing the Subaru, and come to a full stop, the only car at the four-way intersection at Craggy Shore Drive and Milo Avenue Rain beats the roof of my car, syncopated, penetrating, firing straight through my eustachian tubes and directly into my brain. I have uncharitable things I need to say to Ethan.

In our neighborhood, Cicada Flats, our house will be close to the flood but almost certainly untouched. Ours is the oldest home in the area, the original farmhouse for the acreage, and it sits atop the highest point on the city's lowest tract of land, a rise right in the middle of what's now Monroe Drive. Cicada Flats is the northwesternmost sector of the city that's still considered "original," packed with mature trees, brick streets, older homes with small bedrooms, low ceilings, and original woodwork, detached garages, alleyway entrances—not a ranch home in sight. All the essentials of an acceptably hip college town neighborhood.

I pull into the driveway, cut the ignition, get out of the car, and run to the house, the rain coming down so hard it stings my bare arms and shoulders. After yoga last night, Ethan and I didn't speak. I went to bed early while he and his houseguest played Nintendo Wii. I didn't know what to say, didn't know how to apologize when I'm not sorry exactly. Didn't know how to explain that it wasn't about Gary. It was about him, Ethan, and me. That I don't necessarily *not* want to have a baby. It's just that I don't know if I *do* want to have one. And shouldn't I? If I'm going to bring a human being into the world, like it or not, kid, shouldn't I, at the very least, want it? Yearn for it, as I understand people do? As Ethan apparently does?

I switch on the entryway light and see dirty dishes on the coffee table. There are shirts and boxer shorts draped over the arm of the couch, blankets and pillows heaped on the cushions, inside-out socks in the passageway to the kitchen, pants in a ball in the corner by the reading lamp, an open upheaved suitcase at the bottom of the staircase. My phone chimes from somewhere in my purse, and I dig it out, certain it's Suzanne asking for boxes or duct tape or rope. It's a text from Ethan, as if he somehow knew I just stepped into our house. Marital intimacy. Psychic connection. *Gone to help sandbag Beldon Ave. If you get home before us, sorry for the pigsty.*

Again, I picture a pig treading water.

Beldon Avenue marks the easternmost border of Cicada Flats and abuts the river for four or five long blocks. All the homes along that stretch, our neighbors, some of them friends, will flood. All of those families will be displaced, all of their ovens afloat downstream.

Upstairs in my bathroom, I open a middle dresser drawer and root around. Maybe I should join Ethan and Gary on Beldon Avenue. Maybe I should go back to the SVA and help pack or keep inventory or examine our insurance policy. Or maybe I should just sit here in my warm, dry second-story bathroom until someone comes to tell me it's all over. I pull out an old t-shirt, toss it to the armchair, and undress.

I survey my reflection in the full-length mirror. Rain-slick arms, long, dark hair, wet and sticking in loops and tangles against my collarbone and chest, my ratty blue cotton bra, crooked, the right cup scooched up an inch higher than the left, my breast peeking out a little beneath the underwire. I unhook the bra and let it fall to the floor, run my hands over my stomach, push on the curves of my thighs until they're Kate-Moss-narrow, poke at my soft hips. There is no force in this body, no intent. A chill pricks the top of my head and sweeps down my neck, then back, and I look at my forearm as goose bumps rise and the soft hairs go erect.

Over at my dresser, I dig through the lowest drawer for a pair of work jeans I haven't seen, let alone worn, in years, which I find bunched up in a stiff wad and wedged into the vacant space beneath the bottom drawer, technically on the bathroom floor below the dresser. I heave the denim ball to the armchair where my t-shirt lays.

Ethan, I'm sure, did not waver this way. When Karl from a few houses down or Margaret, Karl's burly wife, came knocking and asked if he'd help sandbag, Ethan probably didn't consider making up an excuse not to go. He didn't feel helpless or exhausted. He probably didn't say, "Yeah, sure, I'll be there as soon as I can," and then take his sweet time, maybe not go at all. No, he probably ran inside, peeled off the Contour Core Sculpting Belt, threw on whatever clothes he could find, stepped into his rain boots, and then, with young Gary in tow, flew out the door.

It has always mystified me, Ethan's abiding sense of forward movement, his talent for certainty, his gaping void where impulses to deflect, equivocate, and second-guess ought to be. I have never known him, not once, to engage in the convention of self-doubt meant to follow decisions large and small. He never wonders what it might be like if he'd done A instead of B, if he'd skipped C altogether, if he'd made a move toward D, if only F could have been avoided. He does not look back on his life, half over now, and wonder, *How did I end up in this place? This was not the plan.*

I trot back downstairs picking up articles of clothing as I go—I am disconcerted because I cannot tell which belong to Gary and which to my husband—collecting plates and glasses from the living room. I take my load to the kitchen, drop the dirty clothes in a heap next to the door that leads to our Tales-From-the-Crypt basement and the laundry room, and place the dishes in the sink.

There is an open bag of crusting shredded cheddar cheese on the counter and a stack of staling flour tortillas next to it, no bag in sight. Down the counter, the Griddler is unplugged but slick with hotdog slime, a greasy pair of tongs wedged beneath it. On the kitchen table, amid beer bottles and what look like puddles of salsa, are the seeds and shriveled cores from green and red peppers. I notice a stray tortilla chip in the middle of the floor and am struck by a memory of something that happened a couple years ago, maybe more, prior to Dunbar's restraint from the SVA, well before Ramona read her first bodice ripper. It was a weekday, some regular evening, and I was at the kitchen table reading *Lucky Jim*, which Ethan had given to me the Christmas before. It was chilly out, I was wearing sweatpants and an old zip-up fleece, and when

I ran to get a pair of Ethan's wool socks, the kitchen tile was like ice under my toes.

I had come home from work early that day, a luxury I used to have the professional leisure to indulge, and was reading, drinking beer, probably Goose Island Honker's Ale, eating a tube of Ritz crackers, trying to hold out for dinner until Ethan returned from a faculty meeting. When he finally got home, after 8:00 P.M., I was well into Jim Dixon's berserk tear of self-destruction, a collection of glass bottles on the kitchen table, the tube of crackers long emptied. I was engrossed in some part of the book, I can't remember what, and didn't hear the front door open but gradually became aware of the small sounds of my spouse arriving home—unzipping and hanging up his jacket, sniffling a little from the cold, dropping papers or mail on the coffee table, kicking off his shoes, closing the front door. I pretended not to notice because I wanted to finish reading some scene in the book, and when Ethan walked into the kitchen and came up behind me, he tried to be quiet, tried not to disrupt my absorption. Some movement caught my peripheral attention and I turned to see my husband bend down, pick up something off the floor, stand upright, and put something in his mouth, a cracker, one I must have dropped hours earlier. He took two steps toward me and, still chewing, kissed the top of my head. "Hey, sweetheart." He palmed the side of my neck, his hand cold from outside. "How do you like the book? Funny, huh?"

That moment, the ease and intimacy of it, moved me. It was as much an endearing display of Ethan's inattention as it was a beat of marital communion; of course he could eat his wife's discarded food off the kitchen floor. It was his wife, his kitchen, his floor, his food. It was all the same. I smiled up at him from my chair, put the book upside down on the table to save my place, and led my comely, meeting-weary husband to our bedroom.

Today, if Ethan ate my hours-old food off the kitchen floor, I would not find it sweet. It would not inflame my desire or blind me to the unhygienic fact that my tongue and other body parts would be inside a mouth that just ate from a dirty floor.

I pick up the errant tortilla chip and bring it close to my face, no more than a couple inches from the tip of my nose, and consider eating it as a kind of karmic sacrifice to the Gods of Connubial Amity and Tolerance. But at the last second, just as I'm about to stick it in my mouth, I am grossed out by dirt flecks and fuzz and tiny black hairs I'm pretty sure I see. I toss the chip into the garbage can and brush my fingers off on my pant leg.

Chapter 8

EVERAL SIDE STREETS ARE blocked by police cars with lights flashing. Three or four pairs of officers walk the street, knocking on doors, I assume informing residents of the severity of the situation, telling them they may want, or may be required, to leave their homes. I turn down a still accessible portion of Manchester Avenue and pull to the curb. The sandbagging crew is stationed in an empty lot in the crook of the street, which follows a crook in the river. The far end of a thigh-high burlap wall disappears behind the house to the north; Ethan and Gary are at the other end, the end closest to me, working to extend the wall to the south. Strings of rainwater wing off Ethan's hair and chin, but he doesn't seem to notice. They're working as a team, Gary dragging over sandbags from a pile in the center of the empty lot, Ethan heaving them atop the wall and situating them, airtight and structurally sound. Ethan is wearing jeans and an orange Hawaiian button-down—he obviously did grab whatever clothes he could get his hands on—and Gary is wearing gym shorts and a red and white sweatshirt, a Christmas sweatshirt, it looks like, with snowflakes up the arms and around the collar. My Christmas sweatshirt. It's soaked, the sleeves sagging, misshapen and heavy like old lady upper-arms. The helplessness I felt all morning is replaced with the sting of exclusion then quick annoyance.

My phone rings in my purse, and I dig it out, push the green answer button without looking to see who's calling. Any interruption will do.

"Hello?"

"Nina, it's Mom, are you guys alright?"

"We're fine," I say, and watch as Ethan pushes his hair back off his forehead, slaps Gary on the shoulder.

"Are you flooding? I saw it on the news. It looks awful. Tell me what's happening."

"The house is fine, but we're evacuating the SVA. They're saying we could get ten or twelve feet of water."

"Oh, honey, no, I'm so sorry."

When people ask my mother what I do, she says with pride, 'Nina is an artist.' She has always supported my creative pursuits, almost to the point of covetousness, believing that a life of creativity, particularly for a woman, indicates unconventionality. She and Suzanne are likeminded in this way. In fact, my mother adores Suzanne heartily and wishes, I suspect, that I was more like her. Along these lines, she maintains an impression that I got stuck with my office job. No matter how adamantly I insist I am not one of those disgruntled individuals who believes she was cut out for something better, who feels working as a university staffer does not represent her "full potential," my mother feels slighted on my behalf. I tell her I have a gift for it, *administravia*, an ambition even. The challenges are manageable, and the means of resolving them, available. If the Intermedia grads want to avail themselves of the city's Urban Chicken Policy, I help them do it then revoke their privileges when they start hosting "Peep Shows," live layings and hatchings. Animal-lovers' exhibitionism. Or when a sculpture student wants to make a latex mold of her derrière then cover it in glitter and fit it with a belted harness so that it's a wearable accessory, I explain, in very small words, that she's welcome to proceed, only not in the shared, public undergraduate sculpture loft. What I do not have to do is struggle to summon creative motivation when there is no endgame. No point, really, beyond Suzanne-style do-it-anyway bombast. But my mother continues to presume my position as administrative coordinator, as compared to, say, associate professor, indicates subversion. I was screwed. There's no other explanation. It never ceases to amaze me how oppressive maternal love and support can be.

"We'll be alright," I say.

"Is Ethan helping, I hope?"

My mom likes Ethan, even loves him sort of, but she blames him as well for derailing my once auspicious career. He crippled me with love, blinded me, rendered me incapable of thinking beyond our relationship, made me powerless to create original art. I tell her the same lies I tell Suzanne—I work at home when I find the time, I have new ideas I'm excited about. In truth, her attitude makes me angry and defensive. There is no saboteur, certainly not Ethan. If anybody did any screwing, it was me, of myself. These are my choices she's condemning, not some misfortune that befell me against my will. And deep down, deep deep deep down, when I'm not there and not talking about it and not thinking about it, I still dearly love the School of Visual Arts.

"Ethan is sandbagging our neighborhood." Across the street Ethan turns in my direction, and I almost lift my hand to wave but instead sink low in my seat. As if he could even see me through the rain. As if he wouldn't recognize my car.

"I hope you're not killing yourself for that job," my mom says.

"No, you're right. It's probably time we let the SVA sink into the river."

"I never thought I'd hear you say that."

"I'm kidding, Mother. Of course we're evacuating, and of course I'm going to kill myself helping." It sounds true when I say it aloud.

"Please take care of yourself."

"The river's cresting soon. It'll all be over in a day or two." I watch as Ethan hoists several sandbags across his back, marches along the wall like a soldier. A fresh canker sore flares inside my lower lip.

"Maybe this will be a good time to put your energy into your own work. I mean, it's tragic, no doubt, but maybe this flood will be a good thing." My mom, being supportive. I tongue the canker sore's metallic surface.

"This isn't good for anybody," I say.

"Of course not, that's not what I meant."

I wonder what she'd say if I told her Ethan wants to have a baby—I honestly don't know. If I tried to talk to her about my hesitations regarding motherhood, I imagine my mom, projectionist that she is, would say it's no wonder I'm resistant after what she's been through. She finds it impossible that I do not consume and metabolize her life experiences as my own. She cannot imagine, for instance, that had it been me who had an affair with my much older, married boss and become pregnant with his child then ended up alone after he admitted he had no intention of leaving his wife and children to start a new family with his mistress, I would not have felt betrayed or victimized. I would have felt heartbroken and foolish. And I would not have had the child anyway, out of heartsickness and spite.

"The flood's terrible for us. There's some question whether or not the SVA will even be able to hold fall classes." I'm only saying this to make her feel bad about being dismissive, but I find myself a little crestfallen at the thought of having to cancel classes.

"Are you sure you're safe there? Maybe you and Ethan should drive here for the weekend and wait it out."

"We can't." I almost say, *we've got Gary with us*, but instead, "There's way too much going on. We need to be here."

"Ok, honey, whatever you think."

What comes to mind then, as it does in regular intervals, is my wedding night, sitting at the sweetheart table, my mother across from me, several vodka tonics deep, telling me how happy it makes her that I married the man I loved. It's rare for my mother to be drunk, rarer still for her to be confessional, and I was careful not to disrupt the moment, to keep her going as long as possible, to see what she might say. I remember feeling like Lennie Small with a soft helpless bunny in my hands, stroking it out of affection, trying not to be too rough but knowing it was going to end badly.

"Your father was a sonofabitch," my mother said. "He was a tough guy, you know? But still, he was the love of my life."

"I know, Mom."

"The truth is," she said, leaning in, "if he came back, even now, it's terrible, I know, but I'd leave Richard for him." My stepfather, to whom my mother had been married for twelve years by then, the man who had only a few hours earlier walked me down the aisle, was, at the time, flailing about on the dance floor, arm-in-arm with one of Ethan's cousins. "Your father always told me we didn't match. He said he was Cary Grant and I was Phyllis Diller. He thought I was ridiculous." She looked at me through glassy, made-up eyes. "Do you think I'm ridiculous?"

"I think you're spectacular, Mom. You're Katharine Hepburn."

I told her she felt admiration, not love, for my biological father and that those things were not the same.

"You never knew him," she said, which was true. For some reason when I think of my father, I picture the back of his head, his thick, dark, pompadour. I suppose this was what did my mother in, that luscious black man-hive. I have imagined his bouffant growing silver over the years, first in streaks, then all over, the style never changing.

I told my mother, on my wedding night, "You can't possibly believe I'd be better off if I'd grown up in a household with some macho asshole, just because he happened to have gotten you pregnant. That's not how it works." She didn't say anything, but I will never forget the way she looked at me, her expression as transparent as the tears running down her rouged cheeks: *You might not have been better off*, it said, *but I would have*.

I hear beeping and it snaps me back into the moment. "Mom, hey, I have another call. We'll talk later, ok?"

"Ok, sweetie, be careful. Call with news."

"I will."

"Love you."

I click over to the other line. "Hello?"

"Nina, thank god."

James. Thank god. "What's up?"

"We need you here. It's hitting the fan. Everyone's going apeshit. Campus police showed up." He's panicky.

"Campus police?"

"They say we have to get out today. They're trying to padlock the building."

"Where's Suzanne?"

"She's, uh, indisposed at the moment." An image of the back of Suzanne's fellating head pops into mind, and I wonder if James is breathless not out of panic but another, more corporeal, sensation.

"I'll be right there," I say.

I take a last look at Ethan, shirtless now, standing alongside Gary, the two of them bent together in cooperation, and pull from the curb.

Chapter 9

 MEDLEY OF OVERLAPPING VOICES greets me inside the SVA atrium, Suzanne's alto bark cutting above the protestations of the men she's admonishing. Pete Mustard is there, still wearing the refrigerator box, standing behind Suzanne, and Dunbar behind Pete, the three of them poised single file along the staircase, berating a bunch of campus police officers, lined up perpendicularly against them. A standoff between The Artists and The Man. Dunbar must be in heaven. James is off to the left, close to my office door, and clumps of bystanders are gathered, whispering to one another, taking photos with, and talking on, cell phones. It takes me a second to figure out why Suzanne isn't stomping around—it's not because she is, as I feared, *in flagrante*, but rather, like Dunbar and Pete, she's handcuffed to the staircase railing. She notices me, strains against the handcuffs, flaps her free hand.

"Nina, thank god, these fascists are under the impression we live in a police state, and they can handcuff anybody they want to a staircase." She turns back to the row of cops. "This is a violation of my civil rights, freedom of speech, freedom of assembly..." She cocks an eyebrow. "The First Amendment, motherfuckers. I can say whatever I want." Dunbar is nodding along with Suzanne but looking at me, spiteful and jolly. Pete Mustard looks so tickled I worry he might pee his refrigerator box.

"Suzanne," I say, pointed, abrupt, trying to get her to stop. She keeps her eyes on the cops but doesn't say anything further.

The officer closest to me looks like he's in charge. The personification of mid-life torpor, sixty-ish, his round middle squeezed into a wash-worn uniform, graying hair clipped high-and-tight, an exhausted look on his sun-spotted face. He's doing his best to play the part, but I can tell his heart is not in it. I become aware I did not put my bra back on.

"I'm Nina, I'm the administrative coordinator here." I extend my hand, and he shakes it, his fingers moist, like he's nervous or maybe ill.

"Officer Rick Bigelow," he says.

I smile. "Nice to meet you. I'm sorry for all this trouble," I wave back toward the staircase. "It's been a rough day around here, as you can imagine." I am polite. Beyond polite, I am sweet, an orientation that does not come easily at the moment. I ignore the prisoners, now bickering amongst themselves, hoping to indicate their being handcuffed does not distress me in the least, that I assume they are rightly restrained, that my only objective is cooperation. I too am playing my part: reasonable spoilsport to Suzanne's righteous firebrand. I wonder if Officer Rick Bigelow can tell my heart is not really in it either.

"We're past apologies, ma'am," he says.

I look at Suzanne, swiping at Pete behind her. "I can see that. Can you tell me what happened?"

"The lady," he points to Suzanne, "is being held for assaulting an officer. She became agitated when I told her we were here to evacuate the building. She threatened Michelson over there. Kind of slapped him when he took out the padlock."

"We can't leave, you jackass. We're nowhere near ready. We'll lose everything." Suzanne's voice is strident and airy, getting hoarse from yelling. People in the crowd, which seems to have swollen, applaud. Somebody hoots in support. "It's fucking ridiculous," Suzanne continues, encouraged. "The water's not even up to the building. It'll be at least a day before it's in here. We can't just abandon everything to be destroyed. We won't. We will not." I appreciate that Suzanne is prepared to fight tooth and claw for the SVA, but good god, please, for once, just shut up.

Someone in the growing crowd, some unseen student, yells, "Fuck you, pig!" Applause erupts, more hooting. I picture Officer Bigelow treading water in the filthy, bloated river.

"Ok, alright, hold on a minute," I say, addressing the room but looking at Suzanne. I give her a *be-quiet-let-me-handle-this* look and turn back to Bigelow. "Why do we have to evacuate so suddenly? I thought we had a couple of days."

"President Havercamp's orders, straight from the US Army Corps of Engineers, the governor, the mayor," Bigelow says.

"We'll lose everything." Suzanne is shrieking. "Everything!"

"This flood is coming faster than anybody expected," Bigelow says. "The river could crest today, this afternoon maybe, and this facility is unsafe for occupation. We've been ordered to evacuate everyone, effective immediately."

I feel something like fear, like the taste of metal, a stomach-dropping dive, the ground moving beneath me or the sky opening above. Or maybe that's guilt I feel because now I'm off the hook; here is Officer Bigelow with his badge and his handcuffs and his orders. Evacuate and padlock the building. Nothing I can do to save the SVA, even if I wanted to. We'll lose everything, yes, but it's out of my hands. I don't know if I want to punch him or hug him.

"It's fucking bullshit." Suzanne is still at it. I turn to her again, shoot her the same *be quiet* look. Dunbar grins at me.

"What about those two?" I say. "What did they do?"

"The one, it seems, is trespassing. I've been informed," he jabs a thumb at James, "that he's not allowed in the building. And also he's, you know," he waggles a hand toward Dunbar, "I don't know the official term. Nuts? He was yelling something about his mission and waving a frying pan around. We have to take threats of violence seriously."

"A frying pan?" I say. "Really?" I turn back to Dunbar, and there's that metal taste again, like I have blood in my mouth. I suck the canker sore, hot and painful now, the center a volcanic crater. It's Mount St. Helens 1980 on the inside of my lower lip.

"When I went to restrain him, that's when the other assailant, the joker in the cardboard box, came out of nowhere and accosted me, scratched my arm up with those toys and such. Kept saying, 'unhand him.'" Bigelow snorts in mocking disapproval. I want to hug him. Definitely.

"That's terrible, I'm so sorry, but, honestly, I'm not surprised, knowing the two of them." I wear an extravagant glower, ensuring Bigelow registers my contempt for Dunbar and Pete. "Everybody's under a lot of stress because of the flood. Maybe we can all sit down and talk like the civilized adults we usually are. I'm sure we can figure out what's next." Arrest for violation of a restraining order for starters.

"No offense, ma'am, you seem like you mean well, but I had to restrain them just to keep from getting clocked with a frying pan. I can't just uncuff them, not when we still need to ensure evacuation of the building. I don't think it'd be safe." He grips his belt with both hands and hitches his pants back up to his natural waist.

"Okay, well." I look down the row of officers, five of them, and then over to the chain gang, smug and self-satisfied but at least quieter now. James, over in the corner, is avoiding eye contact but looks contrite, the only person who seems to appreciate the consequence of the situation—we're about to be kicked out of a flooding building, losing millions upon millions of dollars worth of equipment, art, and materials, and our senior faculty are handcuffed to a stairway, hollering nonsense. Hans Mueller joins the crowd and I notice Bunny, standing in the middle of the staircase, a few feet beneath the Pollock, staring at me over the heads of dozens of onlookers, looking stricken.

"I wonder if you might at least consider uncuffing Suzanne. I know she can be volatile, but it's really just a coping mechanism."

"What the fuck, no it's not," Suzanne says.

"It's actually my fault," I say, taking a step closer to Bigelow. "I left her in charge when I knew she was upset and busy, packing her studio and everything. I should never have done that." Bigelow still looks skeptical. Or maybe annoyed. "How about this," I say, lowering my voice, "uncuff Suzanne, and we'll go to the conference room and you can question her or write her up or something. Is that what you guys do? Write people up?"

He rolls his eyes, but I can see he's lost what little energy he had for this nonsense. "The other two stay cuffed until we sort out evacuation," he says.

I nod. "I think that's a good idea."

Bigelow unlocks Suzanne's handcuffs, and she rubs her wrist. The theatrics winding down, people lower their cell phones, go traipsing up the stairs and down the back corridor, talking to one another at regular volume. James, Bigelow and the other officers head to the conference room. Suzanne hurries past me.

"Try to be nice," I say.

She huffs. "Fuck nice."

The elevator chimes, packing tape is pulled from the roll in a nearby classroom, handcarts roll down the back hallway. I go to the staircase.

"What do you think you're doing here, Dunbar?"

"I very much like the gourd arrangement in your office. Are they ordered chronologically or most favorite to least? Either way, it's a lovely display."

I restrain a grimace. "You know you can't be in the building."

"Certainly I can collect my belongings before they wash away in the flood. These are exigent circumstances."

"Where in your restraining order is there an exception for exigent circumstances?" He rattles his handcuff against the steel railing. "Nowhere, and I would know. I've read it a dozen times." I feel focused, in control, like I'm finally equipped to handle this crisis. "You're going to be arrested," I say.

"Tyrant." He's practically hissing.

"Where's the frying pan?"

"I don't know what you're talking about."

"Bigelow told me you had a frying pan. Where is it?" My body feels calm, but my brain soars, like I've just had a triple espresso or a healthy snort of ephedrine.

"Don't tell her," Pete says.

"Why do you get involved in his shit, Pete? It's not worth it. Believe me."

"It's important," Pete says, bewildered, as if I should understand.

"Coming to school in a cardboard box? You think that's important? Really?" My jawbone pulses, a power surge.

"Pete gets the mission. He's my deputy." Dunbar thwacks the refrigerator box causing Pete to stumble forward and torque his cuffed wrist.

I've been shaking my head, I realize, in disbelief. In raging pleasure at finally catching Dunbar. In general anger and specific self-loathing. I bite at the canker sore. "If this is your mission and Pete is your deputy, then here's what's going to happen." I step close to Dunbar, inches from his blotchy potato nose. "For as long as you keep this up," I count off on my fingers, "the bacon, the gourds, harassing Ramona, harassing me, sending naked grad students to meetings, telling them this crap is important, I will take it out on him." I point to Pete who tugs at the rough twine on his shoulders. "Not only him, all of your students, your whole little crew. None of them will pass their courses. None of them will graduate. No funding next semester, no exhibitions, no agreeable MFA committees, no cushy half-time assistantships." I feel composed, even as the professional propriety I've honed and maintained dissolves.

"You couldn't, even if you wanted to," Dunbar says. Spittle flicks from his mouth, his eyes narrow. "You don't have that power."

"Of course I do, I have access to everything. Grades, graduation applications, funding." My voice is strong. I am commanding. "And who would stop me? Ramona? She has no idea what's going on around here. I can't even get her to write a stupid faculty memo. I can do anything I want, and she wouldn't even know, let alone object." Dunbar looks like he believes me about Ramona, like her negligence is old news. I despise him for that and, in this blazing instant, I despise Ramona too, for her failures and her absence, and Suzanne for starting this shit today and Ethan for making me feel deficient and young Gary for existing at all. I feel on the verge of some kind of synaptic malfunction. I do not try to stop it. "They'll all get incompletes," I say. "All your little minions. Incompletes. All of them. Whatever it takes. I don't care anymore. I do. Not. Care." A soggy pant escapes my throat, taking me by surprise, and I swallow it back. "You think you're being so subversive, such a rebel, but you're not. You're a joke. There's no *Man*, Dunbar. There's nothing to fight against. It's over, and I won't be your *foe* anymore. I'm done. Done. Done. Done." I'm not yelling exactly. It's more like a squawk. "Nobody gives a shit about you, Dunbar. You're useless." He looks almost distraught. I notice his shirt is misbuttoned, his hair thinner than I remember. My jaw hinge hurts. "I can't wait until you're fired and I never have to see your face again."

I hear a soft mumble, a snigger. I look up. Mathias Daman, Suzanne's most promising undergraduate student, stands by my office door, right where James had been, pointing an iPhone at Dunbar and Pete. And me.

"Are you filming this?" I move in his direction. "Turn off the camera." Mathias doesn't respond, just backs up and keeps rolling.

"You can't censor us." Pete's voice is cragged with urgency.

"Turn it off," I say again.

"She has no authority," Dunbar says. "You don't have to listen to her. She's a secretary."

I lurch at Mathias. "Come here, you little shit. Give me the camera." I swing an arm toward him, not sure what I'm hoping to accomplish. "You mother*fuck*er." I launch myself, half-run-half-leap, and catch his arm with one flailing hand. He doesn't drop the iPhone but looks a little frightened.

"Get away from me," he says, and scrambles up the staircase.

I move toward him, and my eyes catch on something sticking out from behind the trashcan at the bottom of the stairs. A handle. The frying pan. I run over, pull it out. It's heavy, iron, probably, and still caked with grease from Dunbar's latest escapade. I charge Mathias, holding the frying pan in front of me like a lance. It bobbles a little under its own weight. "Stop filming, you little shit, or I'll do to you what I'm going to do to Dunbar." I jab the pan toward him for emphasis.

"Get away from me with that thing." Mathias scurries backward up the stairs, tripping as his heels hit each consecutive step, fumbling with the phone, still trying to keep it pointed in my direction. I'm practically on all fours, balancing myself with one hand down on the stairs as I go loping after him, some kind of deranged frying-pan-wielding ape.

"Give me the phone." I swing the pan like a tennis racket, aiming for his ankles. "Give it to me!"

Mathias plants his left foot, swivels on the ball, and gallops, three steps at a time, up toward the second floor, the phone down at his side. When he reaches the top step, he doesn't slow down but grabs the banister with his free hand and slingshots himself around the corner. He tears down the corridor toward the library. In a matter of seconds, he is out of sight. I barely have time to right myself and climb a few steps when I hear a door slam. He must have gone out to the balcony where the grad students smoke. I won't be able to get out there before he's gone, down the fire escape and out to the back parking lot, through the rain, through the flooding city, into the world-at-large, where he can do whatever he wants with that video. Where, as far as I know, prior restraint is still considered unconstitutional.

I am seething. My scalp actually feels singed. The sound of rain returns to me, loud and ferocious. I descend the stairs, frying pan in hand, and when I get to the atrium, Dunbar tracks me, watches every step. Despite the handcuffs, he looks triumphant, gloating, as if my confrontation with Mathias is his personal victory. And then I realize it probably is. Dunbar teaches undergrads, most of who have no time for him and his missions, but Mathias Daman could be the exception. There's always an exception. Dunbar put him up to this, to the videotaping. I feel a renewal of disgust. This is all Dunbar's fault. All of it.

I walk over to where he's cuffed and stick the frying pan in his face. "You did this, didn't you? You planned this?"

"What, your nervous breakdown?"

"What do you get out of it exactly? Is it just sociopathic pleasure, or do you actually tell yourself you have an artistic agenda, you fucking asshole?"

"You gave up your artistic insight years ago, Lanning. You couldn't possibly understand my agenda."

"Is that it? Is that what you tell yourself when you're lying there at night, making plans, knowing everything you do is idiotic and pointless? Do you tell yourself you're misunderstood, like some angst-ridden teenager? Do you scribble in your diary? Do you write, *nobody gets me*?" The ridiculing singsong in my voice comes naturally.

"Get that frying pan out of my face."

"With pleasure," I say, flinging around, the pan out in front of me like a bandleader's baton. I march past the staircase and into my office where I drop the pan on the desk, turn, and stand square with the doorway, facing Dunbar, who watches me from the staircase with uneasy relish. I smile and slam the door as hard as I can. On the other side of my desk, I open the middle lateral drawer and get a key. I move quickly, fluidly. I'm angry still but back in control. I'm doing something. Finally.

I take out the key, squat, and unlock the bottom right drawer in my desk then split the front-most file with my index and middle fingers, slip out the restraining order. I move with precision, my limbs working almost involuntarily, my brain racing ahead to the next two, three, four moves. I can see it clearly, Dunbar's demise. A humiliated professor, handcuffed, publically disgraced, his reputation and career ruined for good.

I remove the paper clip, place the document on my printer/ copier and push the big green START button. The machine whirrs to life and in seconds, spits out a duplicate. I return the original to its file, replace the key, walk toward the door, grabbing the frying pan as I pass my desk, and, without a glance at Dunbar or Pete, head to the conference room.

Chapter 10

INSIDE THE CONFERENCE ROOM James is talking. "Yeah, that's true, but I was impressed by the defensive line. They've really improved since December. I mean, they were good last year, but they'll be great by fall."

"Agreed," Bigelow says, "but Aiken needs to work the O line a lot harder. I mean, if Stanley's going to have a fighting chance, he needs better protection. He's quick in the pocket, but he needs more time. A great defense is worthless if we can't put points on the board." I can only assume they're discussing the university football team and the recent spring exhibition game, and I think how even the dimmest of men speak with astonishing coherence when it comes to sports analysis. Some of the other cops chime in, offering their own indecipherable predictions for the fall season.

I hear Suzanne say to the officer on her right, "Have you ever actually had to use your gun?" Her voice has a formal, vaguely British affectation, her *serious* voice, the one she uses when she's trying to be impressive or when she wants something from someone. She touches the officer's belt where the holster dangles against his chair. She's flirting, another favored tactical maneuver, not one she's proud of but usually more successful than her serious voice alone. The cop looks deeply uncomfortable.

The conversational atmosphere concerns me—have they forgotten the fracas in the atrium? Where is Suzanne's outrage? Bigelow's annoyance? "I'm sorry about that," I say loudly. Everybody quiets, looks at me. "Sorry that took so long. Officer Bigelow, as James told you, Bert Dunbar is in violation of a restraining order." I slap the photocopied pages onto the table in front of me, the end closest to the door, farthest from the people, and it slides an inch or two in Bigelow's direction, six or eight feet from his grasp. James, seated across from Bigelow and one chair closer to me, reaches out to try and slide the papers down the table but can't reach them. He scoots closer until his chair is stopped by the one next to it, leans to his left and gropes, walking his first two fingers along the table toward the papers, making a squeaking noise as his fingertips rub the polished wood. This is not how I pictured this moment.

With an exclamatory huffing noise, I walk over, pick up the papers, and take them around the table to Bigelow. Standing next to his chair, I slap the restraining order down once again. "He needs to be arrested," I say and go to cross my arms over my chest but am inhibited by the frying pan, still clenched in my right hand. I grip the pan hard and bring it close to me like a shield, wielding both evidence and weapon.

"I see you found the frying pan," Bigelow says.

"I did, and I think it proves Dunbar intended to cause trouble and, worse, that in the midst of a natural disaster, he was going to fry bacon." It sounds a little innocuous when I say it like that, and Bigelow looks at me like he doesn't have the faintest clue what I'm talking about. "Dunbar is not allowed in the building," I say. "He's breaking the law. He needs to be arrested." I point to the papers on the table.

"Well, I'm not sure what he was planning or what bacon has to do with any of it, but I think the circumstances call for leniency," he says. "I will escort Professor Dunbar off campus, but, given the flood, I think arrest would be excessive."

"Ex*cess*ive?" I raise my voice. "He violated a legally obtained restraining order. You'll see there's no provision for exigent circumstances, nothing about flooding or weather or anything like that. It does include a cease-and-desist addendum that specifically forbids bacon frying in the SVA building." I waggle the pan in Bigelow's direction. He stares. It's like he's not hearing me. "Cease and desist," I say. "Cease and desist. Cease and desist." He looks dumbfounded, so much so I wonder if he's making fun of me. I scan the conference room and see similar expressions on all the other faces except Suzanne's. She looks proud, and for a split second I think of Ethan; he'd probably be proud too. This makes me all the angrier. "What's the problem here? Why is this so hard to understand?"

"Clearly you're very upset. Why don't you put the pan down, have a seat, and we'll talk this through." Bigelow gestures to the chair next to him. I remain standing.

"There's nothing to talk through. A man violated a court order. He should be arrested and fired. It's very simple." I'm starting to feel a sense of alarm, apparently alone in my assessment of the Dunbar situation. "Arrest him," I say, brusque and bossy. "You need to arrest him now, please," barely gentler this time.

"You said yourself, these are extraordinary circumstances," Bigelow says. "Everybody is stressed. I will escort Professor Dunbar to his office where he can gather his belongings, then I'll be sure he exits the premises and leaves campus. I will speak with him about the conditions of the restraining order and be sure he knows the rules. That should be good enough."

"That's the opposite of good enough. Were you not out there just now? Dunbar's a menace. He's a criminal, actually. A real criminal. He orchestrated this whole thing."

"What whole thing?"

"This disruption, the handcuffs, the videotaping. All of it." I swing the frying pan in a rainbow above my head, indicating "all of it."

"What videotaping?" Suzanne says.

"Nina, why don't you sit?" James says.

"And how could he have orchestrated the handcuffs?" Suzanne says. "Nobody knew the cops would show up."

"I'm not sitting. I don't understand why you aren't taking this seriously. Dunbar is a threat to the school. We've been trying to prove it for months, and now, here he is in clear violation, and you're, what? Going to walk him to his office?"

"You need to calm down," Bigelow says.

I take a step back. "I *am* calm."

"I understand your frustration, but I think it'll be best if you let me handle Dunbar. I have a copy of the restraining order now," Bigelow taps the papers in front of him, smiles, placating, "I can take it from here."

"Neens, it's fine. Dunbar will be out of the building and we can focus on evacuation, which is the important thing."

"That's the *least* important thing," I say.

"We need to discuss closing the building," Bigelow says. "I'll have to padlock the doors no later than sundown tonight. Let's call it 7:00 P.M. That's the best I can do." I see Suzanne cringe. She begins moving her lips, noiselessly reciting some New Age mantra she learned at Ramtha's School of Enlightenment, something asinine like, *Trust in the cosmic process, trust in the cosmic process, trust in the cosmic process.*

"Couldn't we get a little more time, maybe until noon tomorrow?" James says.

"The water's already dangerously high. I'm stretching the limits of safety as it is," Bigelow says.

"It's just, we have a lot more stuff we need to pack up," Suzanne says.

"Who gives a shit about stone hammers and fucking clay pots?" I say. "Do you really think that matters? What difference could a few more hours possibly make?" Suzanne looks at me with anger, and I'm glad for it. That's how she *should* look at me, how she should have been looking at me for years. Now, finally, she is. Finally, I'm getting the response I've earned, and it gives me a twisted sense of self-righteousness.

"Let's just agree we have until 7:00," James says.

"You'll need to be cleared out," Bigelow says.

"And what about Suzanne?" James says.

"She's excused with a warning. You should be more respectful of the police in the future, ma'am. We're here to help."

"I cannot *believe* this," I say, turning my attention back to Bigelow. "You have to do something about Dunbar. You have to *do* something. You have to arrest him."

"I'm going to uncuff him and get him out of here." Bigelow scoots his chair back from the table. "That's it."

"That's *horseshit*," I say, fuming, gesticulating, not paying attention when the frying pan, still tight in my declarative fist, swings in a perfect arc, straight toward Bigelow as he stands from his chair, his hangdog mug right in the path of the curve.

It's a direct hit. A face shot. The noise is not the Three Stooges gong I might have expected, more like the last bite of a cake ice cream cone, part mush but with some real crackle at the end. Nasal bone, breaking, I suppose.

The frying pan slips from my grip and clangs to the floor, now with a plangent reverberating ring. Bigelow doubles over, covers his face with both hands, groans, the sound of anger more than pain. Blood squishes out between his fingers. Suzanne, James, and the other officers are on their feet.

"Oh my god!"

"Are you alright?"

"I didn't see what happened. What happened?"

"He's bleeding. Oh my god, he's bleeding like crazy."

"Somebody get a towel."

"Can you talk? Is your nose broken?"

"Get a *towel*!"

"He should sit down. Help him sit."

Bigelow pulls his hands away from his face and holds them out to assess the damage. They're covered in blood and leave smeared finger and palm prints on his cheeks and, somehow, his forehead. His nose is a bulbous geyser, the blood leaking all over the floor, his eyes bugged and watery.

I have never been a violent person, so I'm surprised to be overcome not by disgust or apology but a halcyon calm. It feels, again, like righteousness. You can't blame the train when someone steps in front of it. *If you would have just arrested Dunbar,* I think, and am appalled at myself.

I take two steps backward toward the open door and see James' hands and jeans covered in blood, Suzanne clucking and lifting the hem of her sweater to try and stop the gushing, the campus police officers milling around, upset, awkward, not sure what to do, their leader down for the count, the frying pan, upside down on the floor.

James looks up at me like he might say something but turns back to Bigelow's nose. And then, like I've been horse-kicked in the stomach, I can't get enough air. The adrenaline, the energy, whatever has been propelling me, drains. I feel gagged and weightless. Disincarnate. Like my skull is filled with helium. The white-hot core of my canker sore flames, a blue star burning at 10,000 Kelvin on the inside of my mouth, singeing a hole through my lower lip. I raise a hand to my face as if the sore can be seen from the outside. I want to be elsewhere. I want everyone else to be elsewhere. I want Dunbar gone, Suzanne gone, James gone, Bigelow and his bleeding face, gone. I fight the urge to run.

"Nina, go get some paper towels," Suzanne says. Her regular voice is back, no affectation, no flirtation. I don't say anything. I don't move. "Nina. Paper towels." She looks like she feels sorry for me. I can't imagine she believes this wasn't my fault, clocking Bigelow in the face with a frying pan. No, it's that she sees me, standing there, pitiable. Pathetic.

I nod to her and leave the conference room. I do not go to the bathroom to get paper towels for Bigelow's bloody nose. Instead, I go to my office, retrieve my noise-canceling headphones and walk down the back corridor until I am again outside, moving through the parking lot to my car, which I get into and, as if entranced, begin to drive.

Chapter 11

NEVER DID I CRAVE Suzanne's favor more than at my MFA exhibition. It was the culmination of so much—my years as a student, all that coursework and study, but also my season as an apprentice. I was days away from graduating with an MFA in sculpture and joining the populace Suzanne spoke of three years earlier, on our first day of class, those babysitting artists struggling to make lives for themselves, the ones doing it anyway. I wanted to believe I could be one of them.

My show was an installation in the school's main gallery, the same room from which Mathias Daman's dad's hatchets were stolen. It was a garden, a massive, elaborate, intricate, origami-ish garden, made of wire and thousands of dyed, painted, glossed pages from discarded gossip and fashion magazines. There were delicate Peruvian lilies, tiger striped in deep gray ink; yellow trillium, leaves marbled with diluted whiteout and rubber cement; small-scale redbud tress, riotous pink petals bursting. There were tangled irises, clustered grape hyacinths, bridal tuberoses. The walls were covered in climbing ivy, twisted and knobbed like broken bones, and at the center of it all, a massive amorphophallus titanium in full bloom, a corpse flower, monstrous and gnarled, purplish olive, the smell, that of decaying flesh, created by the years-old rotting magazine paper and some strategically placed rancid beef. It was like some weird kid's art project; after-school crafts taken to an extravagant level. Like so much in my life, it was proficient but somehow meager as well.

It took three-and-a-half semesters to construct everything, and, over that time, the glossy trashed paper began to atrophy and sag. Many of the flowers were bent or crushed in transit or storage. The edges of the older, poorly built blossoms grew soft and gnawed from handling. Some had nickel-sized holes. Many stunk of waste. But when it was time for my show, I hauled it all in to the gallery and arranged it as planned. Originally conceived as a majestic, vibrant garden, it turned out more like somebody's overgrown backyard. A portrait of neglect, rather than beauty.

But Suzanne thought it was brilliant. "They're so grotesque, so exquisite but so flawed, very powerful, and I love that your point is so overt. Finally, somebody who isn't going for abstruse—I feel like most students think opacity is something to strive for—but this is, no, this is different." I don't know what she thought the point was; I don't know what *I* thought the point was. I made the flowers because they were strange, and I used old gossip and fashion magazines because they had the right colors and I could get my hands on them for free by raiding the city's recycle center. As Suzanne complimented construction, arrangement, exact and varying degrees of disintegration, and, above all, the straightforward artistic substance, I felt not fraudulent, as I should have, but proud. Apparently I had done it. I had made art.

As part of the exhibit I was supposed to post a statement explaining conceptual objectives and deeper meanings. I wrote something about inverses, things gorgeous and pernicious, noxious beauty, something about the dioxins in the magazine paper juxtaposing their flowery incarnation, the process of appropriation and recombination, objects losing real-world connotation and taking on philosophical roles when reassigned for artistic purpose, benign and malignant forms, oppositional pairings creating duplicitous environments and conflicting messages. A bunch of big-worded nonsense I didn't understand or mean. But in my haste to arrange the grand, bedraggled garden I forgot to post it. There, on the wall, next to the title of the show, *Top Floor Flora*, was a blank page headed *Artist's Statement*. I didn't even realize I'd forgotten it until Suzanne said, "I love that you chose not to post a statement. Love. It."

Before I could answer, she took me by the hands. "It's perfect, just the art, speaking for itself, no need for elaboration, *that's* your statement, right there, and it's expressive and literal, very on-the-nose, but in a good way, and, you're right. Why fuck it up with a bunch of overwritten crap as if people can't see the meaning and beauty for themselves, and, really, if they can't, they don't deserve to have it spelled out for them." She hugged me. "I'm so proud of you, Neens."

It was the first time she called me that, the moment we transitioned from teacher-student to friends. Peers. Over the years since, as our relationship grew thick from affection and camaraderie, I never corrected her. I never explained that everything she found poignant and adroit about my show was an accident or a mistake or a misinterpretation. All the beauty and meaning she saw was imposed. It was *her* meaning, *her* beauty, projected on to my half-dead flower arrangements. I had been wrong. I'd not made art. Suzanne had.

Something bumps against my chilled arm, and when I move, my neck is sore and tight. I hear roaring silence and consider the possibility that I've drowned.

And then I open my eyes. A wine glass floats in bathwater, colliding now with my bare belly, my noise-canceling headphones, still situated tight against my ears, emitting hollow quiet. My mouth is dry and salty, my head pounding. I've passed the afternoon in soggy, lukewarm, semicataleptic repose. I did not think of the SVA, did not reflect on the events of the day, instead pushed them from my brain and focused on resounding silence and an overfull glass of wine until everything that happened became woolly in my mind, like the vague memory of a surreal dream.

When I sit up, the water cold against my body, I notice through the bathroom window that it's dark outside. The SVA is probably padlocked by now. How strange it is, to feel such hostility for a place and still cherish it. A door closes downstairs, there are footsteps, chattering, and I remember Ethan and the sandbagging. How strange to feel that same discordance for a person.

I fish the wine glass out of the bathwater, turn it upside down to empty what's collected in its bottom, then hoist myself up, pushing against the side of the tub with my free hand. My vision goes spotty, my face flames then gets clammy. I have to sit down in the armchair to avoid passing out.

"Nina?" Ethan is standing at the bottom of the staircase yelling up to me. He won't barge in on me when I'm in the bathroom but he'll stand down there and bellow all night long. I blink, rub my eyes, take a breath, walk to the sink where I turn on cold water, and stick my head beneath the faucet to drink, that metal taste again.

"Nina? You up there?"

I slurp the metallic water for as long as I can, pause, breathe, slurp some more. When I right myself, I towel off and grab my yellow terrycloth bathrobe from the hook on the inside of the door.

"Niiiiiina?" The pitch of Ethan's voice rises and falls, but the volume steadily increases.

I step into the hallway, go to the top of the stairs. "Stop yelling."

"What are you doing?"

"Taking a bath."

"Did you get my messages?"

"About the pig sty?"

"About sandbagging." He looks pickled and satisfied, the way outdoor manual labor makes a man look. "I must have called you ten times," he says. He looks at me, expects me to say something, to explain my absence from his day, my apparent ambivalence toward his neighborhood heroics. "Are you coming down?"

"Let me get dressed," I say.

He smiles, nods. Gary pops into view behind him. "Hi." He's bare-chested and holding my soggy sweatshirt, as, what? Evidence? Admission? Souvenir?

"Yeah, hi," I say. I go back into the bathroom where I replace my robe on its hook and pull on sweatpants and a sweatshirt.

My phone chimes from somewhere inside my purse on the bathroom floor, and when I take it out I see I've just missed Suzanne and, according to the call history, some twelve other incoming calls—a couple more from Suzanne, one from James, a bunch from Ethan, the rest from unknown or private numbers. I can't help but wonder if one of those doesn't belong to Officer Bigelow. The phone chirps again, an impatient Do-Re-Mi, and a text message appears on the screen: *Check your email. Call me. Suz.*

"So we sandbagged all day." Ethan is back at the bottom of the stairs, yelling. "Karl and Margaret came over this morning, and we went with them down to Beldon Ave." He pauses. "Nina?"

"I can't hear you," I yell. Someone says something, presumably Gary, and Ethan walks into the kitchen.

Phone in hand, I ease open the bathroom door and creep down the hallway into our second bedroom. We always thought it would be a guest room, but we couldn't get my old bed frame up the narrow stairs and then we inherited a treadmill from one of Ethan's older brothers. Ethan added a Bowflex home gym a few years after that, which, along with the treadmill handrails, has served as a useful supplement to our bedroom closet—all my hanging clothes now have a home. In the corner farthest from the door, opposite the gym/closet, is a makeshift desk, a collapsible plastic tailgate table and an old folding chair Ethan accidentally welded open as part of a furniture repair experiment. I sit and fire up our little-used laptop.

While the computer starts, I replay the events of the day, focusing on Dunbar, assessing my earlier conclusion that he is to blame for this shit storm. For my erratic behavior and short temper. Bigelow's bloody nose. It makes even more sense now than it did this afternoon, and I feel like an idiot for not realizing it sooner. I used to take art school silliness in stride and so did Ramona. We'd laughed when Dunbar filed a formal complaint with the Office of Equal Opportunity and Diversity, claiming he was discriminated against for his rambunctiousness, that Ramona's fanatical attraction to subhuman espionage and her incessant love of fear-mongering were specially designed to destroy his professional ambitions. "Ramona Holme always knows what's going on, and nobody ever gets away with anything," he claimed. Ramona didn't seem the least bit bothered. But the following year, when the centerpiece of Dunbar's solo show was a collage of Ramona's personal garbage, stolen from her curbside trashcan, she didn't laugh. Dunbar wore her down. Like me, she lost her sense of humor.

"We were out there all day." Ethan's voice is louder now, closer, like he's moved to the middle of the staircase. "What a nightmare. The Stamms, the Williamsons, the Schoolers, that weird guy on the corner with the beard and the dogs. They're going to lose everything. I mean, we did what we could, which, you know, was a lot, but a bunch of houses will be under water and others will get a foot or two. Can you imagine looking around here, knowing it'll all be gone? Everything. Just. Gone." I picture Ethan giving this speech, making a small gesture, *gone*, a swoop of his hands through the air, genuine dismay across his face.

"Terrible," I say.

"What'd you say?"

I turn my face toward the closed door. "I'll be down in a minute." I'm screaming.

The computer chimes, announcing it's awake and ready to go, and I open the browser, pull up my work email. The top message is from Suzanne with the subject line, *You need to see this...* and in the body of the email is a link. When I click on it, the web browser opens to YouTube, a video entitled, *Nervous Collapse at the School of Visual Arts*, and I'm looking at Dunbar and Pete, handcuffed to the stair rail. Then I see myself. I'm yelling. Kind of a screech, really. I hadn't realized I was standing so close to Dunbar, right up in his face. His being handcuffed makes him seem defenseless; if I hadn't been there myself, I would assume I was the aggressor. The sound quality is poor, which only makes it worse as my words come in snippets. *Ramona? She has no idea what's going on around here*, I hear myself say, nasty, snarling, far less controlled than I remember, and then, *I can do anything I want and she wouldn't even know, let alone object.* The camera moves closer, focuses on my face. I appear to be sweating.

Nobody gives a shit about you, Dunbar. You're useless... fired and I never have to see you again. My voice is alien, a cross between a shrieking child and a sputtering chainsaw, and I look wild, unstable, my movements jerky, my fingers in Dunbar's face. The way I remember it, Dunbar was defiant and provocative; in the video, he seems timid, frail almost. Victimized. I see now he was playing to the audience, his favorite role, the martyr. I watch myself turn toward the camera. With the straight-on shot, I look even more out-of-control, almost demented, my face beet red. I can't understand whatever it is I'm saying to Mathias, and then the picture gets shaky and I'm grabbing the frying pan, loping up the stairs.

After one minute and twenty-seven seconds, the video ends. There are only 193 views so far, negligible in badlands of YouTube, but that's 193 people who undoubtedly know me personally, who have now seen me threaten a faculty member and grad student with professional sabotage and attempt to assault an undergraduate with a frying pan. The highest rated comment reads: *No person without a serious mental diagnosis would behave this way. Schizophrenia maybe? Psychopathy? She needs help.* Along the right side of the screen are links to "similar videos" with titles like, *There's a horse in that car!* and *Fat bus driver fights with child.*

"I'm making coffee, you want some?" Ethan has given up waiting and come all the way up the stairs. He opens the guest bedroom door, and I jump, rush to minimize the browser window. "What are you doing in here?"

Panic curls in my stomach. "Just give me a second, I'm coming."

"Alright." Miffed, Ethan walks back out the door toward the stairs.

I wonder if I'll lose my job. The thought of no longer being part of the School of Visual Arts leaves me a little, I don't know, swimmy. And curious. What would my life be like if I didn't have that place? What if *I* was the one ushered out in humiliation?

I click around on YouTube, looking for customer service or a complaint line. I think of other unsuspecting YouTube victims, that poor Star Wars Kid—maybe we could file a class action lawsuit. Or I could sue Dunbar personally. For defamation. Slander. Punitive damages. The computer chimes and a new message pops into my Inbox, this one from Ramona, subject line, *FW: Hello, Handsome!*

Dearest Lucky,

I hope to see you soon! I was thrilled to receive your reply and look forward to our ongoing correspondence until we can meet in person. It's flooding here, maybe you've heard, and I probably won't be able to travel for another week or so but I can't wait to try your Pizza Diablo! Yummy!

I thought about telling you about myself, something about what kind of woman I am and what you mean to me, but I can't find the right words. Instead, please accept the attached photograph and let's just say I hope you find it more exciting than a wordy description!

All my love!
Ramona Holme

I double-click on the attachment. What opens is not the nudey pic I expected, not even a romance heroine recreation, just a full-body shot of Ramona standing in her office, all dolled up. Her thick gray-blonde hair is ratted and loose, her face rouged and painted in bordello pinks and purples. She is wearing the same low-cut, too-tight black dress I saw her in yesterday but has on strappy high-heeled sandals and she's standing at an angle in front of her desk, one foot crossed in front of the other, both hands on her hips. She beams in the photo, going for enticing but coming across more berserk.

From where did she send it, I wonder. I have never known Ramona to email from home, but it couldn't have been sent from her office—the school's been padlocked. Had anybody actually looked for her in the chaos? Certainly she couldn't have been elsewhere in the building, unbeknownst to James and Suzanne, unbeknownst to Officer Bigelow, unbeknownst to anybody. Certainly she didn't reenter later. Certainly she's not still there, locked in. Certainly not.

I call Suzanne, who picks up on the second ring.

"Well, if it isn't our very own loose cannon."

"That video makes it look like Dunbar's the victim."

"Nobody who knows him will believe that. You, on the other hand, look your all-time best." I can't tell if she's being sincere or caustic.

"That little shithead, Mathias. Can you get him to take it down?"

"Highly doubtful, he's calling it 'incidental exploitation.' Very daring. He sent me an email, asked if he could submit it as his capstone project, thinks he's finally found the appropriate creative mode for his application to Carnegie Mellon. He wants to give you co-credit. 'Doing begets exhibition,' he said. He's quite brilliant."

"He's going to get me fired."

"Probably. Hang on." She puts the phone down, and I hear voices, cheering. When she comes back, she says, "Sorry, tequila shot. Have you talked to Bigelow?"

"Where are you?"

"Thirsty Camel, can't get home. All the bridge's are closed. Have you talked to Bigelow?"

"No."

"He and the goon squad are after you. You're in trouble, like, real trouble."

"How'd it go after I left?"

"Fucking horrible, thanks for asking. Bigelow was pissed as hell when you slunk out the back door. He revoked the sunset deadline and cleared the building, had us all out of there in under thirty minutes. We've been here all afternoon, mourning."

"Afternoon morning?"

"Mourning. Grieving." She's quiet a moment. "The Pollock, Neens, it's still in the building. We're mourning the Pollock." I let the phone drop from my ear. The Pollock. I didn't even think of the Pollock. It may be high enough on the atrium wall to avoid submersion, but if the building is sealed, abandoned, and rotting for, who knows, weeks, months, the painting will be ruined. Unsalvageable. Suzanne is still talking. "James called the cops four times. They don't think they'll be able to respond until tomorrow, at which point it'll be too late anyway so what the fuck good is that? The dispatcher said they're expecting *human* emergencies all night. That's what she said, 'human emergencies,' as if art is not an inextricable part of humanity, as if the Pollock itself isn't more valuable than certain human lives, I mean, I personally can think of more than a few people I'd happily bludgeon to death if it'd save that painting." To whoever might be listening on her end, it probably sounds like hyperbole but I hear true contempt. Suzanne loves the Pollock.

"Maybe I should call Bigelow and explain the situation. I'll apologize." I don't blame Bigelow for clearing the building. I wouldn't have been in a lenient mood either if I was him. I'm struck again by the airless sensation I felt in the conference room, and I can't help wondering if maybe some part of this isn't somehow maybe my fault.

"No, they've got city cops looking for you, at least that's what James heard. He's been following your case on Mathias' and Pete's Twitter feeds. I can't believe they didn't come to your house."

"They may have. I fell asleep."

"You can't call Bigelow. He'll take you to the clink."

"Suzanne." What I want to say is something diarrheal like, *I don't know what to do, this was Dunbar's fault but I'm sorry and maybe I can fix it, I kind of hope somebody fires me but also I'm afraid and I can't bear to face Ethan and I think I'm half in love with James, plus I might be having a nervous breakdown.* Instead I say, "I think Ramona might still be in there."

"In where?"

"In the SVA. Padlocked in."

"Holy fuck."

"She just emailed me a love letter, just now, and she never, ever emails from home. The Internet service at her house is spotty at best."

"Ramona is writing you love letters?"

"Not to me, to Lucky."

"Who's Lucky?" But before I can explain she says, "Jesus, Nina, you really think she could be in there still?"

"Yes." I hear fuzz on the line, like Suzanne's got her hand over the microphone. Her voice is muffled, and then I hear a man's voice say Ramona's name, and then collective, muted conversation.

"Ok, get your ass over here," Suzanne says. "We'll figure it out." She hangs up. I do the same.

"You should have seen Gary with the sandbags. He didn't complain once." Ethan is back in the doorway.

I push past him, walk out into the hallway. Gary comes running up the stairs, still shirtless, past Ethan and me and into the bathroom. "I'm go to shower," he says.

"Ok. Hey, great work today, buddy. You want a beer for the shower?"

"Yeah," Gary says, and smiles. He turns into the bathroom, apparently not understanding Ethan's offer, and closes the door behind him.

"Such a great kid," Ethan says. "Can you believe that about Beldon Avenue? We may have some refugees here, needing a place to crash."

"We're sort of at capacity don't you think?"

He shakes his head, makes a brushing motion with his hand. "How was your day?" His hair is a moppy mess. He smells like rain worms. All he wants is to talk with his wife at the end of a long day.

"I have to go out for a while," I say. "And, listen, if the cops show up, tell them you don't know where I am. Say you haven't seen me."

"What do you mean, 'if the cops show up?'"

"Nothing, just more bullshit with Dunbar." Maybe I should post a comment on the YouTube video, defend my actions, explain about Dunbar's restraining order.

"What'd he do?"

I hear the shower turn on, and for some reason, it makes me worry about Ramona. I walk down the stairs, into the kitchen, away from Ethan.

"Nina."

"It's nothing. Seriously, just say you haven't seen me. Say you were sandbagging all day, which is true. Say I wasn't here when you got home, okay?

"Okay but tell me what happened." His voice is bright with excitement.

"It's a long story."

The bathroom door opens upstairs, and I hear footsteps, Gary going into the guest bedroom, opening the squeaky closet door, moving stuff around. "What's he doing up there?"

"You can't tell me the cops may show up and not explain what's going on."

"It's just the school," I say. "It's flooding. They evacuated." I speak with exasperation, as if the flooded, evacuated SVA is a perfectly legitimate reason for not explaining about cops possibly showing up at our doorstep.

"God, of course it is." He looks half stunned. "I'm sorry, Nina. I didn't think about it." He walks into the living room, paces, rubs his palms together, wears that confounded expression of his. "So I guess you sandbagged all day too." He's pleased, as if our both sandbagging would unite us somehow, bond us in the toil of natural disaster. I suddenly wish I still had the frying pan.

"No, Ethan, I didn't sandbag."

"What'd you do?"

"I don't know. I kind of freaked out." A semitruth, the best I can do. "The cops came and padlocked the building. Ramona was missing all day. Is still missing, actually." I imagine where she might be right now, back in her office maybe, our fearless director going down with the ship, armed with nothing but a photo of Lucky and a sopping wet Jackson Pollock.

"So what happened?'

"Nothing happened. I came home, had a glass of wine, and fell asleep in the tub." I step into the kitchen and pull open the fridge, blocking Ethan's access to the room. I look at him over the open fridge door. "I'm probably going to have to go meet Suzanne."

Ethan pushes against the refrigerator, squeezes into the room. "Gary did great today, by the way. I was really proud."

"He's not actually your kid, you know."

"Well." He says this as if the point is debatable.

I close the refrigerator too hard, and the condiments jangle in the door. "You let him wear my sweatshirt."

"What?"

"He wore my sweatshirt today, in the rain, sandbagging."

"I thought you hated that sweatshirt."

"It doesn't belong to you."

"Well, no, but…" he drifts off, confused.

"I wish you hadn't let him wear it," I say.

He purses his lips, rolls his eyes ever so slightly, releases a blustery exhale, impatient, his overreactive wife, worked up over nothing.

"Don't do that. Don't breathe at me like that."

He does it again, breathes at me.

"Ethan."

"Nina, please, I don't want to fight."

"And I do?" He looks at me expectantly, as if the question might be rhetorical, but before I can think of something nasty to say, I hear pounding footsteps on the stairs and Gary comes whizzing around the living room corner into the kitchen. He's wearing my yellow bathrobe, tied loosely at his waist, floating behind him like tux tails.

"Problem," he says.

"Close up that robe," I say.

"What's wrong?" Ethan says, with all the panic of an actual parent.

"Bathroom," Gary says. And then I panic. If he did something to my bathroom, I will have Suzanne bludgeon him. We run up the stairs in a single file stampede, me in the front, then Gary, then Ethan. I grab the banister and haul myself up the stairs two at a time, push into the bathroom, and, one step inside, slip and fall on my right hip. I'm lying in a small pond and the bathtub is overflowing. Gary must not have drained the tub before turning on the shower. He must have let the water run and, while digging around in the guestroom, not realized it was overflowing. Apparently in his panic he didn't turn off the water but instead threw on my bathrobe and ran downstairs to Daddy.

I try to get my feet beneath me and then Ethan is pulling me up. "Are you ok?"

"I'm fine." There is already an inch or so of water on the bathroom floor and still a cascade falls over the side of the tub. Ethan is assessing my sweatpants where they got wet when I fell.

"Are you injured?"

"I'm fine. I'm fine. Turn it off." He taps over to the tub and turns off the water. It takes several seconds after the shower stops for the bathtub waterfall to slow then stop.

I turn to Gary. "You didn't drain the bathtub? Didn't you notice the floor was covered in water?"

"I don't know," he says.

"You don't know? Look at this place." I stomp the water.

"Come on, Nina. It's not his fault. It was an accident. He didn't know," Ethan says.

"Take off my bathrobe," I say, and the kid looks to Ethan because he doesn't understand what I'm saying.

"Leave him alone. He's doing his best."

"How do you know that? Did he tell you? Did he say, 'I'm doing my best, Dad, I promise. Please don't be mad at me.'" I'm using the same ridiculing singsong middle school voice I did with Dunbar.

"Don't be mean."

"I'm not being mean. I'm asking a question. How. Do. You. Know."

"It's been a long day. We should all calm down. I'll mop this up. It'll be fine." He sounds like Officer Bigelow, telling me to calm down, talking to me like I'm dangerous, like *I'm* the crazy one. If I hear any more *you're-losing-it* speak, I actually will lose it. I will beat my husband to within an inch of his life for bringing this disaster into our home then make him watch as I manually strangle his surrogate son.

I splash through the puddle, push past Ethan, move toward the doorway. Gary skitters in front of me. "Get out of the way," I say. He looks back at me, apologetic, scooting out the bathroom door. "Move." A pleasure center in my brain begins to fire. "I can't do this. I cannot stay here with the two of you." I'm whisper-growling, the timbre of hushed fury.

I move into the hallway, and Ethan remains standing in the middle of the bathroom, ready to clean up our own private flood. "There's nowhere to go, Nina, the whole city's shutting down." He sounds resigned, not at all up for a fight.

"I have to go back for Ramona." The moment I say it, I know it's true. I am going back to the SVA. I'll swim if necessary. I'll break in, find Ramona, save her, save the Pollock. I'll fix this.

"What does any of this have to do with Ramona?" Ethan says.

"She needs me."

"So, what, you're leaving, right in the middle of a five-hundred-year flood?" He gestures around the bathroom, indicating the damage already done.

I face him, hands on soaked, bruised hips. "You can stay here and clean this up, or not, or whatever you want, but I have to go."

"Is this about the Christmas sweatshirt?" he says.

"Oh my god, Ethan, are you kidding me?"

He shifts his weight from one foot to the other. "Is it about the baby?"

"What baby?"

"Because I said I want to have a baby. Is that why you're acting like this?"

"This is about getting out of this house before I kill you." I start to walk away. "And helping Ramona."

"I think it's normal to want children, Nina, I think it's understandable, and I think you're being unreasonable. You won't even talk to me."

"Don't be so dramatic." I head into our bedroom where I dig out and pull on an old pair of galoshes. "Not everything is about you," I say.

Ethan throws his arms up and lets them fall to his sides. "I don't understand what's going on. You say the cops are looking for you and won't explain and all of a sudden you're furious and have to go somewhere for Ramona. It doesn't make any sense." He seems truly concerned.

I march out of the bedroom, down the stairs. "I'll worry about me. You worry about you. That's *my* mantra." *It is*, I think. *That's my mantra.*

Ethan is clomping down the stairs behind me. "Fine, just, fine, go."

"And remember, if the cops come, you didn't see me."

I'm out the door, in the car. When I pull from the curb, Gary steps from the house sheathed in yellow terrycloth, the fabric billowing around him like royal garb. He flashes peace signs with both hands and waggles them at me—Ethan's sweet boy, seeing me off.

Chapter 12

WHEN I STEP INTO the Thirsty Camel, I am hit with a waft of beefy smoke—the residue and bouquet of the bar's dumpster-grade cheeseburgers, sizzling on a never-cleaned grill. Standing in the doorway, I breathe in the reassuring scent of unsaturated trans fats and potassium benzoate which, I once read, is not only used in foodstuffs but for the whistle in fireworks. My stomach growls, and I realize I haven't ingested anything other than sour white wine in a day and a half.

The bar is crowded, the atmosphere jovial; the river is expected to crest any moment and yet there is chatter, laughter, midair high-fiving, cheersing. A string of perennial Christmas lights twinkles along the left wall, and the red bulbs in the overhead pendant fixtures are dimmed, their garnet casts swirling with cigarette smoke. Clusters of people, and apparently Thirsty Camel management, are ignoring the indoor smoking ban, presumably in the name of cataclysm.

I navigate to the far wall, the one strung with lights, and as I search the heads for Suzanne's auburn mane, the opening riff of Deep Purple's "Smoke on the Water," that serrated Fender Stratocaster, cries out above the clamor. The crowd erupts in applause and a collective roar of approval. Cutting toward the center of the room, I bob my head knowingly to other patrons, strangers who smile and raise their glasses, throw their heads back to unleash consecrative howls. "We're all in this together," they're saying. "We might as well enjoy our last few hours on dry land. Smoooooke on the water, fire in the sky!" The scene is almost festive but more rambunctiously funereal—it's not a party. It's a wake.

The thick crowd is, as usual, a mix of local alcoholics and the deliberately, dogmatically inurbane liberal arts community, including a respectable contingent from the SVA. Hans Mueller is at a two-top near the bar with a fuzzy redhead, a woman I know to be an affiliate of the English Department, some postgrad groupie. Hans probably comes here for the same reason he attends faculty meetings: to pontificate in front of a captive audience about how much better off the SVA would be with him at the helm. I dodge his gaze and angle my way through the sea of air-guitaring drunks. Suzanne's wild gesticulations draw my attention to a table at the back of the room where she is holding court with James, Bunny O'Brien, and Bunny's wife, Nanette.

I elbow toward them, but stop a few feet away. James sips beer from a glass, Bunny tugs a fleshy earlobe, Nanette pushes up a plaid shirtsleeve that won't stay. Suzanne is mid-diatribe. "... seriously, I wish somebody would please, please," she slaps both palms on the table, "tell me how Dean Reyes is going to explain that to the regents. Forget that it's a spectacular, groundbreaking work of emotional and experiential expression. Forget that its intrinsic creative power is, pardon me, immeasurable. The thing is worth millions, millions, in cold, hard American cash, which, as you may or may not be aware, Dean Reyes, you fuck, can be exchanged for goods and services, millions, probably hundreds of millions. Only a moron would believe he won't end up with his ass in a sling for losing something so valuable, not to mention the inexcusable depravity of sacrificing the painting." Suzanne looks my way, makes eye contact, doesn't acknowledge me or stop talking. "What we need to do is, forget the police, let's contact the press. I've got people at the newspaper and channel nine. Is somebody taking notes? Let's think this through. Who has a pen?" Bunny produces two pens, and Suzanne takes both, one with each hand, then begins to flatten a piece of cheesy wax paper leftover from someone's burger.

When she is cocksure, in the throes of sedition, Suzanne is at her most stunning. Brassy and ferocious, she is a lioness. Conquistadora. Bloodthirsty heroine. Normally, I am by her side, executor, but not tonight. Tonight, I am a trespasser, and Suzanne must work to temper my failings. I take a step backward.

"So we break in here?" Bunny says, pointing to some spot on Suzanne's wax paper.

"I still think the second floor fire escape is our best shot," Nanette says.

"Ok, but first things first. Where can we get boats?" Suzanne says.

"Has everybody had a tetanus shot?" Bunny looks from Suzanne to James to Nanette. "Seriously," he says. "The water is contaminated and not just tetanus. E. coli, West Nile virus, breached septic tanks, decomposing animal carcasses, not to mention whatever might be seeping from the SVA."

Suzanne ignores him. "James, we'll need your kayak. What do you think?"

James nods coolly. "It'll do." He leans back in his chair, crosses an ankle over the opposite knee, watches Suzanne with proud affiliation, as if her performance reflects positively on him. His expression and posture make me wonder if their relationship is more serious than Suzanne led me to believe. I look at her then back to him. I can't believe I didn't see it sooner. This is not Suzanne's usual predation. It's not some fling. This is serious. It's a relationship. I scan my memory trying to think of anything I've said that may have come across as insulting or dismissive. And then I feel the tear of rejection, as if their dalliance, their relationship, rather than my marital status, seals the deal: I will not be the one who ends up with James Brenton.

"Nina, hey," Bunny says, interrupting my mope. "Come on over. We're working on a plan."

I step from the shadows.

"There she is. Our little guerrilla warrior," Suzanne says. It's unclear if the displeasure in her voice is for me or Dean Reyes or the flood or what. "I always knew you still had some of that sweet ass rebellion in you, but, Jesus, Neens, you fucked us today."

"I know."

"Tequila shots all around," she says.

"And two cheeseburgers," I say.

Suzanne raises a forefinger. "Oh, Krissy." And she's off, tracking the waitress. Bunny and Nanette are in conversation, so I sit down next to James.

"How's the lam?" he says. I watch his mouth as he speaks, that bulging, scarred lower lip. "Do you feel like Bonnie Parker?"

"So far the lam has included a lukewarm bath and a marital spat." I touch my hip, bruised from my fall in the flooded bathroom.

James laughs, thinks I'm joking. "Did Bigelow catch up to you yet? He was pretty pissed."

"Not so far. We'll see if Ethan gives me up."

"What'd Ethan say about the YouTube video?"

"Nothing yet."

"I'm surprised he didn't want to join us tonight. Seems like this would be right up his alley. Stupid, a little dangerous, possibly illegal."

Though they've not spent enough time together to become friends in their own right, James and Ethan get along famously. At dinner parties and school functions, they gravitate toward one another. I've always been unsettled at the sight of them, drinks in hand, heads tilted together in conversation and laughter, James most likely describing some SVA shenanigan, Ethan eating it up. It's like watching two strangers who were never meant to meet, all of a sudden in happy cahoots. It disturbs me.

"He stayed home with Gary the Chinese," I say, mean and racist over thoughts of Ethan.

"What is that, like, a television show or something?"

"No, no, it's a kid, this student of Ethan's. He's living with us at the moment."

James' face darkens and he leans away from me, disgusted that I've referred to a real live person as "Gary the Chinese." "You know you can't call him that, right?"

"I don't." I pick up an empty pint glass and fill it from one of three pitchers on the table, drink half, fill it again.

Suzanne comes back to the table, squats down on the other side of Bunny, leans across him, and speaks quietly to Nanette. "She's worried about the boats," James says, nodding in Suzanne's direction. "She keeps weaving these scenarios where we break in, rescue the painting, then accidentally drop it in the river on our way back out. She thinks someone should be stationed downriver to fish it out before it floats to Missouri because, under no circumstances, not even to save the Pollock, will she set foot in Missouri. She'll break into the SVA and rig up a priceless painting between a couple of kayaks, but she will not go to Missouri." The sparkle in his eyes is not excitement over the rescue mission.

"Professor Brenton." I falsify a gawk. "Is Suzanne Betts your girlfriend? Do you love her?" My warbling inflection is teasing, but there is a quaver of ache in my voice.

James chokes on a sip of beer and looks at me like I've admitted being impressed by Adolf Hitler's talent for human resources then regroups and settles into a reluctant look of joy. "She said something to you, didn't she?"

"No. Not really. Just that you guys have been spending time together recently."

"Since last summer," he says. "Almost a year now."

"A year?" And now the feelings of rejection and betrayal are for Suzanne. "I had no idea it'd been that long." So much for giving it all up to the universe.

James senses the hiccup in my response and says, "I'm sorry, it seemed like you knew. She didn't want you to find out like this. We were going to talk to you together." He says "we" like they're a legitimate couple, a unit. "We should talk about it later, when the flood is over, when we're not in a loud bar." The pity on his face tells me he knows about the affair he and I have been carrying on in my mind.

"Why would you have to talk to me about it," I say. My neck feels wormy, my ears hot, from jealousy and humiliation, exhaustion, starvation, grief at the sudden, stupidly electrifying notion I may not have children with either James Brenton or Ethan Lanning. From the accumulated strain of the last twenty-four hours.

"It's just, I know Suzanne will want to be part of this conversation," James says.

"There's no need for any conversation," I say, and consider pouring cold beer over my head but instead sip from my glass and replace it on the sticky tabletop. "Did you know Suzanne doesn't really want children?" I'm half talking to myself but looking James in the eyes. He seems surprised, and I choose to think it's directed at Suzanne, not at me, not because I've raised this private topic. "She's probably too old to have them anyway, or, well, I think her eggs are damaged. I don't know, that's what she said. She probably couldn't have kids even if she wanted to." I peak my eyebrows, indicating I am not too old to have children, that my eggs are healthy and, moreover, that I'd be willing to make available my capable womb, among other lady parts.

This is not exactly what I meant to communicate, but I understand, as James' face constricts and he pitches forward in abhorrence, that it is exactly what came across. And just like that my head is again crawly with heat, this time from shame—I'll betray my best friend by intimating to her boyfriend I'd have his children but won't even discuss the possibility with my own lawfully wedded husband.

Krissy the Waitress arrives with tequila and cheeseburgers then retreats into the mob, now swaying in unison to "Bridge over Troubled Water."

"James," I say, unsure how to continue. He waggles a hand, dismissing me, shushing me. Suzanne notices the exchange, and I give her a don't-look-at-me expression. Suspicion glints across her brow, and she looks away, picks up a shot glass, says, "To saving lives and to extraordinary works of art and to artists on rescue missions. Down the hatch!" She gulps the tequila in a quick swig, and James, Bunny, and Nanette follow suit. They slam down shot glasses on the wooden table. "Another!" Suzanne hollers. She and James clink shot glasses and throw back more tequila.

———————

After several more rounds and a Oneness blessing from Krissy the Waitress, the plan is set and we're ready to mobilize. It's close to midnight by the time we head for the door, a live version of The Who's "Water" coming to dramatic end over the sound system. My phone rings. I take it from my pocket and see it's my mother calling, the third time this hour.

I've been seated for the past hour and now, as I walk toward the front of the emptying room, the warmth of tequila spreads from my belly down my legs to the back of my knees. "Wait a sec," Suzanne says and bounds toward the bar, James trailing in her wake. I feel a tight grip on my upper arm. "What are you morons up to back there? I know you're plotting something, you and that Betts. Tell me." Hans Mueller is drunk and though the alcohol seems to have done nothing to quiet his hostility, it's all but obliterated his accent.

"Let go of me," I say and twist my arm from him.

He loosens his grip but steps closer. "Tell me what you're up to."

"Don't worry about it," I say. "You just get yourself home safely."

"I've been calling Director Holme for hours, Ms. Lanning, and she has been unavailable. I drove all the way out to her house and rang her doorbell seven times, seven times, and then I knocked on a kitchen window. I tried to look in through the doggy door, but apparently it's been nailed shut." He says this like it's my fault and rubs a spot on the top of his head. "I demand to know what's going on with the SVA." He is close enough now that I can see the rosacea on his cheeks purpling with anger.

"Ramona is fine. She's handling things for the SVA. You don't need to worry." My phone rings again.

"I'm on to you, Lanning. I saw you on the Internet, going crazy. Whatever it is you're up to, I'm going to find out. You can't just do whatever you want. There are consequences." He's yelling now. "Consequences!"

"You'll to have to excuse me Hans, I have to take this call. It could be about the school." I take a step away from him. "Confidential. You understand." He growls and I answer the phone. "Nina Lanning, administrative coordinator, School of Visual Arts."

"Are you ok?" Ethan sounds worried. For a second, I wonder if, through spousal ESP, he knows of my uterine proposal to James. Guilt bubbles in my brain, and I break into yet another shame sweat.

"I'm fine. I'm with Suzanne."

"Where?"

"The Thirsty Camel, but we're leaving as soon as we can wrangle everybody." I see Suzanne at the jukebox, flipping through albums, picking coins from James' open palm.

"The cops called, Nina, and it wasn't about the school. It was about you."

"It's fine," I say.

"It didn't sound fine. It sounded like you're in trouble."

Suzanne is pushing buttons on the jukebox. She turns and kisses James. A long, gross tongue kiss. "I'm sorry we haven't talked about having children, Ethan."

Silence on the other end of the phone.

"Ethan?"

"Are you drunk?"

"I've had a few drinks. I'm not drunk."

"Don't drive."

"James is driving. We're taking his Jeep."

"Okay, well, whenever you're done with whatever you're doing, come home. We can talk about…"

The aerobic heartbeat of Bonnie Tyler's "Holding Out for a Hero" drowns out whatever Ethan is saying. "Ethan? I can't hear you."

"… doesn't really matter right now."

"I can't hear you. I'll call you later. Ethan?"

Silence. I hang up.

Across the bar, Suzanne is gyrating, raising her arms overhead, bouncing to the song's opening cadence. I walk toward her; Bunny and Nanette meet me halfway.

The beat escalates, rises to a fever, as hoots and whistles ripple through the bar. Suzanne has done this here before. In fact, she's done this in most of the bars in the city at one time or another. Like many others, Suzanne has a go-to song, her karaoke number, her jukebox favorite. Ethan's is "Bohemian Rhapsody," which he renders with drama and accuracy. I don't know what James' is. I don't have one. Suzanne's is "Holding Out for a Hero" or, really, anything from the Footloose soundtrack except "Footloose."

A chorus of background singers belts out, "Doo, doo, doo, DOO. AAAAH, AAAAH!" Suzanne erupts in verse.

"That woman has balls," Nanette says, suddenly at my side. "Big, beautiful balls."

Suzanne gambols in place, a perfect 1980s popstar. She's got some new, syncopated moves I've not seen before, all knees and jitterbug, and watching her I feel sure she practices this routine at home. As she struts, sings, engages her fans, I picture her doing this in her bathroom in front of the mirror, dancing with her reflection. Suzanne would be a terrific mother. She'd teach her daughter all her best moves, teach her how to be shameless and joyful, and I feel a hollowing loss, for her, for the children she may never have.

She goes jiggling through the bar, and though I can't hear her voice over the song's synthesized gunshots, I see her lips move and her throat tighten as she reaches for the high notes. During the drum solo, she makes her choreographed way over to James, arriving just in time for the song's bridge.

"Up where the mountains meet the heavens above, out where the lightning splits the sea, I could swear there is someone somewhere, watching me." She quivers all over and smiles at James then turns past me to Nannette, points, beckons with a curling forefinger. Nanette shakes her head, but Suzanne nods at her, moves in on her hips, grabs at her hands, sings, "Through the wind and the chill and the rain and the storm and the flood, I can feel his approach, like a fire in my blood." As if against her will, Nanette is wriggling, singing along, shouting at the top of her lungs, and I stand there watching, my real life heroes in action, clamoring to the rescue.

Chapter 13

WE APPROACH THE SCHOOL of Visual Arts from the southwest, through the tree-lined Manford Heights neighborhood, the reversed circuitous route I took home this afternoon after mashing Bigelow's nose. James turns off the Jeep's headlights, and we roll to a silent stop along the curb several blocks up the hill from the school. This is as close as we're going to get—from our vantage point we can see that the SVA parking lot and a good portion of Benson Avenue hill are submerged. The sight is sobering and does not bode well for the building itself, not to mention the Pollock within, farther down the hill, even closer to the river, and still out of view. James puts the car in park, and he and Suzanne get out and begin unloading the kayak.

Down the block, I step from sidewalk to grass, into what is normally the school's expansive side lot, green and hilly, a diagonal path worn through the center. Tonight the slope is almost two-thirds overtaken. As I pad closer to the swamp's edge, groundwater squishes beneath my shoes and foam the color of mustard bubbles up around the rubber soles. It smells like Bunny was right about water contamination; the air, the water, the steaming ground—the whole mess stinks like infection.

My eyes adjust to the semidarkness, and I locate the SVA, thirty or forty yards down the hill in front of me. It is engulfed, swallowed, no longer landlocked but afloat, an island. The boundary where the corrugated steel exterior meets the rising water is seamless, the building replicated in elongated mirror image across the distended river, eerily lit from beneath by the parking lot's barely drowned blue safety lights. The scene is spectral: the building desolate, the water still, almost tranquil from where I stand. For the first time in what feels like months, the sky is clear, a smattering of stars across its inky canvas.

During the city's oft-recounted last flood, The Big Flood, in local vernacular, the summer I graduated from high school, the water reached 100-year levels. This meant, in useful terms, once-a-century flooding, five feet of water right here on this very land, where, seven years after that—just long enough to forget—ground was broken for Karl Stahl's über-modern masterpiece. The SVA. This stupendous, dysfunctional calamity of a building that tonight will be devoured by the cresting river. And though it's tragic, the implications grim, all I can think is, where am I supposed to go when I leave the house Monday morning?

A flock of Canadian geese glides into view and lands silently on the water, the birds pecking at the surface, scavenging, a band of looters with black ski-mask faces and stealth. Sometime in the next couple of hours, the river will crest. I wonder if I'll be able to detect the final, fatal rise. Standing still as a statue, I locate a window frame by which I might measure an increase in water level. I breathe out slowly then hold my breath, both for immobility and protection against the stench. I understand as much about hydraulic engineering as I might expect a hydraulic engineer to understand about American Abstract Expressionism or, more analogously, the School of Visual Arts' scholarship policies and procedures (nepotistic, rigged). But, as Nanette explained to me in the bar between mustardy bites of greasy cheeseburger, the Army Corps of Engineers underestimated the amount of water rushing toward us from the north, from Charles City and Osage and Waterloo, and did not release from our local dam sufficient cubic feet of water to prevent flooding. But, Nanette claimed, even if calculations had been precise, even if release rates had been optimum, there would still be a flood tonight. Perhaps gentler, but still a flood. No matter what. Nothing we could have done. Out of our hands. A force of nature. Karl Stahl would indeed be pleased—his vision of a structure discontinuous from habitat could not be any more realized than what I'm staring at now.

The neon blue subsurface glow and all the streetlights darken, and I am startled by sudden blackness. We've lost power. I can barely see the outline of the building. At once, it's as if I'm no longer in the middle of a neighborhood but adrift in a black boundless ocean, albeit one with traffic lights, an abandoned pickup truck, and innumerable trees, not to mention a 75,000 square-foot building, sticking up out of it. The night seems correspondingly motionless—though we're in a residential area, I hear not a sound, not a dog barking, not a radio blaring, not a single car humming along a side street. I know better than to believe this is the peaceful quiet of a summer night. No, this is the consecrated silence of defeat. If we just left the wake, we've now arrived at the burial.

There are footsteps behind me to my right, and I turn to see Bunny heave in sadness, his eyes moist, his cheeks ruddy and stippled with sweat. I put an arm around his shoulders and squeeze. "It's going to be ok," I say. "When the water recedes, we'll rebuild. It'll be good as new. It'll be better than new." In truth, I find it difficult to imagine how the building will ever be restored. All the damage, all that mold, and hazardous sediment—I wonder if there's a wrecking ball in the SVA's future.

"Let's go get Ramona out of there," I say.

"It's the least we can do," he says.

Suzanne, James, and Nanette come toward us carrying the kayak and a bunch of lifejackets. "Everybody needs to wear one," James says, and flings an orange vest in my direction. "Suzanne and I in the kayak, you guys in the canoe." I pull on the life vest and, snapping the plastic clips together, watch the happy couple head for the water, the kayak swinging between them.

"Ready?" Bunny says. Together we lift the filched canoe and walk it to the newly formed lake where we drop it with a slurp of watery suction. A few yards away, James and Suzanne do the same. At the sight of our seaworthy fleet, I feel invigorated, steeled in our mission, and suddenly impatient to see Ramona. When we were driving to the SVA, we stopped out at her house just to be sure she wasn't there. I rang the bell and banged on the windows but got no response. Her car was not in the driveway, though I don't see it anywhere here either.

"This is the perfect launch spot," Suzanne says, coming up behind Nanette. "You'll have grass beneath the boat instead of concrete, so you should be good, even if you do run aground." She hands me a headlamp, and I pull it down over my hair and turn the lens to the on position. A beam of LED light shoots from my forehead, and I aim it into the canoe where Bunny and James have tossed the rest of our supplies: bolt cutters, duct tape, flashlights, rope, another headlamp, and two wrinkly bags of peanut M&Ms. Bunny adjusts his life vest, Nanette pockets a few extra batteries, James throws back a handful of M&Ms. We look each other over, armed and vested up, battle ready.

"Let's move out," Suzanne says, and we head for the water.

James and Suzanne lower themselves into kayak's holes, and Bunny, Nanette, and I step into the canoe, Bunny sitting stern, Nanette at the bow, and me hunched on the middle bench, arms outstretched gripping the gunwales.

James and Suzanne paddle away in sync with no need to confer or exchange directions, two people who have done this together before. They move in a quick beeline toward the building. We, on the other hand, cannot get ourselves afloat, our collective weight digging us into the soggy lawn beneath the water. I toe into the muck, loose our vessel, then push off and step back in. Once we're drifting, we do nothing but careen about in zigzags and circles.

"Bunny, darling, you have to use your stick," Nanette says and looks back over her right shoulder, trying to make exhortative eye contact with her husband. "Put it out the back of the boat like this, like it's a tail. Yes, exactly, now push left, no right, sorry, right, right, no, honey bunny, right, now harder, you have to push it hard." We spin in a corkscrew and end up facing our point of debarkation.

"You don't have to move it so much," Nanette says.

"I'm not," Bunny says. "I'm hardly moving it at all."

"You have to hold it stiff. Are you holding it stiff?"

"I'm holding it stiff," Bunny says.

I look away, uncomfortable in the literal middle of what feels like a particularly intimate canoe lesson. Suzanne's euphonious laugh unfurls from the depths ahead.

"I don't think I'm cut out to be rudder man," Bunny says, and holds his oar out to me. "You're going to have to drive, sweetheart."

"I don't think you can steer a canoe from the middle," I say. "Just paddle when I do, on the opposite side. We don't need a rudder."

"We'll switch seats," Bunny says. "Stand up and we can sidle."

"I don't think that's a good idea," I say. I look to Nanette for support and see over her head that Suzanne and James have disappeared in the darkness.

"My dear, do you want to get into the building and save Ramona or not?" Nanette employs an expert I'm-not-actually-offering-you-a-choice tone that allows me to imagine how easily she must have bent her three daughters to her maternal will. "Because we will never get there with Bunny Rabbit driving this buggy."

"Fine," I say. "Fine."

I stand and step over the middle bench so that I'm in the back half of the boat, facing Bunny. He rises, wobbly on his feet, and lurches as he tries to step toward me. I reach out and take his hands, and we lean toward one another as he shuffles in my direction. The canoe starts to teeter-totter, left-right-left-right, a buoy in rough water.

"Stand still for a second and let me get by you," I say, but Bunny isn't listening, he's fidgety, eager to return to a seated position. "Stand still, Bunny," I say.

Still squeezing my hands, he takes a clumsy step forward and catches the heel of his boot on the stern seat. As we lose our balance, everything slows down. We're moving so gradually it feels like we should be able to stop ourselves, but when my body tips a little, Bunny gives into the momentum, almost like he wants to fall. In a split second, we're overboard.

"No!" Nanette's voice is a desperate pierce as we, still hand-in-hand, plunk into the water.

Flailing a little, I wrangle my legs beneath me, kick for the ground, and stand without difficulty—we cannot be in more than four or five feet of water. I brush hair out of my face, rub my eyes, pinch my nostrils, spray spittle to clear my lips, adjust the still lit headlamp, gasp at the oppressive stink—it's as if my nose is buried in the scruff of a wet sheepdog. Suddenly my canker sore, which I'd all but forgotten about, throbs.

I look around, disoriented, twist left, right, left, see the canoe rocking in place six or eight feet in front of me. The water is not still, as it seemed from the distance, even from the boat, but has a current. And "water" is a misnomer—this is sludge, full of branches, leaves, disintegrating paper of various size, shape, and color, all manner of debris, including a mostly sunken blue plastic recycling bin, an assortment of flattened cardboard boxes, and what appears to be a chipmunk carcass rippling toward me.

Bunny splashes in my direction. "Are you ok over there?"

I try to answer but am struck by a whorl of vertigo, and the nausea in my throat keeps my voice from rising. I am dizzy, cannot focus on the canoe in front of me, and at first I think, West Nile virus, then, tequila and dumpster burgers, and then I feel, as in all my life I've never felt, alien. Strange. Disaffected. From Bunny and Nanette right there with me, from Suzanne and James skimming along the water, from the School of Visual Arts, flooded and looming large, from Ramona and her conquering adulation of Lucky Savatos, from myself, my conduct, my body. From my husband. From Ethan. Standing here in slimy remoteness, head spinning, inner ears roiling, I am momentarily perceptive of nothing but the abiding lack of generosity that hounds my marriage. I think, it's fine, it just seems bad in this moment, it's going to be fine. It would have been fine. We could have carried on as one of those relentless couples distinguished by doggedness rather than compromise. But now Ethan wants a child. A living, breathing, growing-up, human child. And maybe it's the fact that I'm standing in a cesspool, but when I imagine that child what strikes me is not the potential joy it could bring, not the at-home peek-a-boo Raffi scene, not Gary giddily babysitting, no doubt dressing the child in my clothing, not even my own fears of negligent motherhood. Instead I think only of the gross unfairness of drawing another person permanently into our mess.

I close my eyes, tuck my chin into my chest, and relax my arms, which I hadn't realized were curled and clenched at my sides. As I release the tension from my shoulder blades and feel relaxation descend through my hands, I know it's really fortitude seeping from my fingertips. I am breathless with disappointment at how quickly I let go, at the absolute weightlessness of my limbs.

Never could I have imagined such a circumstance: the building underwater, Ramona trapped inside, the Pollock in peril, Suzanne and James in love in a kayak, Ethan at home playacting fatherhood with an international exchange student, and me, wanted by campus police, staggering around in sewage, a chipmunk carcass thumping against my breastbone as I try to keep from throwing up.

When I open my eyes, I turn my face away from the putrid slop, raise my arms with my gaze, up out of the water, straight overhead toward the clear night sky. Nearby the geese erupt in a honking, flapping swarm, as if something startled them. Wings beat, then the birds cross my line of vision in the sky above. Their trajectory takes them due east over the river, and they are exquisite: uniform and steady, conjoined in implicit communication, the kind of straightforward perfection found only in nature. I shine my headlamp on my raised hands then my forearms covered in goo, and then I watch as half-dollar globs, what I can only assume are nuggets of feculence, slide from my elbows, down my triceps and into my armpits. As they plop back to the water, I note, with all possible connotation and entirely of my own doing, that I am immersed to the chin in shit.

When we land aside the SVA building, Suzanne and James are standing near the top of the second story fire escape stairs, and we pull the canoe into dock just below their feet. I toss the rope to James who ties the canoe to the handrail, leaving plenty of slack in case the water rises further. One at a time, we haul ourselves out of the boat and onto the stairs. Bunny and Nanette unsnap their life vests and toss them back into the canoe.

"I'm soaked," Bunny says. He takes off his short-sleeved button-down, drops it into the canoe. "The last thing I need right now is a bacterial infection."

"Good thinking," Nanette says, and removes her own button-down shirt to reveal a full-coverage white cotton bra. Bunny wolf whistles, and I wonder if he and Nanette have always looked so much alike or if that happened gradually over decades of marriage.

"I like your style," Suzanne says. "Naked rescue mission." She begins to disrobe, at which point I decide to keep my sopping t-shirt and life vest on for the duration.

"What happened to you guys?" James says.

"Nothing a safety shower and eight bottles of Purell won't fix," I say. In the beam of his flashlight, I pick detritus from my body.

When she's down to a pair of opaque purple tights and a pale blue tank top, beneath which she is clearly naked, Suzanne says, "Ready."

"After you," James says, and pushes against the fire escape door, which opens wide.

Chapter 14

THE AIR INSIDE THE school is dank and close, the flood's ripe aroma amplified by enclosure. James yanks at the neckline of his t-shirt and covers his nose, and I'd like to do the same with mine except it stinks. I grab the bottom of my life vest and give it a downward tug.

We file down the corridor past the library to the abbreviated second floor landing and stand in a row along the banister. Through the cavernous center of the building, lit only by the moon, we can see down to what used to be the first floor. The flood has swallowed everything. The atrium below, where only hours ago Suzanne stood handcuffed, is a churning sump. A xylophonic drip-drip-drip tinkles out over hollow thudding—large, buoyant objects gently bumping against doors, walls, windows, other large buoyant objects. My office, the outline of which I can almost discern through the skunky water, is a fish tank, and I find myself wondering if gourds float. Ramona's office, behind mine, must be swamped as well, and I experience a flash of panic: What if she was somehow trapped inside by a stray oven lodged against her door, for instance, or some conscientious person locking up to protect valuables. What if she couldn't get out. She'd be dead. Drowned.

But surely she went upstairs when water began creeping under her doorframe. Surely she grasped the danger. I know she was alive at 7:42 P.M., four hours ago, when the email to Lucky was sent, and this reassures me. Still, seeing the building in this condition imposes a more fateful perspective on our little rescue adventure.

James steps back from the banister. "At least the Pollock's safe. Sort of." We turn in unison to look at the painting, hanging in its usual spot on the wall, directly to our right, even with the second story mezzanine, about three feet above the waterline. For several minutes, nobody says a word. Nobody moves except Nanette who takes Bunny's hand. Together, we regard the Pollock, its uncontrolled, sensual, almost barbaric quality, the slashing color, the dark, vaguely hieroglyphic angles and rounds. The barreling stampede.

It's staggering, really. This magnificent painting, the nascence of a brilliant career, right here in front of us, dangling precariously over a pool of sepsis. The water may not rise much more, but black mold already spots the walls and will reach the painting soon if we don't get it down. I look at Suzanne, standing to my left—I've never seen her like this, stunned into silence.

"Why don't we split up?" James says. "Suzanne and I will find ladders or whatever we can to bridge out to the Pollock. We'll have to make some kind of support rig so we can get it down without dropping it in the water. Nanette, you want to start working on the stretcher so we can ship it out of here in one piece? You guys," he indicates Bunny and I, "want to start looking for Ramona?"

I nod. Bunny nods. "We'll be in the library," I say. I can't imagine where else she could be.

"Ok. But keep in touch. If you go somewhere else, let one of us know."

We look at one other, each of us unnerved. What seemed, in preparation, like customary SVA escapade now feels serious. And stupid. Very stupid. I tell myself our quest is straightforward. Either

Ramona is here or she is not. Either we can get the Pollock out or we cannot. Simple. But that's not how it feels. It feels portentous. It feels like onus, burning a hole in the pit of my stomach. For about the fifth time in two days, I feel like I should apologize but don't.

"Where would you go if you were trapped in here during a flood?" I say.

"The windows," Bunny says. "I'd watch the water come."

I heave open the glass library doors, which normally autolock at 9:00 P.M. but tonight suck open without trouble. Already it smells musty inside, like damp, biodegrading paper, not the immaculate, odorless collection the school has spent decades acquiring and maintaining.

Rising floodwaters have not been Ramona's concern of late. In fact I've never known her to be quite that Old Testament, but this situation seems to have a way of throttling people out of routine.

The art library is L-shaped, the entrance nestled in the right-angled corner. The short leg, directly ahead of the doors, barely contains the SVA's thousands of art books, all jammed together in row after row of too-close shelves. The longer leg, Karl Stahl's most ridiculous triumph, stretches left of the entrance, roughly the size and shape of an Olympic swimming pool, cantilevered above the river. Its glass-paned walls house a smatter of study carrels, rectilinear laminate tables, glaringly uphol-stered armchairs, oversized coffee tables, and, at the very end, sus-pended out over the water, the librarian's work station, all precisely arranged for the appearance of randomness. Bunny is right—this windowed, cantilevered gangway is the best place in town from which to observe the flood. The SVA poop deck. As we walk, I shine my headlamp around the room, checking for our way-ward director and marking in my mind the bacon-frying outlets, their rankings, and whether or not I suspect them of having been employed by Dunbar. In this moment and in this circumstance, his offenses and my reactions to them start to seem the tiniest bit silly. The bacon, the gourds, my insatiable thirst for Dunbar's head on a platter. Our face-to-face quarrel, only hours old, feels like it took place eons ago, and try as I might, I have difficulty mustering the pique that drove me to threaten Pete Mustard and bash Bigelow's nose.

"Do you see her anywhere?" Bunny says.

"Not yet. Do you?"

"No. But look over there. What's that?" Bunny points, and through the glass walls, from somewhere on the short side of the library, I see light, a filmy halation. It's interrupted, on-off-on-off, but the dim glow is evident—flashlight beams. Two of them. Bunny and I, apparently of the same instinct, crouch and tuck in behind a pair of particularly atrocious chartreuse Herman Miller swoop lounge chairs. He grabs my hand while, with the other one, I click off my headlamp. "Do you think that could be Ramona?" he says in a rasping, near silent whisper.

"What would she be doing wandering the stacks with two flashlights?" I say. It's not that I'm scared exactly—mostly perplexed. Who else could possibly be in the building? And why? I think, looters, and picture a flock of ski-masked geese holding flashlights and handguns.

"Maybe she's looking for something to read while she waits for the rescue crew." Bunny says.

"Art books aren't exactly her preferred reading material lately," I say.

"Maybe somebody else reported her missing and the cops came looking for her." He releases my hand and presses his open palms to his bare chest, like he's suddenly modest at the thought of cops.

"If those are cops, why didn't we see their cars or boat?"

"Yeah, I guess," he says, unconvinced.

The flashlights pass the ninety-degree angle of the library's L, their beams crisper now, moving toward us. Bunny lowers to all fours and crawls in the direction opposite the flashlights and, for reasons I can't identify, I follow. We scoot beneath tables and around ugly armchairs, compelled to evade rather than confront the other trespassers here with us in the library. And then the flashlights click off and Bunny and I freeze. Whoever's there stands still, and I cock my head to hear someone shush! someone else. There is murmuring, but it's unintelligible, muted by the sound-absorbent cork flooring, perfect for a library, terrible for eavesdropping. We duck beneath a table for cover, and I stick my head just barely out, hoping to get a look at our companions, or enemies, as the case may be. More mumbling, flashlights click on, quick shuffling, the library door sucking open, then whapping closed. They're gone.

Bunny and I stand and I click my headlamp back on. "Find James," I say. "Let him know there's someone else in the building. Tell him we're not sure who it is, but we don't think it's cops. Maybe looters."

Bunny leaves and I head down the cantilever. Almost at the end, just past a seven-foot-tall cardboard sculpture of a goat (another tour de force by one of Suzanne's brilliant prodigies), the librarian's long low desk sits surrounded by glass and bathed in a faint purplish glow—I can't tell if it's moonlight, refracted off polluted water, or something inside. I walk around the right side of the desk and there she is: Ramona, on the floor, aglow in pastel LED light, a laptop perched on the desk chair in front of her. She has on sneakers again but is still wearing the tight black cocktail dress with its reckless décolletage, the skirt cinched up around her hips allowing her to cross her lean, muscular legs in front of her, and granting me a clear view of her red zebra-striped thong underwear. A triangle of silky fabric is enfolded in her labia, the hint of an elasticized ribbon disappearing beneath her, a tangle of spidery hair crawling out from either side of the narrow garment. With both hands she reaches out to clasp the seat of the desk chair and scoot it closer to herself. I imagine her wondering how the smooth-shaven Internet stars get their private parts to look the way they do, worrying that her dark, twisted patch of hair is a personal failing.

Ramona reaches with her right hand to pick up something from the chair, brings it close to her face—the framed novel cover featuring smooth-chested Lucky flaunting an automatic weapon, which she apparently had the forethought to save from floodwaters. I find this encouraging.

In the moments before she notices me, I think about Ramona from a year ago, five years ago, ten—a reliable, productive, principled woman of serious artistry—and consider whether a person can go through a metamorphosis of this magnitude and have any hope of recovering who she used to be. Whether she'd be capable of the objectivity required to understand her transformation, let alone undo it. Whether there's anything she'd want undone. Whether she has changed at all or if her intentness has just shifted, from art to men. To love. To aloneness. I think of how much I've changed in that same timespan—one, five, ten years—and wonder if there is any hope for me, for the rosy, willing woman I used to be. The artist. Wannabe artist. Abettor of artists.

Looking at Ramona, sitting here, exposed, her willful vulnerability strikes me as exceptional and wasted. I do a mental inventory of everything she has put at risk this past year, and it takes me a moment to identify compounded envy-pity, both for what she's done to her life and the choices she will now get to make. Fight to keep her job at the SVA or let it go; return to her printing presses or abandon them for good; chase Lucky Savatos around Los Angeles or continue stalking him from afar. Maybe she'll write a romance novel of her own about an intelligent, beautiful, scantily clad professor, trapped inside a glass tower, surrounded by a foul moat, slowly going mad as she awaits her hero. Whatever the complications, her aberration will yield certain liberties, and I feel glad for her; that had to have been her objective, at least in part. I want her to look up at me, standing here in sodden t-shirt and life vest, doing my belated best to honor her in her silky red zebra-striped thong. I want her to make eye contact, to exchange with me some kind of understanding, some invitation to join her in her obsession, in her liberation. For her to see that someone has noticed.

She pushes up onto her knees with grace and ease, the way a dancer or an athlete might. The black dress slides down her thighs, and she props the photo of Lucky against the back of the chair, next to the laptop. She sees me. "Nina," she says, not startled, not even surprised.

"Ramona."

"The Internet stopped working." She offers no indication she comprehends what's going on: that this is an emergency, that the building is flooded, that she's marooned in the library and I've come to retrieve her. That I've just shared a personal moment with her vulva. Her apparent incomprehension doesn't disturb me the way it would have in the past. It only makes me feel like an interloper, like I'm invading her privacy. I remove my headlamp.

"The power's out," I say. "Other than that, are you ok?"

"I wish I could get this website going. I was right in the middle of something." She moves closer to the computer, and in the artificial light I notice bags under her eyes, sunken pallidness in her cheeks. She returns to the revealing, cross-legged position on the floor.

"Let me see it," I say and sit down beside her. She pulls the laptop from the chair, hands it over to me, watches as I open the AirPort, check for available networks, double-click on the web browser, get an error message: No Internet Connectivity. I close the laptop and put it on the floor between us. "I think we're going to have to wait for the power to come back on," I say.

Looking down at the computer she nods almost imperceptibly. "It's flooding you know," she says.

"I know."

"It stinks."

"It does." I'm not sure if she means the smell, or if "it stinks" is the sum total of her reaction to the SVA being underwater. Maybe that's the right response.

With her left hand, she caresses the laptop, seems to consider something, then looks at me exactly the way I looked at the Pollock: like she is seeing me for the first time. At least the first time in a long while. She stops caressing the computer and hooks two fingers in the right armhole of my life vest, just below my collarbone. "Nina," she says, tugs at the life vest, grins. "How did you get in here anyway?"

I crave commiseration with this peculiar, lovelorn woman so that together we may identify the ways we've mis-steered ourselves, all the while thinking we were tacking the fairest course. So that we may map routes back to sanity. To happiness. To peace. "I came by boat," is all I say.

She nods. "How did you know I was here?"

"You forwarded me your email to Lucky." Her smile twinges, turns scampish. "Very sexy," I say.

She laughs freely, like she's in on the joke. "I was looking for you earlier, I thought you might be able to work the camera." She puts one hand behind her head, strikes a pose.

"I was at home," I say. "The building was evacuated." I take the Lucky cover down from the chair, look at Ramona. "Didn't you realize you were the only person here?"

"The Internet doesn't really work at my house," she says, and I understand Ramona didn't end up in the building by accident. She chose to be here. Must have hidden from Bigelow and his cohort during the evacuation. I wonder how much she's been perfectly aware of this past semester, how much she manipulated or simply ignored. All of a sudden, her behavior seems calculated and suggestive of the capable woman I used to know.

"What were you planning to do?" I say, a little terse, feeling duped. She shrugs casually, just one of the contingencies of being in love that finds a way of working itself out. "Weren't you worried about being stuck in here?"

She combs her fingers through her hair, looks out the window, down to the flood, takes a sudden, deep breath in and lets it out slowly, like she's trying to meditate or quash tears. She looks at me in that first-time way but dispirited now. "Should I have gone home and sat around by myself, waiting for bad news?" She is honestly asking. "I didn't know what to do, Nina. What was I supposed to do?" I get the feeling she's talking about more than today, more than the flood.

Before I can speak, Suzanne snaps into view on the other side of the desk, appearing with a suddenness that causes me to wonder if she was hiding there, listening to our conversation. "Ramona!" she says. "Look at you! You're alive and all gussied up. Look at that dress! You look terrific!" She is holding a two-by-four in one hand and a screwdriver in the other, both of which she drops on the desk with a thud so loud I'm sure she's dented the polished wooden surface. When she comes around Ramona's side of the desk, I see she's wearing a tool belt over her purple tights. She squats, squeezes Ramona hard, and Ramona squeezes back, welcoming the physical contact.

"Did Bunny find you guys?" I say.

"He and James are tailing the intruders like a couple of private dicks." It's the most Suzanne has said to me since our phone call earlier in the night. "You girls having a little powwow back here?"

"We're just talking," Ramona says.

"About men?" Suzanne says, settling in beside Ramona. "It's always about the men, isn't it." She adjusts her tool belt, glances at me, back to Ramona. "So what's the scoop with this Lucky dude?"

Ramona looks at me, surprised I've broken her confidence or maybe aware how preposterous her crush sounds. Rather than apologetic, I feel haughty; she chose to tell me about Lucky, trusted me enough to confide in me, to believe I wouldn't judge her, even if I have. She turns back to Suzanne. "He's a man," she says with tenderness in her voice. "He lives in Los Angeles."

"You little hound, that's great, I can't believe I didn't know about this. It's so juicy. Do you have plans to go out there and see this Lucky, which is such a perfect beefcake name, by the way. It's like he's a cowboy or something."

"He's more a special agent type," Ramona says, muffling a snigger, taking the framed book cover from me and handing it to Suzanne.

"Yes please," Suzanne says. "Very. Sexy." There is not a hint of mockery or objection in her voice; she is the one Ramona should have confided in. She would have encouraged and guided Ramona's pursuit, taught her about Brazilian waxing. Warmth balloons in my ribcage, a craving for the tribal grace of female friendship.

"We've exchanged a few emails," Ramona says. "Maybe I'll go out there and find him, later this summer once things calm down here."

"Good, perfect, so you'll be out to sunny C.A. with Lucky man, and I'll be here, in the middle of nowhere, forever," she wrinkles her nose, makes a puke face, "where it's either steaming hot or freezing cold but always dull because this is where James is." Suzanne's merciless way of breaking the news, which I deserve. It makes me wonder what James said to her about our exchange in the bar. "But it'll be fine because our little Nina here is planning to make a whole bunch of babies, aren't you, Neens, so don't worry about us. We'll have our own private dysfunctional family circus right here at the SVA." She is mad or hurt or both—passive instigation is not her usual gambit.

Ramona looks me over. "You don't look pregnant."

"Oh god no, I'm not pregnant."

"You never know," Suzanne says.

"Yes you do." I look at Ramona. "I'm not pregnant."

"You could be. You're a robust, sensual being with an apparently gorgeous vagina," she gestures to the open space between Ramona's butterflied legs, and now I'm sure James relayed a more-or-less complete version of my recreant overture. "Unless you've just taken a pregnancy test, you really don't know. You could have a little one squirming around in there right now. It's always a possibility."

"I guarantee you, there is absolutely nothing squirming around in there right now except maybe a few E. coli bacteria."

"But it sounds like there's going to be," Suzanne says and again, inexplicably this time, gestures to Ramona's exposed crotch.

"No," I say. "There is nothing up there, Suzanne. I promise. Nothing at all." A bratty rejoinder, the best I can do.

"Jesus, Neens, what is it with you lately, so petulant and negative. Why can't you say what you mean and get on with it so that you can be yourself again?"

"Suzanne, please, not now."

"Neens, yes, right now, I mean, god, what was that today, with the cops and the running out on us and now the Pollock? It's like you don't give a shit about anything anymore."

"What's happening with the Pollock?" Ramona says, clearer than she's been in months.

"What the fuck is going on with you?" Suzanne says.

"I don't know," I say, huffy, shrugging her off, thinking, evading. "It's Dunbar."

"Oh. My. God. Ok, yes, Dunbar is a ballistic jackass, we know, but that's not what I'm talking about."

I hear steady hammering in the distance and the interminable sounds of water—drip-drop, plunk, sploosh. "It's everything." And then, less in response to Suzanne's insistence, more because of fatigue from this endless day and a selfish desire to purge and Ramona's literal and figurative openness, I say, "It's Ethan."

Suzanne is silent but doesn't look rankled anymore. She doesn't look surprised either; she's been waiting for me to come clean.

"We don't want the same things or the same lifestyle or something. I used to be up for anything, all the crazy shit he always wants to do, but I'm not anymore. I don't want to go along with his stupid adventures, and I don't think he wants me to anyway. I honestly think he prefers Gary." I pull on the straps on my life vest. "It's like he thinks this is just how marriage is, like it's normal for it to be incredibly difficult, all the time, or maybe he's so busy and distracted he doesn't see how disconnected we've become." Suzanne sits back against the glass wall, stretches her legs out in front of her, slides both hands beneath her butt. "It's exhausting living with someone so upbeat. How are we supposed to figure things out when he's constantly making the best of everything?" I scoff—how dare he—then choke a little, realize I'm close to tears. "I'm cruel to him and even that doesn't upset him. He doesn't care. Maybe he doesn't notice." I look at Suzanne and feel measly for what I'm about to say but keep talking anyway. "How can he not notice?"

"Maybe he's trying to avoid a fight," Ramona says.

"I think it's just how he is. I don't know." But I do know. The problem is foundational. Behavioral. It's something I did.

Ethan and I never got past the roles we played for the sake of early impressions. Or, I never did. Never found a way to introduce my knottier, more conventional self. For years, I subverted errant moods and personality kinks to Ethan's better nature, and contrary to hope and love-struck logic, I found myself mangled. Worse than that. Empty. And now there's the resentment. The argumentativeness. The deliberate provocation. Of course there is. "I don't see why he even wants to stay married," I say, aloud but to myself. "How can he possibly want children?"

"I don't know," Suzanne says, and means it.

"How long has it been like this?" Ramona is lucid, almost like herself.

"A while. Years maybe. Even today, with the flood and everything, I couldn't be nice to him. He doesn't even know where I am."

Suzanne pulls her feet beneath her, sits on her heels, rocks onto her toes like she's going to stand up. "It sounds like escape by sabotage."

"I guess," I say.

"Or maybe you're not in love anymore," Ramona says, and I feel like she could be referring to any number of things.

I think about how Ethan would feel if he knew I was having this conversation, about how unfair it is, discussing our life with friends before I talk to him. About how desperately Ramona wants companionship and here I am, disposing of my perfectly wonderful husband like he's a gallon of sour milk. This confession—that I may no longer love Ethan because he's too patient with me, too generous and kind—disgusts me. I am wretched, an ungrateful child who's ripped the arms off her favorite doll and is now crying over the limbless toy. And still, it doesn't change the way I feel. "I don't want to talk about this," I say.

"Back up a second and tell me, who the fuck is Gary?" Suzanne says, and Ramona laughs.

"He's a student Ethan brought home to live with us so we could pretend to be parents. It sounds weird when I say it like that."

"It is weird."

"He wears my clothes," I say.

"He wears your clothes? Is it a transgender thing? Not that I have any problem with that, I'm just saying. Why doesn't he get his own lady clothes?"

"He's not transgender. He's not the problem. He's sweet, actually. I really don't want to talk about this." I unsnap and resnap the top buckle on my life vest.

"Nina."

"Can we change the subject?" Unsnap, resnap, unsnap, resnap.

"You can't bail out, not with the all this poison in your life. This could be the crucial juncture in your psychoemotional journey. You're obviously afraid, fine, but you need to dive in and struggle anyway, assert yourself in your life and take ownership of your trajectory because, Neens, you've been at sea for a while and this could be it, right here, tonight, the turning point in your identity transcendence that leads you to the actualization of your True Self, but you have to be present, you have to be open to it." As Suzanne works herself into a new age prognostic lather, Ramona rolls onto her elbows and knees, leans around Suzanne, and drags over a rumpled leather purse, which she opens and digs through. "Let's breathe," Suzanne says. "Let's absorb what's happening and be mindful of this moment. Feel these feelings. Don't be scared. Put your hands here, on your belly, like this."

Suzanne demonstrates deep thoracic breathing, and Ramona says, "This is all you need," and hands me a book, a worn paperback entitled *Lust of Yore*. "It's was one of my first. Forcible seduction. Very transcendent." She looks at Suzanne then points to the cover, which depicts a longhaired, dark-skinned hulk reclining on a bed, his leg draped suggestively over the side, a silky white sheet barely covering his danger zone. He's making the same scampish expression Ramona did earlier when I mentioned her email to Lucky.

"I'm pretty sure neither of these things are what I need," I say.

Ramona flips the book in my hands. "Just read," she says, and I scan the back cover.

"Aloud," Suzanne says, eyes closed, still breathing deeply.

I read, "'Patricia Spinoza, an independent modern woman, knew that the subject of her deepest fantasy deserved only scorn but, again and again, she drifted away on dreams of a gorgeous villain straight out of an old-timey romance novel. Maybe her scandalous flight of fancy wasn't exactly feminist, but Patricia couldn't resist. And then, somehow, by magic or something, she was cast back in time to the Old West, where she met her brawny outlaw in person. But he refused her, refused to fulfill her deepest wish. Patricia was going to have to use the basest powers of feminine lust to seduce the dangerous gunslinger…and love every minute of it!'"

"So does she time travel?" Suzanne says.

"You have to go after what you want, even if it's scary, even if it seems wrong," Ramona says.

"She's right," Suzanne says. "You need to figure out what you're after."

"Alright," I say and get to my knees. "I'll work on that."

Suzanne sticks her pointer finger up in the air like she's made an important discovery. "You need Muriel. She's your karmic guide. You follow her lead, and you'll be set." Her tone is casual, affirmed, as if I know exactly who and what she means.

"Is she the heroine of *Scantily Ever After*?" Ramona says.

"Muriel. Muriel Kaminski. The rabbits? Don't tell me you've never heard of her. She's incredible. I've been following her for years. How have I not told you about her?"

"It's beyond me," I say.

"Muriel," Suzanne says, her voice purposeful, titular. "She was first arrested in 2008."

"Oh come on, Suzanne."

"Just listen. Her neighbors made this big stink about one or two little rabbit corpses on her front lawn, and when the police came to her house, it turned out she had something like 250 rabbits living there with her, mostly healthy, just hopping about, happy as clams, Muriel and her rabbits, though I should tell you, in the interest of full disclosure, that there were some dead ones in the freezer, maybe seventy or eighty."

"Jesus Christ," I say.

"Anyway, she was arrested and fought the charges, but in the meantime the Lifestyle Gestapo, otherwise known as Tacoma PD, confiscated her rabbits and locked them up as 'evidence,' if you can imagine something so asinine." She pauses, waits for us to signal outrage. Ramona glowers, shakes her head. "Right, so they planned to put the rabbits up for adoption, Muriel's family, just give them away to complete strangers, no matter how painful for her, no matter how absolutely inhuman and wrong, but three days before the rabbits were to be given away, something happened." She pauses again, this time for dramatic impact.

"What?" Ramona says, rapt. "What happened?"

"They were stolen. All 250 of them."

"No."

"Yes. Muriel, little fireball, figured out where the cops were keeping her rabbits, got a moving truck, cut through a chain link fence, and pried open a steel door to get to them. Amazing, right, I mean, that is love." She flicks at the paperback, still in my hands.

Ramona instinctively reaches out to protect the book. "So what happened to her?" she says.

"She took the rabbits to a nearby farm, kept eight or nine with her, and fled for her life. She was desperate, you know, hated being separated from her family, but she didn't know what else to do. She was on the lam for over a week before the police found her. She begged them to let her keep those eight or nine, her special favorites, but of course the fascists wouldn't let her. They took all the rabbits back into custody and threw her in jail. She was despondent. But still, she fought. She took her case all the way to the Washington State Supreme Court."

"Wow," Ramona says, mesmerized, and I wonder if any fantastical story would enthrall her or if it must have daring, mammalian love at the core. "So she won," Ramona says.

"Oh no, she lost, big time. The rabbits were given up for adoption, and Muriel was ordered to stay one hundred yards away from all rabbits at all times."

"Oh," Ramona says. "That's not a very happy ending."

"The point is, Muriel identified the thing she loved and pursued it full throttle, at all cost, just like that time-traveling sex fiend from your book, Ramona, and what's more, she endured. When a probation officer came for a house check, he didn't find any rabbits but he did find a half-empty, ten-pound bag of carrots. Muriel had found some way to keep her love alive, even though it was illegal, not to mention socially unpalatable. You have to envy that kind of profound emotional experience. I mean, that's what we're all after, isn't it, living our emotional truths, no matter what or who or how that may be."

"Yes," Ramona says.

"That could be you, Neens. It used to be."

"A rabbit-obsessed fruitcake?" I say. Funny the way sadness and ignominy turn so easily outward to disdain.

"I think Suzanne's right," Ramona says. "You should get a pet."

"It doesn't have to be a pet. It doesn't necessarily need to be animal-related at all, but the idea holds: passion for whatever it is you decide you want. Love, art, rabbits, whatever. You need to give a shit."

"Maybe, in some very warped way, that's true. But Muriel sounds sick. Clinically. She should probably be in treatment."

"See, that's exactly what I'm talking about, that hostility and criticism. When did you become marshal of anybody whose path is the least bit unusual?" She gestures again to Ramona, "anybody with a little zeal?"

"Muriel's problem is not her zeal."

"I think Muriel is my karmic guide," Ramona says, not without humor.

"Well now, that certainly could be true," Suzanne says.

"Just forget it, please. Forget I said anything about Ethan, forget Muriel, forget my karma, forget this whole conversation." I stand up and my knees crack.

"What, you're leaving?" Suzanne says.

"I think I probably should," I say. "I'm afraid if I sit here any longer you may take my presence as acceptance of this god-awful advice and Ramona will try to buy me a guinea pig."

"This is not a joke, Nina. Don't shut me out," Suzanne says.

"It's a lot to take in, and I haven't even felt my feelings yet."

"Now you're just making fun of me."

"I'm not making fun of you. I just don't want to talk about this."

"Ethan is not your rabbit, Nina. He's a great guy, he's a blast, but it turns out he's not your rabbit. You can't control that. And you shouldn't apologize for it. He's just not your home anymore." Her eyes light up. "Gertrude Stein! That's the name of that wonderful lesbian!" She takes me by both shoulders, stares at me. "There's no there there, Nina."

"I'll think about that." In truth, my thoughts on Ethan are clear and inescapable, and as I stretch my legs I feel the weight of inevitability—this evening will keep moving forward and the moment will come when I return home and tell my husband that I do not want to have children with him and that I think maybe I've destroyed our relationship. "I appreciate your concern," I say. "Seriously."

"Nina," Suzanne says, but James appears on the other side of the desk, across from where I'm standing.

"Hey, Ramona, good to see you," he says and looks down at the SVA director's private parts then over to Suzanne. "We need the screwdriver."

"I know. I'm coming. We were just talking about how Nina's emotionally unavailable."

"Can I take it?" He picks up the screwdriver and the two-by-four.

"Yeah. I'll help." Suzanne stands, straightens her tool belt, and she and James turn to leave. "You two coming?" she says over her shoulder.

"Right behind you," I say. She nods, hooks her left arm around James' right elbow, and they walk away. I turn to Ramona, still crossed-legged, still exposed. "Are you ready?" I say.

"I'm going to sit here a few minutes."

"Ok." I turn to leave. "Why don't you hang on to this for company?" I say, tossing her *Lust of Yore.*

She catches the book, turns it over in her hands, studies the cover. "I'm done with it," she says. She places the book on the floor beside her and looks out the window to the coming flood.

Chapter 15

N THE SECOND FLOOR landing, James leans his left hip against the steel railing, the end of a length of rope hanging down from above, gripped in his right fist, his head tipped sideways and back as he looks up to the third floor. When I step toward him, I feel a queasy bloom of affection, and it reminds me of belly warmth from the tequila at the Thirsty Camel. It's not my usual infatuated moon, rather something closer to kinship, the sort of affinity generated by common love, in our case, for Suzanne. But the feeling is accompanied by the return of shipwrecked disaffection, the sense that Suzanne and James are together skimming away from me.

"Hey," he says without looking over. His voice is scratchy and strained. He sounds tired. I have no idea what time it is. Late.

"Hi." I follow his gaze and the rope up to Bunny who is peering down over the third floor railing. "Is it taut?" Bunny says. "Do you think it's taut enough?"

"It's good," James says.

I track the rope past Bunny to where it wraps around the third floor railing then cuts back down at a diagonal through the open atrium, ending behind the Pollock, eight feet out from James and I.

The moonlight is brighter now, and I can see the school's 28-foot extension ladder standing up in the middle of the atrium lake, maybe a foot in front of the Pollock, the top sticking up a couple of yards above the surface of the water. A second ladder bridges out from the railing, a precarious catwalk, secured in place with yet another length of rope. "What exactly is the plan?" I say.

"It's a hoist job," James says, like I'm a dolt for asking, or maybe just a dolt, period. He gives the rope a little tug, points out to the painting. "We tied one end to the bar across the back of the canvas then looped it around the third floor railing. Bunny insists on manning the fulcrum." I look up and Bunny puffs his chest, lifts his arms in muscleman posture, showcases sagging triceps.

"Is he up for this?" I say, not benignly. James crimps his eyebrows, *you should talk.* "He fell out of a canoe that wasn't moving," I say.

"Did you find Ramona?" Bunny says from overhead.

"Alive and well," I say.

"Excellent!" Bunny pumps his arms, does a little victory hop that sets his belly jiggling.

"See?" James says. "He's good to go." He holds up the rope in his hand. "One strong, steady pull should lift the Pollock off the wall, and then we just have to hope it swings like a pendulum, right over here."

"Isn't that a little risky? Swinging the painting around like that?"

"Better to swing it over to us than try to carry it across the water. We lined it up so it should come to a stop right where you're standing. The key is going to be using enough force to get it off the hooks but not too much or it'll swing high."

I look out to the tied-up Pollock, the latest hostage to SVA madness, and feel impatient to get the painting out of building. "Who tied the rope around it?" I say.

James grins at me, playful, a hint of misadventure creeping back into the evening. "Did you know Nanette teaches yoga to senior citizens on Sunday afternoons?"

"I did not," I say.

"She's surprisingly agile," James says.

"She's a magician," Bunny says, leaning over the railing above our heads. "An acrobat!"

"And," James says, "she happens to know a few nautical knots."

I look at the ladder in the middle of the floodwater and imagine Nanette wearing nothing but her bra and elastic-waist khakis, crawling out there just inches over the waterline, balancing, bending into a deep triangle pose around the painting and tying sailor's knots around the metal crossbar.

Sharp hammering bangs out from the far corner, and I see Suzanne at work on the stretcher that we'll use to bear the painting to freedom. In front of her Nanette is unfolding plastic tarps; she looks up at somebody, says something I cannot hear, makes a shooing motion with one hand. Whoever she is talking to steps away from her and into a beam of moonlight. Dunbar.

My canker sore fires and my jaw seizes, as much from weariness as anger. "What's he doing here?" I say.

"He claims to have come for the Pollock too," James says.

"He was the one in the library with the flashlights?"

"He and Mathias. They were checking the perimeter. For what, I have not a clue." I see Mathias Daman in the far corner behind Suzanne, iPhone in hand. I give him a look of warning, but he's not paying any attention.

Suzanne notices me, stands, moves in my direction. Dunbar sees her moving, looks over. "Lanning," he says, his voice thick with malfeasance. He looks battier than ever, wearing a knight getup, green knee-high rubber rain boots, black tights, fake chainmail beneath a sleeveless maroon tunic with some kind of crest on the front, all squeezed over his lumpy middle, making him even more potato-shaped than usual.

"Dunbar," I say, trying to match his assurance. Nanette stops what she's doing and watches as Dunbar and I size each other up. He takes a few sure steps toward me, and I see he has a jousting helmet under one armpit and a plastic sword in the opposite hand. As he gets closer, I make out the image in the crest on his tunic: a green semiphallic gourd brandishing a shield and broadsword of its own. He takes another step toward me, and Suzanne scurries, cuts Dunbar off, stands square in front of him, blocking his path to me. She adjusts her tool belt, steps her right foot forward, and sets her shoulders, a southpaw fighter waiting for the bell.

"I hope you're looking forward to a night in jail," I say.

Dunbar lets out an eruptive guffaw. "Priceless!" he says. "The intensity of the rage, it's so *vibrant*. Very potent. Very combustive. You're a true artist, Lanning. Welcome back."

"This is not art, Dunbar, and you're not an artist."

"You're right. You shouldn't always have to be the antagonist. Who should play the part this time?"

"This time?"

"We're rolling." Dunbar gestures with his sword to Mathias who nods at the phone out in front of him. "This," Dunbar says, strutting across the landing, "is the perfect encore to this afternoon's digital exhibition. It's the final execution." He makes sinusoidal swoops with the sword. "Me against the murderous administration, fighting to save *Art itself* from the gallows." He switches the helmet to his other underarm and tries to grab the rope from James, but James yanks it away and gives Dunbar an openhanded shove to the chest. Dunbar trips and staggers backward, exaggerating for the camera. He walks to Suzanne, leans close to her, lifts the helmet to block his mouth from the camera's view, and says in a hush, "The Pollock is about to be martyred, Suzie Q. Hung then drowned in the name of the cause. Far more effective than saving it, don't you think? Tragic. Maybe even epic." He turns to the camera, pulls the plastic helmet down over his head, reaches his sausage fingers through the opening to push frizzy tufts of gray hair from in front of his eyes. He brandishes the plastic sword and chops at the air.

Suzanne stomps a stocking foot. "Dunbar, you animal, just once in your sad little game of self-promotion and egomania why don't you take a step toward humanity, just one teeny tiny step. Do think you can manage that, you overblown assbag, or are you afraid you might cease to exist if you're not stirring up everyone else's shit and recording yourself doing it?"

"Mathias, did you get that? Is there enough light? Focus on her face."

"Don't you dare film me, Mathias," Suzanne says. Mathias lowers the phone to his side.

"Do you need me down there, Suzanne?" Bunny says, feeling bold from behind the third floor railing, hands at the ready in case the situation escalates to fisticuffs.

"Stay where you are, honey," Nannette says. She moves next to Suzanne, widening the blockade in front of me. "We've got this."

"Okay, let's all calm down," James says. "We all want the same thing here, so how about we just get the painting off the wall without soaking it?"

"You're missing great stuff here, Mathias, come on, keep rolling, keep rolling." Mathias tentatively raises the phone, looks at Suzanne who gives him a death stare, lowers it, looks at Dunbar who flaps his free hand in urging, raises it, lowers it slightly, then finally raises it again.

"The Pollock," Dunbar says, gearing up for his sermon, his voice reaching a theatrical decibel. "Strung up like an Ipswich sorceress, suspended over waters most foul, the physical manifestation of creative persecution." He skips toward Mathias, arms perched in front of him like a T. Rex, sword bobbling, and lowers his helmeted face to the camera. "Reprehensible, yes, but poetic, no?"

"Why don't we tie him up and leave him here to drown?" I say. "That'd be poetry."

"Let's not give him an actual cause for complaint," James says, and tugs on the rope in his hands, making the painting shiver on its hooks.

"This," Dunbar booms again, "is the monster's ball. Look around you, friends, witness the death squad, the lynch mob, behold, the executioners' song." Mathias lifts the phone and pans from one end of the landing to the other, capturing our faces on film. "And here I am, witness to the horror, with no recourse but to hold fast to a belief in the everlasting power of Art and lovingly administer the last rites." He stands the sword tip down in front of him, crosses his hands over the hilt, bows his head, and starts mumbling unintelligible nonsense.

"Enough of this," Nanette says, looking like she might launch herself at Dunbar.

"Don't," James says. "It's what he wants."

We stand our ground, silent, united. After a few moments, Dunbar stops mumbling and peeks at us from half-closed prayerful eyes and, seeing he's not instigated confrontation or capitulation, raises his sword overhead like He-Man and says, "Mathias, good lad, rouse yourself for we shan't stand by and do nothing! We may not be able to stop our foes, but that does not mean we cannot call in the cavalry. There's a burglary in progress."

Mathias looks confused, unsure if he should stop filming and call whomever Dunbar's cavalry might be, Pete Mustard maybe, or Glory Hedgeman.

James hands me the rope and I take it. "Hold it tight," he says, then moves next to Suzanne. "Get the stretcher ready, Nanette."

Nanette walks past Dunbar, toward the stretcher, and then there she is, Ramona, standing a few yards from us, her neckline somehow tamer than before, the picture of Lucky tucked under her elbow almost like an afterthought. Not forgotten but not the trophy it once seemed. She too seems changed. Not restored exactly but sober, like she knows something good has come to an end. "What's going on out here?" she says, looking at us, her chin jutting to indicate Dunbar, *what is this madman up to, please tell me you're not cooperating with him.*

"Ramona," I say. I want to beg her not to engage, tell her to go back to the library and wait, let us handle this, but her steady expression impels me to silence.

"Director Holme, what a delightful surprise, I had no idea you'd be joining us." Dunbar is gleeful, his neck reddening with ill will. "We were just discussing the role of antagonist for tonight's film."

"You should not be here." Ramona is intent, and it makes me nervous; the few times I've seen her this way lately she's been stalking a retired male model. But there is nothing jaunty or coquettish about her demeanor now. She is resolved, rather like the SVA guardian she used to be.

"What is that you have there?" Dunbar says, swishing his sword at Ramona's picture frame.

"Nothing I'd deign to discuss with you," Ramona says, and holds the photo down by her side, Lucky's face against her thigh.

"Something from the lords on high, no doubt, Official University Business." He speaks in a lowdown mocking tone. "Probably an operation manual, *How to Sell Your Artistic Soul for Career Success and Still Live with Yourself.*"

"I'd stop right there if I were you."

"Why? Are you going to tattle on me again? Tell the big bad general counselors I've been naughty?"

"I'm done playing fair, Dunbar."

A tight arrhythmia flutters in my chest, an indication that something featherbrained is afoot and I ought to interfere, ought to stop Ramona. But I don't. For some reason—final abdication maybe or, finally, trust—I stand there and watch her seethe at Dunbar, sword wagging by his side.

"Film is my preferred form these days," he says. "It's just so flexible, so immediate. Perhaps you were you able to catch our earlier foray, the work we did with Ms. Lanning?" Ramona is taken aback, rattled. "Or, maybe I should say, the work we did *on* Ms. Lanning." And then Ramona is enraged.

"I swear to god, if you did anything to harm her, I will take you down." I can see her actually quaking with fury. I know the feeling.

"Not before I take *you* down," Dunbar says. "Oh, forget you, let's return to the Pollock. I shall singlehandedly battle your gang of pretenders and bring down the painting, right straight into the muck." He swipes his sword at all of us, points the plastic tip at my face. "You look like you know something about muck, Lanning."

Ramona blanches in anger. She grips the picture of Lucky with both hands. "You really should not have come here," she says, her voice trembling and low.

"Tonight is the night, Madame Director. Say goodbye to your compatriots. Say goodbye to your precious school. And say goodbye to the Pollock."

Ramona jabs the picture frame out in front of her. "I'm going to end you," she says, and seems to mean it literally. Physically.

For one terrifying moment, the landing is silent except the distant, doleful thudding of buoyant office supplies. Nobody says a word, our speechlessness indicative of concern and irresolution; we're unsure if Ramona has finally lost it completely or has at last recovered her faculties.

Dunbar glances at Mathias Daman and his iPhone, nods sharply, turns back to Ramona. "I'd love to see you try," he says.

And Ramona is upon him, slinging herself with months, years, of pent up aggravation, taking it all out, it seems, on Dunbar's throat. They're a wriggling tangle of arms and legs, yelps and slaps, and I can barely breathe from the schoolyard spectacle. As they storm toward us, scrambling and shoving, Ramona brandishes the photograph of Lucky, jabbing it at Dunbar, corner first, in menace.

"You're a fucking maniac!" I've never heard Ramona use the f-word before. Her face is contorted in violence, her hair fuzzy and askew, pulled loose in the fray. She doesn't at all resemble the composed director who minutes ago emerged from the library, all precision and mettle, nor the dreamy-eyed sap I came upon earlier, cross-legged and bare. This is Ramona unbound, free at last.

"You'll never be anything but a puppet." Dunbar is spitty and hissing, batting at the picture frame with forearms and elbows.

"Don't *call* me that."

"You're a puppet. A *puppet!*" They're to us now.

"I'm not letting you *near* the the Pollock, you monster. You're a parasite, a cretin!"

Dunbar wings his arms out at his sides and moves in on her, a chimp, circling, ready to attack at the slightest provocation. Ramona drops into a boxer's stance, bobbing about on the balls of her feet. "You twisted wench," he says, in keeping with the medieval motif, "you think you can stop me?" He's snarling when Ramona winds up with her free hand, preparatory for what would no doubt be a powerful left jab to his unprotected chin.

James and I yell simultaneously, "No!" while Suzanne and Nanette, dropping the wooden stretcher, run to Ramona and grab her by the elbows, attempting to restrain her with an improvised full nelson. Ramona twists against them, turns to face Suzanne, and actually bears her teeth and growls as the stretcher crashes to the floor with an airy *thwack!* Ramona starts at the sound, looks up, and sees Mathias, filming.

"Turn off the camera, you little prick," she says.

"Ramona." I gasp, shocked at her language, as if that's the primary issue of concern here.

"Stay out of this," she says to me, then to Suzanne, "get *off* of me." She shoulders Suzanne hard then comes toward me, and I actually feel afraid. She uses the photo of Lucky as a kind of mini-battering ram, thudding me in the chest, grabbing at the rope in my hands.

"Ow, Ramona, stop." I give her a look of hurt, which she either doesn't notice or chooses to ignore. She pulls hard on the rope in my hands, burning a track through my closed fist. I loosen my fingers in pain, and she wrenches the rope away from me.

"Wait, not really," Dunbar says, abrupt, fearful. "The painting is seriously in danger." He looks worried something might happen to the Pollock, and I realize his taunting was only for the video, that he never intended to let the painting come to harm. "Give me the rope," he says.

Ramona looks blissfully demented, all hopped up on adrenaline and retaliation, and I know exactly how she feels. There's no quelling Dunbar-induced hysteria. "Give *you* the rope? Are you out of your mind? You are the bane of my existence, Dunbar, the curse of this school. Give you the rope. Just hand it over to the devil incarnate. You're not getting anywhere *near* the Pollock." Suzanne steps tentatively toward Ramona. "This whole thing, the evacuation, the Pollock, this insanity, this is *your* fault, *you* did this." Her wild contention, identical to my own earlier in the day, sounds absurd. Of course this is not Dunbar's fault. This night. This insanity. Maybe these things—the flood, the evacuation, the Pollock, the romance novels, Lucky, Ethan—are just things that happened, not things somebody did. "You'll get this painting over my dead body," Ramona says, facing Dunbar down, stance strong. With one hand, she lifts the rope, daring him to test her, and with the other she wields the photo of Lucky.

We stand in silent awe. Ramona is sensational in her self-destruction. I am relieved and sorry that it's her this time, losing it in front of a crowd, and I get that metal taste in my mouth. James steps in front of Nanette and me, his arms out, low and wide like a crossing guard, then backs us up, away from the fight.

"Ok, alright, you're right, I'm usually inciting rebellion in order to bring down your reign of terror, I'll give you that, but that's not what this is about. I want the same thing as you this time." Dunbar seems to be trying to reason with Ramona, and I actually feel a little sorry for him. "I'll put down my weapon," he says. Through the slit in his plastic helmet he keeps his eyes on Ramona and lowers his plastic sword to the ground, shows her his empty, surrendering hands. "See? We can work together. Cooperation can be sensationalized too. Just give me the rope."

"You want the Pollock?" She jerks away from him, gnashes her teeth. "Then you'll have to fish it out of the Mississippi." Dunbar lets out a little bark, lurches, and Ramona flinches, down and away, the top of her dress flopping open, the rope snapping alongside her. The painting shudders on its hooks, and as Ramona ducks and skitters, evading Dunbar's bumbling clutches, the Pollock twitches a few times then finally jerks from the wall.

"No!" Suzanne yelps and hurls her body between Ramona and Dunbar, grabs Ramona's closed fist and leans, trying to hoist the painting before it dips into the water or collides with the wall. James, Nanette, and I stand mesmerized.

Suzanne squares herself with the railing and pushes down fast and hard on Ramona's hand, giving the rope one final heave, jolting the painting up, clearing it of the water. The Pollock sails through the air, a quadratic missile, and, on a fierce upswing, crosses the railing where Dunbar stands. When the painting's bottom right corner collides with his helmeted head, it makes a plasticy *crack*, like a cinematic tibia snapping. Something clatters to the floor, part of Dunbar's orbital bone or a piece of the jousting helmet that's broken off.

"My eyeball!" His voice is shrieky. The painting, knocked from its pendulum trajectory, wonky from impact, wobbles and twists back out over the water. Bunny lets out a moan of dismay. Suzanne pushes Ramona, who seems to have lost her fevered steam, and takes control of the rope, steadies the painting, lets it swing once more to and fro above the water then, the oscillations slowing, clasps the canvas tenderly as if it were the wounded one.

"You gouged my eye out," Dunbar says. There is a surreal, full-circle completeness to the moment. Ramona has now bashed somebody in the face, and Dunbar has finally gotten what he's always wanted: actual victimhood, and at the hands of the evil overlord no less. I look at Mathias, still filming from the corner, and, with gut-souring dismay, feel certain this fiasco will mark Ramona's last act as director of the School of Visual Arts.

Suzanne takes a deep breath, calmer now the painting is dry and safe, propped against her hip, and turns to Ramona. "There are a lot of things I can forgive, and there's a lot I can understand, particularly from a woman in love, but this," she gestures to the Pollock then over to Dunbar, "this is inexcusable." Ramona doesn't say anything but looks satisfied, as if she's achieved something to be proud of. "Nina, come help me with this," Suzanne says.

I step to Suzanne's side and go to work on the knots at the back of the painting.

"You're through," Dunbar says, holding his eye through the knight helmet. "I'm pressing charges. This is assault."

"Oh please," Ramona says. "Who would believe you? Look at that outfit. What are you supposed to be anyway? You look like a homeless circus clown. And besides, it was self-defense. You attacked me."

"I was trying to get the Pollock, not you, and you know that. If it hadn't been for Suzanne, you'd have dropped it in the water."

"That's preposterous."

"I was disarmed and you attacked me with a painting."

"You came at me with a sword. I was afraid for my life."

"A plastic toy and I lowered it to the ground!"

"Just stop, both of you." Suzanne's tone is emphatic, but her pitch is flat and tuneless, entirely devoid of the empathy that normally sweetens it. "Look at you," she continues. "You've made this whole thing about yourselves, not at all about the art, and you very nearly destroyed everything." With both hands, she lifts the painting upright off her hip. "This is over. It's totally and completely over." Neither Ramona nor Dunbar responds. "Nanette, will you get the stretcher back up and see if it's ok?"

"I'll help you," James says, and he and Nanette raise the stretcher from the floor and check it over for damage.

"Nina, hold the painting while I grab the blankets and tarps so we can wrap it up."

"Yep," I say.

"I'm pressing charges," Dunbar says, and points to Mathias, nods a few quick times.

"What do you expect *me* to do?" Mathias' voice is all nerves, thin and quaky, reminding me that he's just a kid, barely older than young Gary, and doesn't belong in the middle of all this.

"Call the police!"

Mathias looks to me, the one who, as far as he knows, is in charge of SVA law enforcement. As little as I want to see policemen right now, there's a part of me that feels comforted at the thought of them. Cowardly, but comforted. It would again be the police interfering, not me. It would be them saving Ramona from herself. I look at James. He raises his eyebrows and shrugs, a mix of *why not* and *I have no idea what we should do*.

"No," Suzanne says. "You're waiting until we get the painting out of here. I don't care what you do after that." She looks at Ramona. "Call the cops. Tell them whatever you want. I don't care. But we're getting the painting out."

Ramona stands in the center of the group, conspicuously silent and looking aloof, like it's somebody else we're talking about who's going to be arrested and charged with a felony. After a beat that feels like a moment of silence, James says, "How are we going to do this?"

"We'll carry it to the canoe then Nina, you, and Nanette will have to hold it upright as we boat back to the cars," Suzanne says.

"Who's going to row?"

"Bunny." Suzanne looks up to him and he shakes his head.

"I'm useless," he says. "No boating duties for me unless you want that thing underwater. I can hold the painting though."

"He's right," Nanette says.

"Okay, well, Nanette, maybe you could kayak, and I could canoe?"

"Yeah, maybe, but you'll need more than one person to row the canoe," Nanette says. A bewildered moment passes as we realize we focused so intently on getting into the building and retrieving the painting, it never occurred to us to figure a way out.

"Shit, how are we going to do this?" James says.

"You don't have an exit worked out?" Dunbar says, cocking his maimed head in disapproval. "That's B-and-E 101."

"Like you're some criminal mastermind," Suzanne says.

I think how, in nine months, I've been unable to catch Dunbar in the building and how, from a criminal perspective, his escapes are slippery and impressive. He looks over at me like he knows exactly what I'm thinking. I get a phantom whiff of bacon and resist the urge to look away.

"Do you have any suggestions?" James says

Dunbar picks up the sword from the floor and twirls it, considering whether or not to help us. He pretends to be reluctant when he says, "I suppose I could allow you use of my knarr."

"Don't be disgusting," Suzanne says.

"It's a Viking ship," Dunbar says.

I know the ship he means, part Nordic merchant ship, part dragon boat, the same one from which he launched human waste cannonballs at the building a few years ago. At the bow stands a six-foot-tall serpentine monster that will serve perfectly to brace the Pollock as we row ashore.

"It's over on the side of the building," Mathias says. "We parked it beneath Professor Mueller's office window."

"We'll bring it around to the fire escape and load the Pollock there," Dunbar says.

Suzanne nods grudging consent. "Let's get the hell out of here," she says.

Chapter 16

$\mathcal{I}$T'S AFTER FIVE IN the morning when we pull into my
driveway and come to a stop in front of the detached
two-car garage. Out the side window of James' Jeep, I see
a slice of fuchsia against a navy sky, the sun's atmospheric refrac-
tion just beginning to glow above the neighbors' roofs. There is a
feathery spray of clouds, but it's mostly clear. No rain. I think of
Ramona and wonder how she's doing.

When I last saw her, several hours ago, she was huffing off to
the SVA library, refusing to help us carry the painting, miffed that
nobody had taken her side against Dunbar and, I suspect, embarrassed and tired, that hardscrabble exhaustion that comes after
any big blowout.

Once we got the Pollock into the knarr, roped and raised, mast
and mainsail, James, Suzanne, Bunny, Nanette, and I stepped into
the hull. The whole operation was so heavy, it required all hands on
deck. As we prepared to shove off, restiveness ricocheted between
us; we were as eager to get away from the building as we were nervous about what would happen once we left. I felt heartless and
hypocritical abandoning Ramona to Dunbar's mercy, a virtue of
which I know he has none.

James undid our moorings and Dunbar, standing on the fire escape stairway above us, said, "So we're clear? Row downriver, stay away from the building, then take my truck, cut back through the neighborhoods to avoid the cops. The whole area is flooded. You should have plenty of side streets to wind through, although the power is out everywhere and it'll be dark, so be careful." Dunbar tapped the gunwale with his sword. "I expect my vessel returned in the same pristine condition it's in now." James looked at Suzanne, smirked, raised an incredulous eyebrow, mouthed, vessel?

Dunbar continued, "Get the painting to safety and then, Suzanne," she turned from her exchange with James, "call me the moment you've got it loaded in your vehicle. Mathias and I will take your kayak and the canoe when we're done here. I'll come back later for my knarr."

"Can't you just call it a boat?" Suzanne said.

"What about Ramona?" I said.

"I imagine by then she'll be in police custody where she belongs." Dunbar produced a cell phone from some fold in his garb.

"Is that really necessary?" I asked.

He lowered the phone and made a show of gaping at me. "Is that some kind of joke? Look at me." He pointed to his eye, which he'd covered, atop his helmet, with a makeshift construction paper patch.

"We got the painting out. Isn't that what matters?" I said.

"My eyeball is what matters. And seizing the opportunity to oust Ramona. That also matters."

"Can we get out of here?" Bunny said. "It's starting to get cold." He hugged himself and rubbed his bare arms, the night's festivity long drained.

I looked to Suzanne for support regarding Ramona's fate, but she pretended to have some business with her oar. I should have argued further, should have made the case for clemency or refused to let the Pollock leave the site until Ramona was in the knarr with it, but I didn't have the energy to fight, and anyway I got the impression my strategic input was not as indispensible to this group as it had once been.

"Let's row people," Nanette said.

As James and Bunny pushed us away from the staircase, Suzanne said to Dunbar, "You'll hear from me," and when she nodded at him, it seemed to me something was confirmed between them.

Dunbar headed back up the stairs, lifting the phone to his ear. We weren't more than fifty yards from the building when we heard sirens.

———

From the backseat of James' Jeep, I study my house, check the windows for signs of light or life, look to see if the front door is ajar. My insides wring, the twist of dread and what feels like faithlessness.

"I'll give you a hand," James says. He hops out of the Jeep, walks around the side of the car, and opens the back hatch. "Slide it toward me so I can get a grip."

Kneeling, I push the Pollock toward James until it sticks out the back of the vehicle and he can get his hands beneath it, then I crawl alongside the painting and step out of the car. I help James lift and carry the Pollock into the garage where we lay it across a doublewide worktable. "It'll be fine here until Monday," he says.

I look down at the bundle of tarps and blankets, nod, walk back to the car. James trails behind me, goes around the Jeep to close the back hatch, and I step to the passenger side where Suzanne rolls down her window, climbs to her knees on the seat, leans her elbows on the windowsill, and sticks her torso outside. "Do you want me to come in with you?" she says.

"No," I say. "I'll be fine. I'm sure he's sleeping."

"What a night," she says.

"The worst," I say.

She laughs hard, wraps her arms around my neck, squeezes. "The best."

"I'm so sorry," I say, finally, sincerely, without ceremony.

"I know you are." Her arms fall away from me, and she sits back in the car. "We'll post Ramona's bail as soon as the courthouse opens." She looks overcome but resolved, like she's preparing to do something she really doesn't want to do, and I can see her making the delicate calculations: what she'll say to Ramona, how she'll be kind but unapologetic, how she'll attempt to counsel her on what to do next.

When she called Dunbar an hour ago, he confirmed he had pressed charges and Ramona had been arrested for battery with a dangerous weapon. It was unclear whether the cops considered the Pollock or the photo of Lucky weaponry. Apparently three policemen boated to the SVA building, issuing instructions through a bullhorn—put the romance novel on the ground and your hands in the air—which must have delighted Dunbar to no end. When the cops landed, they took custody of their perpetrator and led her out in cuffs and a life vest with POLICE stamped across the chest, Mathias filming the whole thing from some covert corner. When Suzanne heard the details, she became overwrought and, for the rest of the morning, reiterative—she should have never allowed this travesty. She didn't know what she'd been thinking. "It's not fair," she kept saying. "It's just so unfair. Not at all what I thought would happen. How is this justice? Tell me. How is this justice?"

She seems more collected now. "Are you sure you're up for a bail bondsman and the jailhouse? I could go," I say. She shakes her head, reaches out, and brushes a lock of hair from my face, tucks it behind my ear. "That's sweet, but I need to be the one to do this. It's partly my fault she's in there, and besides, you need to stay here and talk to your husband." I hesitate, look toward the house, don't move, grip the windowsill with both hands. "It's going to be fine. I promise. Don't worry about Ramona. You know her. She can handle anything, and anyway, there's nothing you can do about it now, just guard that painting, ok? I'll call you later." She smiles a consoling smile, and I look past her to James who smiles in the same way. They back out of the driveway and turn down Monroe Street, and I stand there watching until long after they're out of sight.

Plodding back to the garage, my shoulders and neck feel stiff, my legs heavy, the balls of my feet sore. My skin is tight from being dunked in floodwater, my hair crusty, my clothes stinking and stale. Exhaustion from the day shudders through me; I want nothing but a hot shower and twelve hours of uninterrupted sleep.

Inside the garage, I push the button to lower the overhead door and switch on the light. The painting covers the worktable and more, sticking off several inches front and back. I hold my hands out, palms down, hovering above the tarp and blankets. It makes me nervous having the painting in my garage, but I'm also staggered by it, honored to have this work of art in my possession, if only for a couple of days. It was a group decision that the Pollock be stored here—since it's stolen property and since I'm already wanted by the law, we figured it'd be lowest risk. Or rather, lowest additional risk. The last thing we need is another member of the SVA community getting arrested.

The backdoor of the house opens into the kitchen, and when I step inside, I'm choked by the alkaline tang of Clorox. The place is spotless. Ethan has scrubbed, swept, waxed, and deodorized, and this dismays me; it's either nerves or apology, the only two reasons he cleans, and neither seems like a fitting response to all that's happened the last couple of days. Hurt, maybe. Anger, certainly. But not apprehension. Not penitence.

Through the kitchen doorway I see Gary, still wrapped in my yellow bathrobe, and Ethan, both asleep on the living room couch, one head on each armrest, their legs and a few blankets entangled in the middle. I am revisited by the sense of inevitability I had in

the library, though I find myself wondering if the clarity I felt—
that my marriage is irreparably damaged—wasn't caused by delirium from swallowing too much floodwater. Maybe I was wrong,
misguided by Ramona, Suzanne, Muriel and her rabbits, flood-
induced stress, tequila, sleeplessness. Perhaps Ethan is my rabbit
after all. Watching him sleep, I want this to be the case. I want
it to be the case that Ethan finds he understands me again, and I
find I understand him, and our marriage becomes, as it once was,
inextricable. I want it to be the case that we are forever thankful
this flood swept through the city, through our home, and rescued
us. I want it to be the case because the alternative is unimaginably
difficult.

Walking through the living room, I don't deliberately make
noise but I don't try to be quiet either. Ethan is normally a
heavy sleeper, but he wakes with a start, as if an alarm sounded.
"Hey," he says.

"Hey."

"What time is it?"

"A little after five."

"In the morning?" He blinks, looks down his body to Gary,
smiles adoringly, rubs his eyes then raises them to me. "Are you
alright?" he says. It doesn't surprise me that this is his first question. It's not as if I expect him to say, "Where have you been all
night? How dare you go out for hours during a natural disaster
and not even call." Still, I feel disappointed and wonder how it's
possible he has no sense of marital apocalypse.

"I'm fine," I say.

He extracts himself from the body-blanket knot, puts his finger to his lips, and makes a shhh face, nods to Gary. "Come in
here," he says in a whisper, and I follow him to the kitchen. We
sit at the table, and I look at my husband, his eyes red and rheumy
with sleep. For the first time in awhile, I find I have no appetite
for spousal brinkmanship. I do not wish to goad or provoke him.

Rather, I want to be kind, and it's a strange, uncomfortable feeling. I'm not sure if it's affection or a parting gesture or, more selfishly, a ploy so that when he thinks back to the days when everything fell apart he remembers me as compassionate rather than heartless.

"I'm sorry about tonight," he says.

"I'm sorry," I say. "It was terrible of me to storm out like that."

"You needed it, whatever it was."

I don't say anything just run my hand back and forth across the tabletop as if I've got a rag and there's something to wipe up.

"So, is everything okay?" he says. I can't tell if it's fatigue or resignation in his voice, so I pretend he means the School of Visual Arts, not me, us.

"Ramona's in jail," I say.

"Oh god."

"And James is in love with Suzanne."

"Well, that I saw coming."

"Really?" I say. He nods. "I think they're happy. They seem to balance each other out." It sounds corny when I say it aloud but it also sounds right.

"You had quite a night," Ethan says. He doesn't ask follow-up questions and there's no inquiry in his tone, nothing to indicate he wonders what exactly I've been doing or why Ramona is in jail or how I feel about the flooded SVA, no tension telling me he's mad and pretending not to care but is actually eager to know more. He speaks the sentence flatly, inattentively, like exactly what it is—chitchat.

For some reason, what begins to play in my mind is the conversation I might have with my mother. "Mom, Ethan and I are getting divorced." "Oh sweetheart, that's awful. You must be devastated. Do you want to talk about it? What happened? Did that bastard cheat on you? He did, didn't he? Well, good riddance. Men are dogs. What will you do? Will you finally quit that job, for god's sake?" Her voice would be frayed with all the things missing from Ethan's: sorrow, conjecture, anger, superiority.

"How can you not be furious with me?" I say.

He releases a heavy sigh like he's worn out by the question. "I don't know your reasons, Nina. I don't need to. I'm not sure I'd understand if you tried to tell me. But I'm sure you have them, and that's good enough. You're doing what you need to do, and I have no problem giving you that space. You're doing your best." I understand the words coming from his mouth and, in theory, I admire his aplomb, but in reality I find it insulting. How can he be so nonchalant? I wonder if he doesn't repeat this time and time again— everybody is doing their best, everybody is doing their best—not as a Zen mantra, but as a method of disengagement. If everybody is doing their best, then he doesn't have to be bothered, cannot, in fact, be bothered.

"Come with me," I say. "I want to show you something." I take his hand and lead him to the garage where I flick on the light.

"What's that?" he says.

"Unwrap it."

He walks to the worktable and unwraps two plastic tarps from the Pollock, peels back blankets until a corner of the painting is exposed. With its somehow corporeal quality, its almost blinding dabs of yellow amid swathes of rich purple, its caked and knobby surface, the painting possesses me. I've never seen it up close like this—in the building tonight it was dark, and, once down from the wall, the painting was almost immediately wrapped in blankets, and anyway I was distracted by Ramona and Suzanne and Dunbar's bleeding eyeball.

"Please tell me this isn't the Pollock from school."

"It is," I say.

"What's it doing here?"

"I'm keeping it for now." I want him to understand my reasons, the ones he thinks he doesn't need to know. I want him to see them in this incredible painting and, more so, in the act of rescuing it. I want him to ask me how we managed it, how we got it down, brought it safely ashore. What it means to me. As I watch him for reaction, I acknowledge I'm testing him, unaware, and it makes me feel openhearted and deceitful. Here is your chance. Please don't get it wrong.

"I thought you were at a bar," he says.

"We were, but then we went to the school."

"Isn't it flooded by now?"

"Yeah. The whole first floor."

"So how'd you get there?"

"By boat."

"Who has a boat?"

"James and this neighbor of Bunny's."

"Bunny's neighbor went with you?" He doesn't say this like it's unfair, like if Bunny's neighbor got to go, surely Nina's husband should have been invited. He just says it like he's confused.

"No, we just took his boat."

"Oh."

"Nanette did, actually. She stole it."

"Nanette?"

"You've met Nanette. Bunny's wife? She teaches yoga?"

"Is she the one who came to the Christmas party in overalls?"

"Could be."

"Huh."

"It's beside the point."

"So what happens now? Are we going to hang it in the living room or something? Because if we are, that's fine, but we'll probably have to find a new spot for the Klimt prints. I'm not sure they'd go with this."

So maybe he doesn't understand. Maybe we're not two peas in a pod, or in a kayak, like Suzanne and James, but isn't that what marriage is? Two strange people jamming their lives together, hoping to find companionship and comfort? And am I really prepared to rip that apart because Ethan isn't asking the right questions? Because he's not bowled over by this spectacular work of art, right here in our garage? Because, ok, fine, maybe he's not my rabbit?

"It'll only be here until Monday," I say. "I guess the cops or somebody will take it after that, the dean maybe, or the insurance company. I'm not really sure. But at least we saved it, Ethan. We didn't lose it to the flood."

"Yeah." He doesn't seem moved.

"It's incredible, isn't it?" I reach out and uncover more of the painting.

"It's nice. Very colorful." And then he says, "Maybe Gary would like to see it. Can we show it to him, even though it's contraband? I'll tell him he can't say anything to anybody." From the eagerness of his question, I understand I was wrong. Ethan isn't unmoved by the Pollock. He just can't connect with me over the painting, over this night, this flood. He has, in the space of a day and a half, become more emotionally involved with Gary, and that is whom he wants to share this experience with. And I realize I've done the same thing, with Suzanne, Ramona, James, Bunny, Nanette. Even Dunbar.

Hopelessness drills down through my chest, and I understand that continuing together in this way would not be resilient or adult or normal but an act of cowardice.

"Sure," I say. "We can show him later today." Ethan nods and looks at the painting, and I can tell he's imagining what he'll say to Gary when he shows him. "I think we should talk, Ethan."

He looks up at me, startled but clearly cognizant of what it is we should talk about. It's the first real sense of connection I've felt with him in I don't know how long.

"We should," he says, "but not now. It's been a long night. I'm beat. You've got to be beat. Let's go to sleep. We can talk tomorrow when we're thinking clearly. We'll sort this out. Everything will be ok."

He reaches out to caress my arm in comfort, and his knowing expression hits me like a firebolt. All at once I understand. It's not that Ethan has infinite tolerance. It's not that he's enduringly generous or pathologically disengaged. It's that he's been patiently waiting, allowing me to come around to this moment on my own. It's that he's known, all this time, years maybe, what I now grasp: that what he and I have is no longer worth fighting for.

Chapter 17

*E*THAN AND I MET shortly after I started working at the SVA, at a university function for newly tenured faculty, a congratulatory dinner in a windowless mauve ballroom, hosted, in absentia, by President Havercamp. Suzanne invited me as her plus-one—she was cavorting with a first-year grad student in painting at the time, Mateo, his name was, of Cuban descent but born and raised in Gary, Indiana. For Suzanne's benefit, Mateo donned the guise of Latin Lover, affecting an accent and greasy disposition, all of which she ate up but couldn't take public. Ethan was seated at our table, talkative, dateless, and handsome. He seemed to tremor beneath a package-creased button-down, like he was struggling to keep himself from getting up and peeling out of the costume clothes and false party atmosphere. I remember his shoulders, broad and round like clamshells, remember imagining them bare, with my teeth sunk in. There was a throwback of sexism in the way he looked at me that took me by surprise; Suzanne was usually the one on the receiving end of chauvinistic attention. From the very start, Ethan seemed like a man set on getting something done but unsure how to go about it, like the precise moves were not necessarily in his skillset but he was going for it anyway.

Full speed ahead. I've always thought of him that way—abiding, and all sinewy for it.

When he took me home, a couple weeks and several dinners later, I knew why—he found me just the right shade of reckless. Basically unbridled but with a balancing dose of practicality. I presented that way, both deliberately and not. In turn, I thought Ethan was antidotal to the listless, browning relationships I saw among my administrative colleagues, the kind I feared was in store for me. Ethan was different. Brasher, stranger, more energetic. More interested in sex. I made the mistake of thinking these traits translated into aliveness, a necessary romantic ingredient, the absence of which, I was certain, bred stagnation. He made the mistake of letting me believe all that.

But I really was crazy about him. He was intelligent and almost obtusely nonjudgmental. And as a true believer in the power of the academy to do good, he was possessed with momentous professional ambition that I admired and envied. And he was kind. Genuinely, deeply kind, to me, to his family, to his colleagues and the students in his classes, to waitstaff and bus drivers, to small children and passing strangers. And then there was the intense, corkscrew chemistry, driving the two of us half insane. When we married, there was not any possibility I could have been persuaded our relationship was faulty. I believed we were pure and exceptional. Maybe everybody thinks that way when they're first in love.

We sleep most of Saturday, waking in the late afternoon to a gamy, sulfuric smell coming from downstairs. Ethan gets up to investigate while I shower for the second time and put on clean clothes.

When I'm decent, I head downstairs and hear Ethan talking, the sing-songy trill of praise. I step into the kitchen and, in the millisecond after we've made eye contact, before either of us speaks, before Gary explains what reeks like limburger curry, concordance forms. Ethan doesn't smile or nod, in fact his face doesn't change at all, but something passes between us. Surrender, freighted with affection and grief.

"Dinner," Gary says.

"Gary cooked." With a flashing glance, Ethan indicates the kitchen table. Gary grins and, like a Price is Right model, showcases an overfull serving tray—the apparent source of the foulness. He looks comfortable in the kitchen, wearing Ethan's Real Men Don't Use Recipes apron atop a navy blue button down Ethan got from his sister for Christmas but, when it was too small, regifted to me. It seems endearing now, seeing Gary in our clothes, and I feel a swell of appreciation, if not regard, for the boy. I'm glad he's been here keeping Ethan company.

"Delicious," I say, without a trace of sarcasm or discontent, and now Ethan smiles at me.

We take the tray and a stack of plates, napkins, and silverware into the living room, and Gary dishes up what turns out to be an atrocious garlic-soaked pork, green pepper, chili flake gravy concoction, which apparently spent the afternoon stewing in a crockpot I didn't know we had. Gary seems to have tidied the house as well and in such a way it makes me wonder if it wasn't him who cleaned the kitchen in apology while I was out saving the Pollock. I can't help thinking, like father, like son.

Over dinner, I do my level best to be affable, and it comes easier than expected. In fact, aside from the pork mash, which tastes exactly as it smells, it's a pleasant meal. In one great outpouring, I tell Ethan and Gary all that happened at the SVA. The events sound to them like some wacky adventure rather than a harrowing tale of professional and emotional undoing, which is distinctly how they sound to me, even as my audience crows and guffaws. Ethan explains the incomprehensible particulars to Gary—the two have developed their own lexicon since I saw them last—and together they exclaim over Dunbar's impetuousness. It feels familial and warm and even as it's happening I find myself longing for it, like it's intimacy I'm dreamily aware of but not actually experiencing.

Between Ethan and I, there is conviviality. He doesn't shift in his seat, and his shoulders sit low and move freely beneath his threadbare t-shirt. He is relaxed as I've not recently seen him, chatting, getting loud, teasing, mostly with Gary, who beams from the attention. I am the same, my bare feet tucked up beneath me on the couch, my laugh loose, conversation unguarded. We now share the burden of that exhausting secret—that it's over—and the parity acts on us like a tonic. Just as everything is about to fall apart, peace finally descends.

After dinner, Ethan takes the dishes to the kitchen, then he and Gary go to the garage to look at the Pollock. While they're out there, Suzanne calls to say she paid the $500 bond and took Ramona home, that all's well, Ramona is fine, almost giddy at what she considers a spectacular triumph.

"You should hear her. She sounds like Dunbar. Emancipation, she's calling it, like it's some performance piece. She's not even pissed at me for ditching her, or anyone else for that matter, I think she's thrilled she stood up for herself. Otherwise, in terms of the painting and the ass-whipping, we're basically on hold until Monday, apparently they're convening some kind of powwow with all the big wigs—Reyes, Bigelow, there's even a chance President Havercamp will make an appearance, should he deign to be in the presence of art faculty, the bigot—and I guess they plan to ream us all at once, which, if nothing else, is pretty efficient. You've got to grant them that, although one would think, at a moment like this, with eleven buildings skunked and molding into putrefaction as we speak, they'd have better things to worry about, but I suppose it's a defense mechanism, dealing with us first, denial, you know, which makes sense, the whole grieving process and whatever. Anyway, when I sprung Ramona from the clink, she acted like she'd been grilled by the SS but was tough and kept her trap shut, refused to tell them anything about the painting, and, Neens, you should have seen her. She was a proud little puppy, so pleased with herself, as well she should be when you think about all she's risking…"

After Suzanne finally hangs up ("Shit, I have to run, the blender's exploding."), I call Ramona but there's no answer, no voicemail, nothing. I try again a couple of hours later before crawling back into bed, but it only rings and rings.

———

Sunday morning I make coffee and spinach tomato omelets for the three of us, then retire to my bathroom. Ethan sits downstairs following flood news on the television and reporting it to anyone within earshot, repeating in a yell everything the newscasters say, screaming updates to me, huddled in my chair in the bathroom, flipping through old magazines, and to Gary in the guestroom playing computer games on the laptop.

"They've announced that the university will be shut down for at least the coming week, maybe longer depending on power outages," he hollers. "'Do not report for work Monday morning, no matter your position,' they say." And then four minutes later, "City officials request that residents remain in their homes to keep streets clear for emergency and rescue vehicles. If you must travel to get foodstuffs or other supplies, please do so on foot and avoid major thoroughfares and flooded areas,' which doesn't make sense since all the stores are either underwater, without power, or closed." And then, "They're saying it's the worst hydrological event in the state's history. Jesus, you guys should come see these aerial shots!"

Around 8:00 P.M., the phone rings.

"Hello?"

"Is this Mrs. Lanning?"

"It is."

"Mrs. Lanning, this is Oscar Reyes, dean of the College of Arts and Sciences. I suppose you know why I'm calling."

"If it's to let me know the university is closed for the week and I shouldn't report to work under any circumstances, though I appreciate it, the call was unnecessary. I saw the announcement on channel seven."

"Well, yes, the university is officially closed, but we're going to need you to come in anyway."

"Oh?"

"There are some disciplinary matters that must be addressed."

"Will there be a hearing?"

"More of a junket for fact finding. We're hoping to avoid an official hearing."

"May I ask what this is regarding?"

Dean Reyes is quiet for a moment, presumably in stupefaction. "You mean aside from a stolen painting and a charge of felony battery against the director of the School of Visual Arts?" He pauses for a rhetorical beat of disparagement. "We will also be discussing your own delinquent behavior, including threats you made to faculty and students, captured on video and posted on the Internet by, as I understand it, an undergraduate student." He says this like I've sexually violated a toddler. "As well as an alleged attack on Officer Rick Bigelow. Does any of this sound familiar?"

"Vaguely," I say.

"We'll expect you at 9:00 A.M. in the dean's conference room."

"Is that your conference room or another dean?"

"It's my conference room, Mrs. Lanning. My conference room."

Ethan is undressing, slinging clothes to the corner where a pile has grown, flood-related casualties, stinking and moldering. He looks to me unchanged from the day we met, not a pound heavier, not a hair grayer, though I know it's an illusion from having been all the time at his side so that the changes, however major or slight, are immeasurable.

"I need to do laundry," he says. With one hand, he turns off the overhead light, with the other clicks on the bedside lamp, then slides into bed beneath the top sheet.

"Me too." I unbutton my jeans, step out of them, fling them with a toe to the corner pile.

"Who was that on the phone earlier?"

"Dean Reyes. There's a meeting tomorrow morning, supposedly about the painting." I don't say anything about my own delinquency. Ethan doesn't know about Bigelow or the YouTube video and, at this point, I see no reason to change that. "I think they mostly need to figure out what to do with Ramona." I cross my arms in front of my chest and reach each hand into the opposite shirt sleeve, slip my bra straps down and off, then spin the undergarment around at my waist, unhook it, and let it fall to the floor. Ethan glances at the bra as it lands on the floor, averts his eyes, then settles a soft-focus gaze somewhere between my breastbone and belly button. He seems uncomfortable now we're alone, unsure whether he should keep his distance or be tender.

"Do you have any idea what they'll say?" he says.

"Not really, not about Ramona. Suzanne thinks we should bring the Pollock, have it in the room before everything gets started so we're not forced to produce it at some later date, so that I am not forced to produce it at some later date and take the blame. That's her thinking, but I'm not ready to part with it, and besides, why not make them sweat a little?"

He laughs. "Suzanne's right. You can't keep it indefinitely and since you're going to have to let it go at some point, you might as well avoid the blame."

"I like having it."

"Naturally." He shows me a smile that's more a leer, apparently going with suggestive rather than distant or tender.

"We'll see what happens," I say.

Ethan pats the sheet beside him. "Come here," he says. I sit sidesaddle on the edge of the bed, legs over my way, torso twisted toward Ethan. He tightens his lips and levels his eyebrows, reading me with that knowing look. "I know it's hard to believe right now, but it's going to be alright. It'll take time, and it may be awful, but it won't always feel the way it does tonight." He means everything, the SVA, Ramona, our marriage.

"I'm fine," I say, fear and heartache rising in my throat, the internal floodgates ready to burst, total collapse only one more kind word away.

"We're going to figure everything out," he says. "People do this all the time, weaker people than you, and they survive." Now he's talking about divorce.

"I know that."

"Come here."

I get to my knees on the bed, feeling like a small child in need of comfort. Ethan leans up on one arm and hugs me tight with the other, pulls me close to him, holds me for a moment then releases me, brushes my hair back off my shoulders. When he kisses me, it is with the force of certainty. He tastes savory, like green tea, and it makes me salivate, but his skin smells the way it always does: earthy, like rosemary and mulch, but underneath something stronger, rich and oily, a mix of kalamata olive and sunscreen. As he pushes his tongue harder into my mouth, I breathe him in and know that his scent will haunt me long after he's gone for good.

We stay that way for a while, kissing, then he rises to his knees, lifts my shirt over my head, presses his chest and stomach against mine, takes my face in his hands and kisses me again. His whole body is pulsating now, his energy corporeal, urgent, final, his need visceral.

He is not gentle. He closes his hands tight around my neck, my shoulders, jerks me by the elbows. He bites my nipples and pushes up against the underside of my breasts, where there's flesh and weight. He buries his face, inhales, grabs with both hands around my ribcage, and squeezes the breath from my lungs. My fingers rake his scalp as I gasp for air, and he moves his grip to my hips, his mouth to my abdomen, wrests me to the bed, flat on my back.

Between my open legs, he yanks down my underwear, takes me by the back of the thighs, the back of the knees, puts his lips to my lips, and I raise my pelvis, press myself to him so he can barely breathe.

"Use your fingers," I say, and he does, straining against me from the inside. He applies pressure to my clitoris with his thumb and tongue, his shoulders kneading bruises inside my thighs. When I'm about to come, I arch away and he slides up my body, slick with sweat and saliva. Compressing me with his full weight, he sucks my clavicles, finds my open mouth with fingers that were just inside me, clutches my right hand with his left, pins it above my head.

When he finally pushes into me, it is with headlong force. He fucks me as hard as he can, and when I cry out, it is in gratefulness. What other way is there to oblivion? How else can we hope to create a moment within which it's acceptable to be profoundly lost? To find ourselves, side-by-side, blind and blundering but, for this instant, unafraid?

And so we drive into one another as if we still have something to lose, determined to suspend time, if just for a short while, and stave off the end, even as we feel it shudder toward us, unstoppable and devastating.

Afterward we lie together, breathless. We do not talk. There is no discussion of our marriage or its termination. Ethan seems to understand I need to sort out the mess at school before addressing the mess at home. One disaster at a time.

That we've come in carnality to what feels like our penultimate moment doesn't surprise me in the least. From the start, we've allowed the heavy lifting in our relationship to be attended to by something chemical.

Ethan begins to snore lightly, sprawled on his back on top of the sheets, comfortable in his nudity and dried perspiration. I turn off the bedside lamp and measure my breathing, try to match it to Ethan's snorts. As if he can sense the attention, he rolls onto his left side, facing me, and becomes quiet.

I don't know why I propagated our origins myth—that it was Ethan's obligation to be forward-moving and irreproachable and mine to be tart but compliant and that the composite was conjugal dynamite. Now look at us.

I climb beneath the top sheet and curl into the fetal position on my right side, facing Ethan. I reach out to his forehead but do not to touch him, just hover, my hand above his temple, cheekbone, mouth, centimeters from his skin. I put my fore and middle fingers beneath his nostrils and feel streams of hot air against my fingernails. He doesn't stir.

I tell myself our degeneration has been complex and painstaking, so much so we couldn't possible identify one single cause or culprit. But I was the one who fucked it up. Ethan tried. He tried to outgrow those initial polished roles, tried to be himself, imperfect and cheerful, asked me to be myself, crankier, artsier, unconstrained and self-serving. He begged me, begged me to be fearless enough to be myself. Begged me to find comfort in our shortcomings. I refused, until finally our marriage deformed into something else. Something joyless. There remains no doubt in my mind: You cannot do this kind of damage and hope for repair. After years of chipping away at affection, what you lose becomes permanent.

I turn away from Ethan and roll onto my other side, slide both hands together beneath my pillow, pull my knees in tight. He deserved better. He deserved a partnership that wasn't endlessly trying but, rather, freeing. He deserved reciprocity. He deserved reverence. And that he patiently strung along, gallant and good, only makes the dismantling worse.

I scooch back toward him until my butt reaches his belly and fit my legs against his, tuck into the spoon. Ethan sleepily wedges a warm forearm against my back, and I am heartwrenched. All these years of reckless ignorance when remedy was right there, surrounding me, within my reach and under my control. I have been senseless and wrong—the fool, standing out in the pouring rain, screaming of thirst.

Chapter 18

O N MONDAY, I WAKE up feeling miserable. After six hours of fitful semiconsciousness, my eyelids are heavy, my skull throbs, and for some reason, I'm sore all over, muscle to bone, like I lost a bar brawl.

As I move through the morning—coffee, shower, awkward exchange with Gary when he walks in on me wearing my yellow bathrobe and acts like I hijacked it from him—the weekend's strange, homey suspension dissipates entirely and by 8:00 A.M., when Suzanne and James arrive to pick me up for our meeting with Reyes, I am swamped with dread.

After I've convinced Suzanne to leave the painting in my garage until we know what they decide to do with us, she and James hop back in the car, and Ethan and Gary come outside to say goodbye.

"What's the worst case scenario?" Ethan says.

"We're toast."

"Fire a bunch of people who just saved a, what, hundred million dollar painting, immediately following the worst flood in the state's history? Hopefully even Dean Reyes can recognize how bad that'd look. Besides, it's no easy feat, firing state employees, particularly you artists. You're an intransigent bunch of assholes."

He's trying to keep it light, make me laugh, make me believe the situation isn't dire, but I can't bring myself to crack even a polite smile. "Be that as it may, I'm not faculty, so if Reyes feels like firing somebody over this, it'll probably be me."

"Would it be so terrible if your job were on the line?" Ethan says. I'm annoyed at the suggestion and make a face indicating as much, but then he says, "I'm not saying I want you to lose your job, I know how much you love the school, but you've got to admit, it's been pretty miserable lately. Maybe it's time for a change." I continue to look at him like he's suggesting I might get leniency if I were maimed so I might consider sawing off a finger or two. "I'm just saying, I hope Dean Reyes knows you've been single-handedly running that place for over a year. That's your leverage. You can use that."

"Yeah, I'm sure the plan is to reward me for this."

Ethan smiles wryly. "You're not in the worst possible position. That's all I'm saying, even if you did threaten an undergrad with a frying pan."

I feel an icy searching sensation that I recognize as the impulse to lie, but it's clear there's no point. "You saw me on YouTube."

"As of last night, I think sixteen people have forwarded it to me."

"Shit."

"I'm very proud."

"Yeah, my finest moment."

Suzanne dog-whistles, then makes a gentler, more human let's go expression and flaps a hand out the car window.

Ethan looks at me weakly. "Everything will be fine," he says. "And if it's not, then it's not, and you'll deal with it." He hugs me, quick and tight, then takes a step backward and I feel him let go. In the past, he might have joined me or intervened on my behalf, but today he is leaving me, without pity, to repair this on my own. I feel surprised at my relief that he'll be uninvolved.

Suzanne leans her elbows on the Jeep's windowsill, sticks her head out as far as she can, says, "Come on, Neens, time to face the music."

As I start toward the Jeep, Gary scampers over and wraps his arms around my neck. My immediate instinct is to stand stock-still and pretend it's not happening, maybe fake hug him, arms encircling but not actually in physical contact, but he squeezes a little harder and I find myself leaning in, squeezing back.

"It's okay," he says, letting me go. "It's quite okay."

"Thanks, Gary," I say, unsure exactly what he means but comforted nonetheless. "Sorry I've been so mean to you." He nods, uncomprehending, and steps back to Ethan's side. I get into the backseat of the Jeep, pull the door closed, and for the third time in as many days, pull away from Ethan and Gary.

Driving through town, we are treated to a daylight horror show of the flood's destruction. The first thing I notice is abandonment. Houses are more than just dark and empty. They're forsaken. It's like a scene from some global pandemic B movie—the streets desolate but for the wreckage, the sky vivid blue, big-winged birds of prey circling overhead, squawking.

As we turn from Cicada Flats onto a main artery, I see that the homes to the east, the ones with backyards abutting the riverbank, are completely underwater. The sandbag levees Ethan and Gary worked so hard to build easily breached. Down the hill toward the river—though "river" is a now misnomer, it's become a ten-tacled swamp—the water is outhouse-brown, mucky, debris-filled, populated not only with conifers, but cars, stop signs, streetlights, floating bicycles, drifting propane tanks. Buildings. Houses. It occurs to me that somebody could have remained inside one of these swallowed homes, mistakenly or stubbornly, and could be dead, bloated, and bobbing like a buoy amid the refuse and bacteria. I wonder who is checking on these residents, confirming their safety, worrying about their possessions, their flood insurance, where they'll stay for the foreseeable future, what they'll eat, what they'll wear, how they'll ever recover. The dread I felt this morning is replaced with despair and fear.

Up front, James and Suzanne talk strategy for the meeting with Dean Reyes but our problems seem incidental. None of us lost our homes, let alone our lives, and the disaster we're about to face is of our own making. I tune out the strategizing and keep my focus out the window. There will be no quick cleanup for the people whose lives were in these houses, no weekend restoration, no fact-finding session followed by an under-the-rug resolution. It'll be days before the water even recedes and months, years probably, before the homes, the neighborhood, the city itself, are restored.

James drives in the direction of the School of Visual Arts but when he gets to Benson Avenue, continues south then turns left onto Perkins Drive, heading out of town. In order to find a traversable bridge, we have to skirt the heavily flooded areas, seven or eight miles south, then loop back up on the east side of the river. Even with the detour, we arrive ten minutes early. When we get to Dean Reyes' office, we hear chatter; we are not the first to arrive.

Around the conference table sits a who's who of my recent misery: Officer Bigelow is at the end nearest us, his face showing no obvious sign of having been recently mashed with a frying pan, and next to him is Charlie Miller from general counsel, a lovely workaday family man, father to infant twins, and tolerant campus advocate who once pursued in earnest an SVA student's lawsuit against Jay-Z for stealing cover art for The Blueprint 3. At the head of the table, looking like a stuffed peacock, is Dunbar, no longer in the knight outfit, instead wearing a faded sage green tuxedo with a yellow polka dot bowtie, hair mussed like a mad scientist's, a black vinyl eye patch partially covering the bluing contusion Ramona gave him. When I meet his good eye, he fingers a wooden gavel on the table in front of him then looks to the corner of the room, directing my attention to a media cart upon which a flat-screen television looms large. Mathias Daman, the little fink, is dancing around the machine, pressing buttons, working remote controls, plugging in cords, preparing, I can only assume, for the premier of his latest work.

"Motherfucker," James mutters, but Suzanne shushes him.

"Play it cool," she says. Her hooligan confidence gives me hope that maybe the fix is in.

James starts to say something, but Bunny walks in and Suzanne is up, pulling at his shoulder and whispering in his ear.

"Do you know if she's got something planned?" James asks me.

"Not a clue," I say.

We sit down in a row—James, Suzanne, me, Bunny—on one side of the conference table, as far away from Dunbar as possible, across from Bigelow and Charlie Miller. I run my tongue across the canker sore. It's flat and smooth now, no longer singeing a hole through my lower lip, and the recovery feels wrong; the pain was merited, the healing ill-gotten.

I scoot my chair to the table, and Dean Reyes walks into the room, followed by President Havercamp, who I have never actually seen in person. He's taller than I thought he'd be, rangier, his skin pulled, like he's suffering from the effects of sun damage or an overzealous plastic surgeon, and he has a gray-brown dappled mustache. He reminds me of a stretched out version of Michael Caine in Dirty Rotten Scoundrels, so much so I half expect a British accent. The men are followed by Havercamp's toady, an unfortunately undersized man who infamously endures ritualistic abuse from the individuals he serves. Whether this is fact or legend I do not know but, in any case, it's earned him the half-sympathetic, half-sneering behind-the-back moniker, Peanut. Poor Peanut. I've never seen him in person before either and he is a stunning anthropomorphization of his nickname. I can't help picturing him with a monocle, top hat, and cane.

The men walk behind us through the room, and we don't stand or speak. Peanut shoos Dunbar out of the head seat and brushes off the chair as if cooties might remain then gestures to President Havercamp to sit. Dunbar snaps up his gavel and moves down the table to one of the empty seats, across from Bunny and up one, next to where Dean Reyes is pulling out a chair for himself.

As people adjust suit jackets and scoot in chairs, I think how if only Ethan were in attendance I could settle my criminal, professional, and matrimonial legal matters in one fell swoop. Talk about efficiency.

"Are we all present?" Havercamp says. No British accent but a hint of something Cajun, a slight bayou twang.

"We're waiting for Ramona Holme," Peanut says. Havercamp looks at him like he doesn't have the slightest clue who Ramona Holme is, and, furthermore, how dare Peanut put him on the spot like that by not specifying title and rank.

"Director of the School of Visual Arts and, as of this past Friday night, alleged felon," Peanut says.

Havercamp looks pointedly at Dean Reyes. "In the meantime."

"Yes. Let's review today's points of discussion. I'll repeat what I told each of you on the telephone. This is not a formal disciplinary hearing. Our purpose is fact finding, so there'll be no official record."

Dunbar smacks his gavel on the tabletop, and Peanut jumps in his seat.

"Do that again and Officer Bigelow will escort you out of here," Havercamp says.

Dunbar lifts the gavel to his patched eye and salutes. Havercamp takes a long moment to glower at Dunbar like he's a stinking hunk of dog shit smeared on the underside of his shoe. He turns to Peanut. "No minutes," he says, and Peanut closes the laptop on the table in front of him.

Dean Reyes proceeds with a rundown of Friday night's events, stopping now and then to look reprovingly at one of us or simperingly at Havercamp. He gets it mostly right except that he's not sure who was there when Ramona attacked Dunbar nor does he have any idea how the painting was removed from the building or where it ended up. This last bit clearly aggravates him most of all. Just as he concludes his summary, the door opens and Ramona saunters in, looking like herself in t-shirt and slacks the same pea shade as Dunbar's tuxedo. She is followed by Pete Mustard, similarly cleaned up, no longer wearing a decorated refrigerator box but instead an ill-fitting black pantsuit with a ladylike sheen.

"How about this flood," Ramona says, like she's exclaiming over a downtown parade that's really impeding traffic. "I apologize for our tardiness. It's horrendous out there. Half the streets are closed." She's an altered version her old self, using mostly complete sentences, more or less coherent, but bubbly and loose. I become, for what must be the twentieth time in four days, terrified of what she'll do or say. She and Pete find empty seats across from Suzanne and James, and as Pete bends to pull out a chair for Ramona, I realize his suit looks ladylike because it is—it's Ramona's, her good one, the one she saves for formal occasions.

"Please allow me to introduce Mr. Black," Ramona says, gesturing to Pete, who sits down beside her, "my legal representation." Charlie Miller, from general counsel, mumbles something and scribbles on a pad of paper in front of him. I catch Ramona's eye to give her a worried look, and she winks at me, causing that now familiar chest-squashing sensation that lately precedes colossally stupid behavior.

"So pleased you could join us," Havercamp says. "Are we at last ready to begin?"

"I call to order this meeting to address and investigate infractions perpetrated by Ramona Holme, Nina Lanning, Bert Dunbar, and possibly other offenders as yet unidentified." Reyes frowns suggestively. "James Brenton, Suzanne Betts, and Professor Emeritus Bunny O'Brien are also present. Officer Rick Bigelow, victim, witness, and arresting officer, has graciously agreed to join us and shall provide detail as he is able. We'll address the primary matter of concern, the missing Jackson Pollock painting and, only as necessary, the related attack by Ms. Holme on Dunbar..."

Dunbar interrupts, "I'll ask to be referred to as professor, as is my right, or, if you prefer, I'd be comfortable with Don Dunbar." Dean Reyes and Peanut look to Havercamp who slowly closes his eyes for momentary relief from the sight of us then opens them again and gestures to Reyes to continue.

"The attack on Professor Dunbar," Reyes says, "that led to a criminal charge of battery with a dangerous weapon and Ms. Holme's subsequent incarceration. We are here today in cooperation to resolve these issues quietly in a manner favorable to all parties and to recover the missing painting. Again, we'd like to keep this meeting unofficial and off the record." Dean Reyes seems anxious, and I get the distinct impression I'm missing some subtext.

Pete rises. "Before we get any further, the defense would like to enter a plea of not guilty by reasons of self-defense and extreme emotional disturbance."

Dunbar raises the gavel to give the table another whack, but Havercamp stops him with a glare and then turns to Pete. "Mr. Black," he says. "Do you see a judge in this room?" Pete looks at the faces around the table as if he might actually locate a judge among them. "Do not be misled by Don Dunbar's gavel." Havercamp's voice is low with ridicule, and for a fleeting moment, I actually feel defensive of Dunbar and Pete. "This is not a court of law. There is no defense and there are no pleas. Be glad for that. Sit down." Pete sits.

"Shall we proceed?" Dean Reyes says.

"Yes, for god's sake. Let's get this over with," Havercamp says.

"A series of phone calls were placed in the early hours of Saturday morning by Hans Mueller to campus police, myself, and President Havercamp. Professor Mueller, though inebriated, made credible claims about a plot against the School of Visual Arts. We were, of course, eager to come to the aid of the building and the invaluable Pollock." Dean Reyes seems nervous. "Well, I mean, not technically invaluable, more like highly valuable, monetarily speaking, like, $143 million, give or take."

"Hans Mueller identified you, Professor Holme, as well as you, Mrs. Lanning, as the perpetrators. I suspect others were involved," Havercamp says.

Next to me, Suzanne removes her hands from the tabletop and places them in her lap. Her stubborn expressionlessness gives her away. The only people reacting are Charlie Miller, whose exhausted impatience is as plain as the infant spit up across the breast of his wrinkly suit jacket, and James, who looks guilty as hell.

"I'm going to assume from your general lack of surprise or outrage that the rest of you already know about this," Havercamp says, his twitching mustache the only betrayal of how volcanically furious he is. "Listen closely to the following: The Pollock belongs to the university, and its disappearance constitutes larceny. If we leave this meeting without resolution, you can expect criminal consequences, along with professional."

"It sounds to me like you're threatening faculty and staff," Ramona says, unfazed. "And that seems ill-advised, given the fact that, as far as you know and as far as you can prove, they've done nothing wrong."

Havercamp stares at her. "Very well, Professor Holme, let's fact-find, shall we?" He crosses his long left leg over his right, his knobbed knees sticking up above the tabletop.

"Officer Bigelow, we'll begin with you," Dean Reyes says. "You responded to an emergency call placed by Bert Dunbar in the early hours of Saturday morning. Is that correct?"

"Yes, sir."

"Please explain to us your understanding of the events that preceded this call."

"After receiving several calls from Hans Mueller and then the 911 emergency call, I travelled by boat to the School of Visual Arts and took a statement from Bert Dunbar, who, at the time, was trespassing on evacuated property and was also in violation of a restraining order." Bigelow holds up a copy of the restraining order, the one I gave him Friday, and hands it over to Charlie Miller. "He told me Ramona Holme had assaulted him with a painting, 'The Pollock,' he called it, which didn't mean anything to me at the time. He had what looked to be a minor wound to his eye, more or less corroborating his statement, and Ms. Holme made no denial of her involvement. Professor Dunbar said he wanted to press charges, so I cuffed her and took them both in."

"And where was the painting at this time?"

"It wasn't anywhere on the premises, not that I saw anyway. I questioned Professor Dunbar about its location, thinking I'd need it as evidence since he claimed it was Ms. Holme's weapon of choice, but he couldn't locate it either."

"Professor Dunbar? What do you have to say about that?"

"I have no idea what happened to the painting after she crushed my skull with it. I was practically blind in one eye and had to tend my wound."

"Director Holme?"

"My client pleads the fifth," Pete says.

"I won't tell you again, Mr. Black..."

Bunny pushes back in his chair and shoots up. "Dunbar knows exactly what happened to the painting," he says.

"That's an outrageous lie." Dunbar stands. "I couldn't tell you the location of that painting if my life depended on it." This is, in fact, the truth.

"So you were present at the time of the attack?" Havercamp says to Bunny.

"Proudly," Bunny says, with barely repressed glee at finally defending the SVA against university leadership. In this moment, despite mounting terror, I am delighted for him.

"Who else was there?"

"Nobody. Not a single soul. I accompanied Ramona to the building to help her save the painting. Professor Dunbar was already there when we arrived."

"That isn't what Hans Mueller said," Dean Reyes says. "He saw all of you at the Thirsty Camel, planning your intrusion into the School of Visual Arts."

"Hans is a liar and a traitor," Bunny says. "He can't be trusted. He has a personal vendetta against Ramona. He'd say anything to bring her down."

"So after the attack on Professor Dunbar, you singlehandedly removed the painting from the building before the police arrived? Is that what you're claiming?"

"I'm claiming only to have been there at the time of the assault, which was not Ramona's fault, and that Dunbar knows exactly what happened to the painting."

"Outrageous!" Dunbar says. "I'm the victim, not the perpetrator."

Havercamp looks over to Peanut who rolls his eyes. I'm so sorry these abhorrent peons are wasting your precious time, m'lord. "I have a hard time believing your involvement ends there, Bunny," Havercamp says, "and I promise you, it's in your interest to tell me exactly what happened."

"That sounds like an unfounded accusation and, yet again, a threat," Ramona says. "Perhaps we should be taking minutes after all."

"I think now would be an appropriate time to review the evidence," Dean Reyes says. "I understand there is a video recording of the events?"

Pete stands again. "The defense renews its objection to the video evidence as hearsay."

"A video recording is the opposite of hearsay," Havercamp says. "And, as I've already informed you, this is not a courtroom; there are no objections. What kind of lawyer are you?"

Pete remains standing and smoothes the shimmery lapels of his lady suit.

"Play it," Dean Reyes says.

The video is shaky, the sound garbled, not the same high quality as the masterwork Mathias posted Friday on YouTube. It opens with a shot of Dunbar ranting about the gallows and the execution of Art itself but cuts quickly to Ramona followed by a shot of Bunny overhead and then back to Dunbar talking about Ramona selling her artistic soul. After a few seconds of Bunny flexing his muscles from over the third floor railing, Ramona and Dunbar come marching toward the camera, screaming at one another, too far away to be audible. The shot cuts again, and Ramona is wielding the photograph, looking furious, then there is an unfocused image of what appears to be Dunbar raising his sword overhead then lowering it in a chopping motion, something I don't recall actually happening. Cut to Ramona's face, full of fear, as she pleads, "Don't hurt me, Bert," then the shot changes again, and she's ducking, pulling the rope with her, and Dunbar moves in on her in a blurry jumble of flailing limbs. The screen is black for half a second and there is a close-up of Dunbar's face in hyperbolic surprise as he is struck, in slow motion, by the painting. Fade to black, roll credits.

Across the table Dunbar applauds. "Extraordinary work, young man, just extraordinary." I, however, am baffled—the video does not at all resemble what actually took place. It is a highly edited, highly fictionalized montage of something only vaguely reflective of real events and entirely exclusive of Suzanne, James, Nanette, and me. When did Ramona say, "Don't hurt me, Bert?" When has she ever called Dunbar "Bert?" The two of them must have made some arrangement—not to mention footage—after we left with the painting. I wonder what promises Ramona had to make for Dunbar to delete us from the final cut. This was her final act as director, this remake, this deed of sacrifice and guardianship, for us, for the Pollock.

Pete smacks the table with open palms. "Clearly my client was acting in her own defense, and the collision of painting and helmet was nothing more than a happy accident." Ramona looks composed and resigned, all this theater for the sake of what, and who, she loves.

"That is not at all clear to me, but neither is it my concern." Havercamp makes a dismissive brushing motion with his right hand, identical to one of Ethan's favored gesture. "I want the painting back." His voice is like distant thunder, and I understand that in his blinkered perception the only thing that matters is recovery of the Pollock. Not the painting itself, just its safe return. Not the flooded school. Not Dunbar or Ramona or their squabble, not any of us, not any of our actions. All that's at stake here is presidential protection from scandal generated by the loss of valuable artwork. But rather than assure me we're not worth firing, this only makes me feel all the more disposable.

Havercamp continues, "What I cannot tell from this video is what happened to the painting after it struck Dunbar in the head. Can someone please speak to that? Bunny?"

"I'll never talk," Bunny says, raising his voice, hands on hips, getting a little carried away.

"Who made the video? Was it the student? Professor Betts?" Havercamp says. Suzanne crosses her right leg over her left, mimicking Havercamp's posture, implicitly daring him, like this is all a game of chicken. "I understand from Professor Mueller that you were the one leading the charge at the Thirsty Camel."

"I have no knowledge of what happened to the Pollock, and I resent any implication that I do," Suzanne says.

"What about my eye?" Dunbar says. "I demand to discuss Ramona's punishment."

"That's not my concern," Havercamp says.

Dunbar stands and flips the eye patch up onto his forehead displaying a slightly swollen eye and a short, crusty red-brown laceration across the bottom of the socket. "This is not concerning?" he says. "I'm Cyclops!"

"A salient point, professor, but your disfigurement is nevertheless not at issue today," Havercamp says.

"I shall sue!" Dunbar says.

"We shall countersue," Pete says, and I swear Dunbar mouths along, as if silently reciting lines from a script.

Dunbar lifts the gavel overhead and shakes it. "I demand justice and restitution. Ramona Holme shall be put away."

"You scurvy dog," Pete says, and now I know Dunbar wrote the dialogue. "You'll never take our freedom."

"Try and stop me," Dunbar says, loosening his bowtie like he's preparing for a fight.

"Enough," Havercamp says. "Jesus Christ, you people are morons." He doesn't raise his voice, if anything he lowers and deepens it, almost to a growl. His stretched face, that thin mustache, the southern edge to his speech, command our attention. The room becomes quiet. "I want the painting," he says, spitting out the words as if he's discussing venereal disease rather than a great work of art. "And let me tell you what happens if I don't get it. For suspected faculty—that includes you, Professor Betts—we'll begin with one semester of leave without pay, pending the outcome of an investigation, which I can guarantee will not resolve in your favor. For Dunbar, there'll be further punishment for violating the restraining order. Let's say one full academic year of leave without pay, plus criminal penalties. The same for Ms. Holme, one full academic year, dismissal from her position as director, and whatever comes of the felony battery charge. For staff," he looks at me and I can't take my eyes from the twitching mustache, "it'll be termination of employment. If you're lucky, Ms. Lanning, I'll allow you to resign rather than be fired so that you have some prayer of future gainful employment. If you're lucky."

Havercamp strikes me as a man true to his threats, and this one leaves me feeling physically ill. Unemployed divorcee. Terrific.

Ramona lets out an airy scoff. "I'll fight you every step of the way, publicly if necessary. If you want the Pollock back, there will have to be guarantees. For my faculty, for Nina. You can't do a thing without cause." This is Ramona, playing her hand—she'll go down for stealing the Pollock if Havercamp lets the rest of us off the hook.

"I have cause," Havercamp says in that low growl. "I have a mandate from the chairman of the State Board of Regents to ensure the Pollock's safety and prepare it for auction. Have you any idea how far the money from that painting will go toward recovery? I'm not going to let a bunch of artists interfere with that."

Ramona is silent, thunderstruck. Auction. She had no idea. There is an atmospheric shift in the room from mischievous to menacing. We have no move here. If before we were hopeful of escape with reprimand and a bit of self-righteousness, it seems now we'll be lucky to leave the room with our freedom, let alone our jobs. Let alone the Pollock.

"What does that mean, 'prepare it for auction'?" Suzanne says.

Havercamp grins.

"The painting is to be sold," Dean Reyes says, the insistence in his voice an expression of joy at crushing our collective spirit.

I'd have thought nothing could make this worse, nothing could compound the losses, but this does it. We are uniformly horrified. Bunny's lower lip actually begins to quiver.

"You can't," Ramona says.

"It's already done," Havercamp says. "After the river crested Friday night, the regents spent the weekend in an emergency session reviewing expendable assets. That painting is at the top of the list. Once it's recovered, it goes to straight auction."

"You're fucking with us," Suzanne says.

"We've already been in touch with Sotheby's," Dean Reyes says, taking obvious pleasure in Suzanne's agony.

"You're out of your minds if you think we're going to let that happen," Suzanne says. "You think you can just hock the Pollock to the highest bidder and nobody will try to stop you? You're deluded, and even if that were a realistic possibility, it doesn't matter. You will never get your hands on that painting, ever, and just so you know exactly how serious I am, Dean Reyes, allow me to outline for you the various ways in which I will personally make your life a living hell if you continue to let even the thought of auction drift around in your otherwise empty skull..."

Suzanne rages on, but her words distort into a screamy blur and enter my lizard brain as meaningless noise. I can't hear it anymore. The scene before me seems to stand still and the instinct to retreat comes on strong. I find myself in a hyperaware Matrix moment, attentive to all that's happening, as it's happening. I am aware of how barbaric it would be if the Pollock were sold at auction, not only because of what we went through to save it but because of what it means to the school and where it could end up— in a Plexiglas hallway encasement at some casino or posh department store, forever dismissed by an endless stream of tourists and shoppers. I am aware of how terribly I want to keep my job and perpetuate my codependence with the SVA and everyone there, how I want to protect and enable Ramona, Suzanne, James, Bunny, even Dunbar. I am aware these are my primary relationships and that these people deserve better from me, as a friend and steward. I am aware we're going to need something stronger than an indignant diatribe to save ourselves from Havercamp's wrath.

An image flickers to life in my mind. Ethan, drowned, floating face up in a flooded house. Our house, filled nearly to the ceiling with mucky floodwater. He's alone—in my imagination, he was waiting for me to come home and became trapped by rising flood-water—his Hawaiian shirt swirling around his lifeless body like fog, his eyes open, his mouth closed, his arms rolling on small ripples independent of his torso, as if amputated, rotted through by the spoiled water. What I think is, where is Gary? Why isn't he there, helping Ethan? And then something inside me yields. Some combativeness. The choleric fervor that fueled my pursuit of Dunbar and made Suzanne angry and pushed Ethan away and left me artless and miserable.

Havercamp, I realize, is talking again. "...and seeing as the SVA building is underwater, the school will remain closed for the coming academic year. It'll go to the bottom of the recovery list. Do you understand me? The bottom. No students, no courses, no equipment, not this year, not the next. Unless the painting is returned, immediately and unharmed."

His tone still vibrates with that low roar, but I recognize the exigency in his threats, virtually identical to those I made to Dunbar when he was cuffed to the staircase Friday afternoon. This is the cry of a desperate man. A man grasping. A man who has yet to inform the chairman of the Board of Regents that he did not save the Pollock before the river crested, that the painting is not in his possession, and that he does not, in fact, know where it is. Next to me, Suzanne is fuming, her jaw clenched, brow knit, earlobes an inhuman fuchsia.

"Mr. President, if I may," I say, preempting Suzanne's next outburst. "You might want to consider how it'll look, you firing a handful of faculty and staff immediately following the worst flood in university history, particularly for their attempted rescue of a painting your administration let drown. I doubt that's really something you want to have to tell the Board of Regents—that we should be punished for trying to save one of the university's most valuable assets, which you neglected, or rather, refused to rescue."

All eyes are on me now except Suzanne's, which bore holes through Dean Reyes. "Suzanne," I say, trying to snap her out of that fire-stare, "how many calls did you make to campus police trying to get help rescuing the painting?"

"Dozens," she says, exaggerating beautifully. "And to campus safety. And to city police. They all told me the same thing: The painting wasn't a priority." To prove her point, she turns her contemptuous gaze to Bigelow.

"And how many times did you try to reach somebody at the university who could facilitate the Pollock's rescue? Some high-level administrator, for instance?"

"At least as many," she says, steely now, under control.

Havercamp narrows his colorless eyes. "What is your point, Ms. Lanning?" he says.

"Your administration made no attempt to save the painting. If this situation was brought to the attention of the regents, you would be in just as much trouble as we are, that is, if we had been involved in the painting's rescue, which I'm not admitting we were." I wait a beat. "But what if the painting was lost in the flood?"

"That would be a serious problem," Havercamp says. "I'd have no choice but to impose the penalties previously outlined and to explain to the regents your sole responsibility for the Pollock's demise."

"I think Nina made clear why it'd be better if nobody hears about our alleged involvement," Suzanne says. "Were you not listening carefully?"

Havercamp froths at being forced into a corner not of his making. He speaks through clamped teeth. "I don't know what you're hoping for here, but I'm about out of patience."

"I suppose you already know that if you went to the School of Visual Arts right now you'd find the Pollock gone," I say. "It was, tragically, lost in the flood. It fell into the water during an attempted rescue and was swept out to the river, probably halfway down the Mississippi by now. This can be documented." I gesture to the big screen television. "But more importantly, it can be filed with the insurance company as a claim for the loss. And the Board of Regents can get their recovery money."

Charlie Miller speaks up for the first time all morning. "You're talking about insurance fraud," he says.

"That would be true only if the painting survived this unprecedented natural disaster. Does anybody have any specific knowledge that it did?" I am speaking to the room generally, and the room remains quiet.

"I don't know where that painting is," Charlie Miller says, "and I don't have any idea what really happened Friday night," he tosses his pencil down on the legal pad in front of him, "but I cannot be party to this." There is no conviction in his tone, no judgment, no blame, just indifference; he seems to be looking for an excuse to leave more than disentangling himself from conspiracy. "I'll be available by email if you need me," he says to Dean Reyes, "but I advise you not to need me."

When the door closes behind Charlie Miller, President Havercamp says, "So we were unable to remove the painting because the building was evacuated and padlocked. The rush to do this came from the US Army Corps of Engineers and a violent outburst by a staff member." He's thinking aloud, giving my explanation the sniff test, searching for something rotten. "And there wasn't time to collect everything, is that correct? Many items were left in the building?" He looks at Bigelow.

"Yes, sir," Bigelow says, looking like he hasn't slept in days, like he'd rather be anywhere but here and will agree to anything in order to be excused.

Havercamp is quiet for a few moments. His mustache stops twitching. "Professor Dunbar would have to drop the charges against Ms. Holme," he says. "This cannot become a scandal, not if we lost the painting. It was a botched rescue, plain and simple.

I'll prepare a press release saying we did everything we could, I'll commend you all for your efforts, I'll be magnanimous."

Dunbar half-stands from his chair. "Outrageous," he says, but he sounds unconvinced. We've gone off script, and he seems to be struggling with the improvisation—this is still a scheme against the administration but he's uncomfortable with Havercamp's assent. He's not sure if he should play infuriated or complicit. "I will not be censored," he says, his go-to battle cry. And then, for good measure, "That video is a work of protest, destined for public consumption and, for resolution, for revolution. Ramona Holme must be punished. Off with her head!"

"What about a demotion?" Ramona says, spookily calm. "Somebody has to take the blame for this, right? Publically, I mean, like a fall guy? Why not the director of the School of Visual Arts? It should have been my job to make sure the painting was safely out of the building. I failed." The price of our salvation.

I feel the hot rush of heartache, and I'm not sure if it's at hearing Ramona admit personal liability or the thought of her demoted or that she will shoulder the blame for the lot of us. Before I can think of what to say, Dunbar speaks. "I'll agree to nothing short of imprisonment."

"No," Havercamp says. "You will drop the battery charge, and in exchange, you'll get the comfort of knowing you've not lost your job or been jailed yourself for extorting the president of the university and breaching, for at least the second time, the restraining order your own school has against you." His tone is more regulated now, his speech rapid but not with desperation, as before, rather with logistics. "Ramona Holme," he says, his voice formal, official. "For not going through proper channels to successfully save the Pollock, I remove you from your post as director of the School of Visual Arts. You're demoted to professor and will be on leave for the coming semester or until the insurance claim is settled. In the press release, we'll call it a long overdue sabbatical. Perhaps you have some out-of-country research to do, hmm? Unavailable for comment?"

I open my mouth to object but, with speed and apparent inconsideration, Pete Mustard says, "The defense accepts the deal."

Ramona sits quietly, her fingers interlaced, hands resting lightly on the edge of the conference table. Tranquility and relief settle over her like melting butter, and I realize she has just become free. Free from the constraints of her SVA duties but, better, free to chase Lucky all over Hollywood, or whatever else she has in mind to do.

"Officer Bigelow, do you see any problem with these solutions?" Havercamp seems to have only just remembered there is an officer of the law in the room.

"No, sir. Insurance claims aren't really my area of expertise. It sounds like Ms. Lanning has it figured." For all he knows, the painting really was lost in the flood.

"Excellent," Havercamp says. "That's excellent." He seems so delighted with our conniving. I almost expect him to twirl the end of his mustache and toss his head back to cackle. He does neither of those things, and there seems to be little else to say.

In the silence, accord takes hold, and there is another barometric shift in the room, this time to the strained after effects of high stakes collusion; we've gone all in and we're each thinking through what we could lose, how it could go wrong, what we need to do to make sure the arrangement sticks.

"Suzanne Betts should be director," Bunny says.

Dean Reyes, who has been silent since we foiled plans to auction the Pollock, says, "No, absolutely not, out of the question, we will not be handing out promotions for this unmitigated nightmare."

"Anybody who knows anything about administration will understand this is a punishment, not a promotion," Havercamp says, making it sound like a personal insult to Dean Reyes. "She'll be interim director, and at this time next spring, there will be a faculty vote on permanent directorship, subject to my approval. Can we agree on that?" Havercamp turns to Suzanne.

"Yes," she says, taken aback. "Agreed."

"Mrs. Lanning." Havercamp faces me now. "We need to deal with you. You'll be issued a formal reprimand for your involvement in the incident precipitating the hasty evacuation of the SVA building and the threats you made against one undergraduate student." He nods toward Mathias, looks at Peanut.

"Mathias Daman," Peanut says.

"Your actions directly contributed to the loss of the Pollock. I'll waive the disciplinary hearing, but this official reprimand will remain in your personnel file and will come with a two-week suspension without pay. Do you understand?" Peanut is scribbling furiously, taking notes for the paperwork he'll have to complete and attach to my university file.

"I understand," I say. I'd have thought when punishment was doled out I'd be furious or ashamed, but I feel nothing.

"Officer Bigelow, as Ms. Lanning's victim, is this acceptable to you?"

"She didn't mean to hit me with the frying pan, if that's what you're talking about. We never intended to charge her with anything."

"Excellent. Then I believe our business here is complete. Ms. Lanning, when you return from suspension, you will be the point person on the insurance claim, and you will keep me apprised of all developments." He looks at me dispassionately, and his mustache twitches one final time. "Is that understood?"

"Yes, sir," I say, sealing my professional fate with Havercamp's.

He pushes back in his chair and stands. "Meeting adjourned," he says, and Dunbar smacks the conference room table with his gavel.

Chapter 20

E STAND TOGETHER OUTSIDE the building's main
entrance, Bunny and James bent together in agitated
whisper, retracing the events of the past hour, trying to
sort out who won and who lost and whether or not their understanding of the outcome is correct: The Pollock is ours.

Dunbar steps out of the building followed by Mathias and Pete
Mustard. They turn to walk down the sidewalk, but when he's a few
steps away, Dunbar stops and turns back to me, lifts the eye-patch.
"Nicely played, Lanning, very nice. I didn't see that coming. But
this isn't over. Consider yourself warned." He wrenches the side
of his face into what appears to be a wink with the pulverized eye,
flips the eye-patch back down, and heads off with his devotees, no
doubt to plan their next escapade. I repress a smile.

"Mathias recorded that whole thing," Suzanne says and I start;
I hadn't realized she was standing beside me.

"What whole thing?"

"He recorded the meeting. Oh please, you can't tell me that
surprises you. The kid records everything. I have a feeling my
SVA administration is going to have a very productive working
relationship with Dean Reyes and President Havercamp once

those two assholes know we've got all that on tape." She jags her eyebrows up and down, and in that moment, I decide not to ask her how much of this she was in on—from now on, I'll leave the scheming to Suzanne.

She tilts her head, senses I'm holding back, and, confusing my unresponsiveness with sentimentality, says, "Sweetie, are you ok? Is it Ethan? Was it awful with him this weekend?"

"It was actually fine," I say. She looks me over but doesn't push, offers me a comforting, discerning look, like she's unsurprised but still sorrowful. Like she understands Ethan said he wanted children as a way to force the conversation, because he does want them, just not with me, and that makes her sorry. Like I can say aloud as much or as little as I choose. She hugs me.

James and Bunny walk over to where we're standing. "That was incredible," Bunny says. "I'm shaking all over. Did you think of that on the spot?"

"It seemed like the only way to keep the painting from auction," I say.

"Are you sure this is a good idea?" James says to nobody in particular. "You realize we are now actually stealing a painting."

"Are you fucking kidding?" Suzanne says. "A little insurance fraud and honest-to-goodness thievery to keep the Pollock from going to auction? Yes, god yes, ten thousand times yes, this is a good idea. It's a great idea. It's the only idea. It may be the best idea we've ever had." I flush at her use of the plural pronoun—it makes me feel less responsible, less alone.

James shrugs one shoulder and nods, as much accepting our crime as he is Suzanne herself. "Okay." He's talking to Suzanne but looking at me, sideways, like he's expecting me to say something, like there's one final piece still missing.

"Bunny and Nanette should take the painting," I say.

For a split second, nobody responds, then an enormous, giddy smile winds up Bunny's face.

"Yes!" Suzanne is whooping. "Bunny, Bunny, Bunny, Bunny, Bunny! You will take it, you and Nanette. Not only will it be safe at your house, you deserve it, for your bravado, for your swagger, big man," she swats him on the shoulder, and he beams. "But maybe, eventually, just to be safe, we should take turns with it so that no single person is totally liable. Get it on some kind of rotation. Move it around town under the cover of night, like a secret society with a pact and a treasure, gathering in private on the anniversary of the flood, wine and dinner parties. We'll tell people the painting's a fake, a print we had made in memoriam, but we'll all know it's real. Can you imagine? A real Pollock, hanging in your house!" She is exuberant, and as she talks, we each imagine where in our homes we might hang the Pollock, what kind of lighting and care it will require, how we'll always share this great secret. I cannot fixate on a specific image of the Pollock in my house other than beneath blankets in the garage—I'm unsure how long I'll be living there or how the rooms will change if Ethan is the one to go.

"I don't think we should talk about this here," James says. "Let's go somewhere else. Let's get some breakfast. I'm starving."

"You're right," Suzanne says, startled, looking around to see if anybody could have been listening. "Let's get out of here."

As I watch Suzanne, James, and Bunny walk away, still talking, tittering, staggering from thoughts of the Pollock hanging permanently above their fireplace or bed, I notice that the crystalline awareness I felt in the conference room has escaped me and in its place is seasick confusion. Astonishing, the way an impression can coalesce in such sharp relief and then, within a matter of moments, scatter and blur. Was manipulating the situation really any better than fighting against it or is this just one more massive undoable mistake? Is keeping the Pollock in the illicit possession of four private individuals really better than selling it for recovery money or waging a public campaign to keep it from auction? Or was I, still yet, being impulsive and reactionary? What will I tell Ethan about what's happened? What is my obligation to him now? I am filled with doubt and fear. About all of it. About what I'll do next, once breakfast is over and I have to go home.

I hear footsteps to my right and turn to see Ramona. She looks good. Happy. She comes toward me and without a word we hug. We stay that way for a long moment.

"Congratulations," I say to her, and she smiles. "Are you heading out to Hollywood?"

She blushes, chuckles. "I'm going to back to my studio," she says. "And I think I'll try online dating." We hug again, then she takes a few steps back, ready to get going. "Rebuild that place into something better, ok? Make it what it always should have been. Get rid of all that glass and steel. Make it warm. Make it a place people actually want to come and spend time."

"We will," I say.

She smiles once more, then turns and walks away. I watch her until she's around the corner then follow after the others. As I walk, I am struck by a rising sensation, as though the ground beneath me is surging. I too anticipate what's ahead but not like Ramona—this is not my liberation. What's in store will be more difficult than what's passed. Scarier. The ripping down of relationships and places, rather than constructing them anew. Maybe I should have seen this coming, been better prepared. Or maybe this was the only way, being caught off guard, swept off my feet, rocked, billow to billow, until there was nothing left to keep me from finally understanding how much needed to change.

I turn the corner and see Suzanne, James, Bunny, and Nanette, who, I gather, was waiting in the car while we met with Havercamp and Reyes. They're standing together in a circle, holding hands, laughing, shaking their heads, stomping their feet, swaying to a soundless beat. Suzanne is giving instructions of some kind, and James seems to be teasing her, while Bunny, giggling, watches them flirt. Nanette sees me and lets go of James' hand, breaking their human chain. "Nina," she says, flailing her free hand in my direction. "We're doing a chant Suzanne knows. Come on. Get in here."

"It's an incantation, not a chant," Suzanne says to Nanette, then looks at me, radiant, loving. "Move it, sister, we're waiting for you."

I go toward them, my head clearing, my steps surer as I resign myself to the uncertainty in front of me. For however indefinite the future may be, however dismantled my world is about to become, the fact is, I won't be navigating alone. I have a loyal cabal of trustworthy advisors who will support and guide me with all possible prudence. Just look at them, hand-in-hand, calling out to me with magic in their hearts. How could anything possibly go awry?

ACKNOWLEDGEMENTS

This book exists only because of the guidance and energy of others. I deserve the blame, but these people get the credit.

My editors at the Unnamed Press, Olivia Taylor Smith and C.P. Heiser, believed in this novel and gave it a home, then worked and worked and worked to make it better.

Mark Winegardner inadvertently corrected a gross detour by being unbearably insulting and mostly right.

The hysterical, the remarkable, the bighearted Tod Goldberg walked me step-by-step through the writing process and a first draft, while David Ulin inspired me with unassuming brilliance, and taught me about finding the deeper meaning. Mark Haskell Smith—where do I even begin? In Nebraska City, I suppose, of all places. This book is all yours.

Steve McGuire and Annette Niebuhr, I had such a blast with you and everybody else at the SAAH. You know it all comes from a place of great affection, right? So we're cool? Still friends? Guys?

All the innocent people who had the misfortune of working alongside me, standing within earshot at the grocery store, sitting behind me on an airplane, or otherwise crossing my path, all of you, whose personal details, anecdotes and quips I swiped, then disfigured for narrative fiction, you have my great appreciation and, in some cases, apology.

My family, who never once uttered disapproval but instead illicitly repurposed office supplies to print and bind hard copies of this novel. I am so grateful.

To my mother, for many things but most pertinently that she actually believed me when I told her I was going to write a book. At the time I thought it was gullibility but I know now it was yet another instance of incredible maternal generosity.

To my father for his influence as a shrewd and tireless reader, and for once pulling me gently from a years-long cliffhung cycle of murder mysteries with his personal copy of *Women in Love*. I'm not giving it back.

To my three brothers, Sean, Timmy and Brian, who have been complicit, or more often instigative, in all my questionable decisions, including becoming a writer.

To Oliver and Miles, who demand my best just by existing, and to my dearest Bradley, who convinces me I can do anything, then quietly makes it all possible. There'd be none of it without you.